The Rosie Project

A NOVEL

GRAEME SIMSION

HarperCollins*Publishers*Ltd

The Rosie Project
Copyright © 2013 by Graeme Simsion.
All rights reserved.

Published by HarperCollins Publishers Ltd

Originally published in Australia by The Text Publishing Company: 2013
First published in Canada by HarperCollins Publishers Ltd in an
original trade paperback edition: 2013
This mass market edition: 2017

HarperCollins books may be purchased for educational, business,
or sales promotional use through our Special Markets Department.

HarperCollins Publishers Ltd
2 Bloor Street East, 20th Floor
Toronto, Ontario, Canada
M4W 1A8

www.harpercollins.ca

Library and Archives Canada Cataloguing in Publication
information is available upon request.

ISBN 978-1-44345-444-5

Printed and bound in the United States of America
QUAD 9 8 7 6 5 4 3 2 1

To Rod and Lynette

1

I may have found a solution to the Wife Problem. As with so many scientific breakthroughs, the answer was obvious in retrospect. But had it not been for a series of unscheduled events, it is unlikely I would have discovered it.

The sequence was initiated by Gene insisting I give a lecture on Asperger's syndrome that he had previously agreed to deliver himself. The timing was extremely annoying. The preparation could be time-shared with lunch consumption, but on the designated evening I had scheduled ninety-four minutes to clean my bathroom. I was faced with a choice of three options, none of them satisfactory.

1. Cleaning the bathroom after the lecture, resulting in loss of sleep with a consequent reduction in mental and physical performance.
2. Rescheduling the cleaning until the following Tuesday, resulting in an eight-day period of compromised bathroom hygiene and consequent risk of disease.
3. Refusing to deliver the lecture, resulting in damage to my friendship with Gene.

I presented the dilemma to Gene, who, as usual, had an alternative solution.

'Don, I'll pay for someone to clean your bathroom.'

I explained to Gene—again—that all cleaners, with the possible exception of the Hungarian woman with the short skirt, made errors. Short-skirt Woman, who had been Gene's cleaner, had disappeared following some problem with Gene and Claudia.

'I'll give you Eva's mobile number. Just don't mention me.'

'What if she asks? How can I answer without mentioning you?'

'Just say you're contacting her because she's the only cleaner who does it properly. And if she mentions me, say nothing.'

This was an excellent outcome, and an illustration of Gene's ability to find solutions to social problems. Eva would enjoy having her competence recognised and might even be suitable for a permanent role, which would free up an average of three hundred and sixteen minutes per week in my schedule.

Gene's lecture problem had arisen because he had an opportunity to have sex with a Chilean academic who was visiting Melbourne for a conference. Gene has a project to have sex with women of as many different nationalities as possible. As a professor of psychology, he is extremely interested in human sexual attraction, which he believes is largely genetically determined.

This belief is consistent with Gene's background as a geneticist. Sixty-eight days after Gene hired me as a post-doctoral researcher, he was promoted to head of the Psychology Department, a highly controversial appointment that was intended to establish the university as the Australian leader in evolutionary psychology and increase its public profile.

During the time we worked concurrently in the Genetics Department, we had numerous interesting discussions which continued after his change of position. I would have been satisfied with our relationship for this reason alone, but Gene also invited me to dinner at his house and performed other friendship rituals, resulting in a social relationship. His wife Claudia, who is a clinical psychologist, is now also a friend. Making a total of two.

Gene and Claudia tried for a while to assist me with the Wife Problem. Unfortunately, their approach was based on the traditional dating paradigm, which I had previously abandoned on the basis that the probability of success did not justify the effort and negative experiences. I am thirty-nine years old, tall, fit and intelligent, with a relatively high status and above-average income as an associate professor. Logically, I should be attractive to a wide range of women. In the animal kingdom, I would succeed in reproducing.

However, there is something about me that women find unappealing. I have never found it easy to make friends, and it seems that the deficiencies that caused this problem have also affected my attempts at romantic relationships. The Apricot Ice-cream Disaster is a good example.

Claudia had introduced me to one of her many friends. Elizabeth was a highly intelligent computer scientist, with a vision problem that had been corrected with glasses. I mention the glasses because Claudia showed me a photograph, and asked me if I was okay with them. An incredible question! From a psychologist! In evaluating Elizabeth's suitability as a potential partner—someone to provide intellectual stimulation, to share activities with, perhaps even to breed with—Claudia's first concern was my reaction to her choice of glasses frames, which was probably not even her own but the result of advice from an optometrist. This is the world I have to live in. Then Claudia told me, as though it was a problem: 'She has very firm ideas.'

'Are they evidence-based?'

'I guess so,' Claudia said.

Perfect. She could have been describing me.

We met at a Thai restaurant. Restaurants are minefields for the socially inept, and I was nervous as always in these situations. But we got off to an excellent start when we both arrived at exactly 7.00 p.m. as arranged. Poor synchronisation is a huge waste of time.

We survived the meal without her criticising me for any social errors. It is difficult to conduct a conversation while wondering whether you are looking at the correct body part but I locked on to her bespectacled eyes, as recommended by Gene. This resulted in some inaccuracy in the eating process, which she did not seem to notice. On the contrary, we had a highly productive discussion about simulation algorithms. She was so interesting! I could already see the possibility of a permanent relationship.

The waiter brought the dessert menus and Elizabeth said, 'I don't like Asian desserts.'

This was almost certainly an unsound generalisation, based on limited experience, and perhaps I should have recognised it as a warning sign. But it provided me with an opportunity for a creative suggestion.

'We could get an ice-cream across the road.'

'Great idea. As long as they've got apricot.'

I assessed that I was progressing well at this point, and did not think the apricot preference would be a problem. I was wrong. The ice-cream parlour had a vast selection of flavours, but they had exhausted their supply of apricot. I ordered a chocolate chilli and liquorice double cone for myself and asked Elizabeth to nominate her second preference.

'If they haven't got apricot, I'll pass.'

I couldn't believe it. All ice-cream tastes essentially the same, due to chilling of the tastebuds. This is especially true of fruit flavours. I suggested mango.

'No thanks, I'm fine.'

I explained the physiology of tastebud chilling in some detail. I predicted that if I purchased a mango and a peach ice-cream she would be incapable of differentiating. And, by extension, either would be equivalent to apricot.

'They're completely different,' she said. 'If you can't tell mango from peach, that's your problem.'

Now we had a simple objective disagreement that could readily be resolved experimentally. I ordered a minimum-size ice-cream in each of the two flavours. But by the time the serving person had prepared them, and I turned to ask Elizabeth to close her eyes for the experiment, she had gone. So much for 'evidence-based'. And for computer 'scientist'.

Afterwards, Claudia advised me that I should have abandoned the experiment prior to Elizabeth leaving.

Obviously. But at what point? Where was the signal? These are the subtleties I fail to see. But I also fail to see why heightened sensitivity to obscure cues about ice-cream flavours should be a prerequisite for being someone's partner. It seems reasonable to assume that some women do not require this. Unfortunately, the process of finding them is impossibly inefficient. The Apricot Ice-cream Disaster had cost a whole evening of my life, compensated for only by the information about simulation algorithms.

Two lunchtimes were sufficient to research and prepare my lecture on Asperger's syndrome, without sacrificing nourishment, thanks to the provision of Wi-Fi in the medical library café. I had no previous knowledge of autism spectrum disorders, as they were outside my specialty. The subject was fascinating. It seemed appropriate to focus on the genetic aspects of the syndrome, which might be unfamiliar to my audience. Most diseases have some basis in our DNA, though in many cases we have yet to discover it. My own work focuses on genetic predisposition to cirrhosis of the liver. Much of my working time is devoted to getting mice drunk.

Naturally, the books and research papers described the symptoms of Asperger's syndrome, and I formed a provisional conclusion that most of these were simply variations in human brain function that had been inappropriately medicalised because they did not fit social norms—*constructed* social norms—that reflected the most common human configurations rather than the full range.

The lecture was scheduled for 7.00 p.m. at an inner-suburban school. I estimated the cycle ride at twelve minutes, and allowed three minutes to boot my computer and connect it to the projector.

I arrived on schedule at 6.57 p.m., having let Eva, the short-skirted cleaner, into my apartment twenty-seven minutes earlier. There were approximately twenty-five people milling around the door and the front of the classroom, but I immediately recognised Julie, the convenor, from Gene's description: 'blonde with big tits'. In fact, her breasts were probably no more than one and a half standard deviations from the mean size for her body weight, and hardly a remarkable identifying feature. It was more a question of elevation and exposure, as a result of her choice of costume, which seemed perfectly practical for a hot January evening.

I may have spent too long verifying her identity, as she looked at me strangely.

'You must be Julie,' I said.

'Can I help you?'

Good. A practical person. 'Yes, direct me to the VGA cable. Please.'

'Oh,' she said. 'You must be Professor Tillman. I'm so glad you could make it.'

She extended her hand but I waved it away. 'The VGA cable, please. It's 6.58.'

'Relax,' she said. 'We never start before 7.15. Would you like a coffee?'

Why do people value others' time so little? Now we would have the inevitable small talk. I could have spent fifteen minutes at home practising aikido.

I had been focusing on Julie and the screen at the front of the room. Now I looked around and realised that I had failed to observe nineteen people. They

7

were children, predominantly male, sitting at desks. Presumably these were the victims of Asperger's syndrome. Almost all of the literature focuses on children.

Despite their affliction, they were making better use of their time than their parents, who were chattering aimlessly. Most were operating portable computing devices. I guessed their ages as between eight and thirteen. I hoped they had been paying attention in their science classes, as my material assumed a working knowledge of organic chemistry and the structure of DNA.

I realised that I had failed to reply to the coffee question.

'No.'

Unfortunately, because of the delay, Julie had forgotten the question. 'No coffee,' I explained. 'I never drink coffee after 3.48 p.m. It interferes with sleep. Caffeine has a half-life of three to four hours, so it's irresponsible serving coffee at 7.00 p.m. unless people are planning to stay awake until after midnight. Which doesn't allow adequate sleep if they have a conventional job.' I was trying to make use of the waiting time by offering practical advice, but it seemed that she preferred to discuss trivia.

'Is Gene all right?' she asked. It was obviously a variant on that most common of formulaic interactions, 'How are you?'

'He's fine, thank you,' I said, adapting the conventional reply to the third-person form.

'Oh. I thought he was ill.'

'Gene is in excellent health except for being six kilograms overweight. We went for a run this morning. He has a date tonight, and he wouldn't be able to go out if he was ill.'

Julie seemed unimpressed and, in reviewing the interaction later, I realised that Gene must have lied to her about his reason for not being present. This was presumably to protect Julie from feeling that her lecture was unimportant to Gene and to provide a justification for a less prestigious speaker being sent as a substitute. It seems hardly possible to analyse such a complex situation involving deceit and supposition of another person's emotional response, and then prepare your own plausible lie, all while someone is waiting for you to reply to a question. Yet that is exactly what people expect you to be able to do.

Eventually, I set up my computer and we got started, *eighteen minutes late*. I would need to speak forty-three per cent faster to finish on schedule at 8.00 p.m.—a virtually impossible performance goal. We were going to finish late, and my schedule for the rest of the night would be thrown out.

2

I had titled my talk *Genetic Precursors to Autism Spectrum Disorders* and sourced some excellent diagrams of DNA structures. I had only been speaking for nine minutes, a little faster than usual to recover time, when Julie interrupted.

'Professor Tillman. Most of us here are not scientists, so you may need to be a little less technical.' This sort of thing is incredibly annoying. People can tell you the supposed characteristics of a Gemini or a Taurus and will spend five days watching a cricket match, but cannot find the interest or the time to learn the basics of what they, as humans, are made up of.

I continued with my presentation as I had prepared it. It was too late to change and surely some of the audience were informed enough to understand.

I was right. A hand went up, a male of about twelve.

'You are saying that it is unlikely that there is a single genetic marker, but rather that several genes are implicated and the aggregate expression depends on the specific combination. Affirmative?'

Exactly! 'Plus environmental factors. The situation is analogous to bipolar disorder, which—'

Julie interrupted again. 'So, for us non-geniuses, I think Professor Tillman is reminding us that Asperger's is something you're born with. It's nobody's fault.'

I was horrified by the use of the word 'fault', with its negative connotations, especially as it was being employed by someone in authority. I abandoned my decision not to deviate from the genetic issues. The matter had doubtless been brewing in my subconscious, and the volume of my voice may have increased as a result.

'Fault! Asperger's isn't a fault. It's a variant. It's potentially a major advantage. Asperger's syndrome is associated with organisation, focus, innovative thinking and rational detachment.'

A woman at the rear of the room raised her hand. I was focused on the argument now, and made a minor social error, which I quickly corrected.

'The fat woman—*overweight* woman—at the back?'

She paused and looked around the room, but then continued, 'Rational detachment: is that a euphemism for lack of emotion?'

'Synonym,' I replied. 'Emotions can cause major problems.'

I decided it would be helpful to provide an example, drawing on a story in which emotional behaviour would have led to disastrous consequences.

'Imagine,' I said. 'You're hiding in a basement. The enemy is searching for you and your friends. Everyone has to keep totally quiet, but your baby is crying.' I did an impression, as Gene would, to make the story more convincing: 'Waaaaa.' I paused dramatically. 'You have a gun.'

Hands went up everywhere.

Julie jumped to her feet as I continued. 'With a silencer. They're coming closer. They're going to kill you all. What do you do? The baby's screaming—'

The kids couldn't wait to share their answer. One called out, 'Shoot the baby,' and soon they were all shouting, 'Shoot the baby, shoot the baby.'

The boy who had asked the genetics question called out, 'Shoot the *enemy*,' and then another said, 'Ambush them.'

The suggestions were coming rapidly.

'Use the baby as bait.'

'How many guns do we have?'

'Cover its mouth.'

'How long can it live without air?'

As I had expected, all the ideas came from the Asperger's 'sufferers'. The parents made no constructive suggestions; some even tried to suppress their children's creativity.

I raised my hands. 'Time's up. Excellent work. All the rational solutions came from the aspies. Everyone else was incapacitated by emotion.'

One boy called out, 'Aspies rule!' I had noted this abbreviation in the literature, but it appeared to be new to the children. They seemed to like it, and soon were standing on the chairs and then the desks, punching the air and chanting 'Aspies rule!' in chorus. According to my reading, children with Asperger's syndrome frequently lack self-confidence in social situations. Their success in problem-solving seemed to have provided a temporary cure for this, but again their parents were failing to provide positive feedback, shouting at them and in some cases attempting to pull them down from the desks. Apparently they were more concerned with adherence to social convention than the progress their children were making.

I felt I had made my point effectively, and Julie did not think we needed to continue with the genetics. The parents appeared to be reflecting on what their children had learned and left without interacting with me further. It was only 7.43 p.m. An excellent outcome.

As I packed up my laptop, Julie burst out laughing. 'Oh my God,' she said. 'I need a drink.'

I was not sure why she was sharing this information with someone she had known for only forty-six minutes. I planned to consume some alcohol myself when I arrived home but saw no reason to inform Julie.

She continued, 'You know, we never use that word. Aspies. We don't want them thinking it's some sort of club.' More negative implications from someone who was presumably paid to assist and encourage.

'Like homosexuality?' I said.

'Touché,' said Julie. 'But it's different. If they don't change, they're not going to have real relationships—they'll never have partners.' This was a reasonable argument, and one that I could understand, given my own difficulties in that sphere. But Julie changed the subject. 'But you're saying there are things—useful things—they can do better than…non-aspies? Besides killing babies?'

'Of course.' I wondered why someone involved in the education of people with uncommon attributes was not aware of the value of and market for such attributes. 'There's a company in Denmark that recruits aspies for computer applications testing.'

'I didn't know that,' said Julie. 'You're really giving me a different perspective.' She looked at me for a few moments. 'Do you have time for a drink?' And then she put her hand on my shoulder.

I flinched automatically. Definitely inappropriate contact. If I had done that to a woman there would almost certainly have been a problem, possibly a sexual harassment complaint to the Dean, which could have consequences for my career. Of course, no one was going to criticise *her* for it.

'Unfortunately, I have other activities scheduled.'

'No flexibility?'

'Definitely not.' Having succeeded in recovering lost time, I was not about to throw my life into chaos again.

Before I met Gene and Claudia I had two other friends. The first was my older sister. Although she was a mathematics teacher, she had little interest in advances in the field. However, she lived nearby and would visit twice weekly and sometimes randomly. We would eat together and discuss trivia, such as events in the lives of our relatives and social interactions with our colleagues. Once a month, we drove to Shepparton for Sunday dinner with our parents and brother. She was single, probably as a result of being shy and not conventionally attractive. Due to gross and inexcusable medical incompetence, she is now dead.

The second friend was Daphne, whose friendship period also overlapped with Gene and Claudia's. She moved into the apartment above mine after her husband entered a nursing home, as a result of dementia. Due to knee failure, exacerbated by obesity, she was unable to walk more than a few steps, but she was highly intelligent and I began to visit her regularly. She had no formal qualifications, having performed a traditional female homemaker role. I considered this to be an extreme waste of talent—particularly as her descendants did not return the care. She was curious about my work, and we initiated the Teach Daphne Genetics Project, which was fascinating for both of us.

She began eating her dinner in my apartment on a regular basis, as there are massive economies of scale in cooking one meal for two people, rather than two separate meals. Each Sunday at 3.00 p.m. we would visit her husband at the nursing home, which was 7.3 kilometres away. I was able to combine a 14.6-kilometre walk pushing a wheelchair with interesting conversation about genetics. I would read while she spoke to her husband, whose level of comprehension was difficult to determine but definitely low.

Daphne had been named after the plant that was flowering at the time of her birth, on the twenty-eighth of August. On each birthday, her husband would give her daphne flowers, and she considered this a highly romantic action. She complained that her approaching birthday would be the first occasion in fifty-six years on which this symbolic act would not be performed. The solution was obvious, and when I wheeled her to my apartment for dinner on her seventy-eighth birthday, I had purchased a quantity of the flowers to give her.

She recognised the smell immediately and began crying. I thought I had made a terrible error, but she explained that her tears were a symptom of happiness. She was also impressed by the chocolate cake that I had made, but not to the same extent.

During the meal, she made an incredible statement: 'Don, you would make someone a wonderful husband.'

This was so contrary to my experiences of being

rejected by women that I was temporarily stunned. Then I presented her with the facts—the history of my attempts to find a partner, beginning with my assumption as a child that I would grow up and get married and finishing with my abandonment of the idea as the evidence grew that I was unsuitable.

Her argument was simple: there's someone for everyone. Statistically, she was almost certainly correct. Unfortunately, the probability that I would find such a person was vanishingly small. But it created a disturbance in my brain, like a mathematical problem that we know must have a solution.

For her next two birthdays, we repeated the flower ritual. The results were not as dramatic as the first time, but I also purchased gifts for her—books on genetics—and she seemed very happy. She told me that her birthday had always been her favourite day of the year. I understood that this view was common in children, due to the gifts, but had not expected it in an adult.

Ninety-three days after the third birthday dinner, we were travelling to the nursing home, discussing a genetics paper that Daphne had read the previous day, when it became apparent that she had forgotten some significant points. It was not the first time in recent weeks that her memory had been faulty, and I immediately organised an assessment of her cognitive functioning. The diagnosis was Alzheimer's disease.

Daphne's intellectual capability deteriorated rapidly, and we were soon unable to have our discussions about genetics. But we continued our meals and walks to the nursing home. Daphne now spoke primarily about her past, focusing on her husband and family, and I was able to form a generalised view of what married life could be like. She continued to insist that I could find a compatible partner and enjoy the high level of happiness that she had experienced in her own life. Supplementary research confirmed that Daphne's arguments were supported by evidence: married men are happier and live longer.

One day Daphne asked, 'When will it be my birthday again?' and I realised that she had lost track of dates. I decided that it would be acceptable to lie in order to maximise her happiness. The problem was to source some daphne out of season, but I had unexpected success. I was aware of a geneticist who was working on altering and extending the flowering of plants for commercial reasons. He was able to supply my flower vendor with some daphne, and we had a simulated birthday dinner. I repeated the procedure each time Daphne asked about her birthday.

Eventually, it was necessary for Daphne to join her husband at the nursing home, and, as her memory failed, we celebrated her birthdays more often, until I was visiting her daily. The flower vendor gave me a special loyalty card. I calculated that Daphne had reached the age of two hundred and seven, according to the number of birthdays, when she stopped recognising me, and three hundred and nineteen when she no longer responded to the daphne and I abandoned the visits.

I did not expect to hear from Julie again. As usual, my assumptions about human behaviour were wrong. Two days after the lecture, at 3.37 p.m., my phone rang with an unfamiliar number. Julie left a message asking me to call back, and I deduced that I must have left something behind.

I was wrong again. She wanted to continue our discussion of Asperger's syndrome. I was pleased that my input had been so influential. She suggested we meet over dinner, which was not the ideal location for productive discussion, but, as I usually eat dinner alone, it would be easy to schedule. Background research was another matter.

'What specific topics are you interested in?'

'Oh,' she said, 'I thought we could just talk generally...get to know each other a bit.'

This sounded unfocused. 'I need at least a broad indication of the subject domain. What did I say that particularly interested you?'

'Oh...I guess the stuff about the computer testers in Denmark.'

'Computer *applications* testers.' I would definitely need to do some research. 'What would you like to know?'

'I was wondering how they found them. Most adults with Asperger's syndrome don't know they have it.'

It was a good point. Interviewing random applicants would be a highly inefficient way to detect a syndrome that has an estimated prevalence of less than 0.3 per cent.

I ventured a guess. 'I presume they use a questionnaire as a preliminary filter.' I had not even finished the sentence when a light went on in my head—not literally, of course.

A questionnaire! Such an obvious solution. A purpose-built, scientifically valid instrument incorporating current best practice to filter out the time wasters, the disorganised, the ice-cream discriminators, the visual-harassment complainers, the crystal gazers, the horoscope readers, the fashion obsessives, the religious fanatics, the vegans, the sports watchers, the creationists, the smokers, the scientifically illiterate, the homeopaths, leaving, ideally, the perfect partner, or, realistically, a manageable shortlist of candidates.

'Don?' It was Julie, still on the line. 'When do you want to get together?'

Things had changed. Priorities had shifted.

'It's not possible,' I said. 'My schedule is full.'

I was going to need all available time for the new project.

The Wife Project.

3

After speaking with Julie, I went immediately to Gene's office in the Psychology building, but he was not there. Fortunately his personal assistant, The Beautiful Helena, who should be called The Obstructive Helena, was not there either and I was able to access Gene's diary. I discovered that he was giving a public lecture, due to finish at 5.00 p.m., with a gap before a meeting at 5.30 p.m. Perfect. I would merely have to reduce the length of my scheduled gym session. I booked the vacant slot.

After an accelerated workout at the gym, achieved by deleting the shower and change tasks, I jogged to the lecture theatre, where I waited outside the staff entrance. Although I was perspiring heavily from the heat and exercise, I was energised, both physically and mentally. As soon as my watch showed 5.00 p.m., I walked in. Gene was at the lectern of the darkened theatre, still talking, apparently oblivious to time, responding to a question about funding. My entrance had allowed a shaft of light into the room, and I realised that the audience's eyes were now on me, as if expecting me to say something.

'Time's up,' I said. 'I have a meeting with Gene.'

People immediately started getting up, and I

observed the Dean in the front row with three people in corporate costumes. I guessed that they were there as potential providers of finance and not because of an intellectual interest in primate sexual attraction. Gene is always trying to solicit money for research, and the Dean is constantly threatening to downsize the Genetics and Psychology departments because of insufficient funding. It is not an area I involve myself in.

Gene spoke over the chatter. 'I think my colleague Professor Tillman has given us a signal that we should discuss the finances, critical as they are to our ongoing work, at another time.' He looked towards the Dean and her companions. 'Thank you again for your interest in my work—and of course that of my colleagues in the Department of Psychology.' There was applause. It seemed that my intervention had been timely.

The Dean and her corporate friends swept past me. She said, just to me, 'Sorry to hold up your meeting, Professor Tillman. I'm sure we can find the money elsewhere.' This was good to hear, but now, annoyingly, there was a throng around Gene. A woman with red hair and several metal objects in her ears was talking to him. She was speaking quite loudly.

'I can't believe you used a public lecture to push your own agenda.'

'Lucky you came then. You've changed one of your beliefs. That'd be a first.'

It was obvious that there was some animosity on the woman's part even though Gene was smiling.

'Even if you were right, which you're not, what about the social impact?'

I was amazed by Gene's next reply, not by its intent,

21

which I am familiar with, but by its subtle shift in topic. Gene has social skills at a level that I will never have.

'This is sounding like a café discussion. Why don't we pick it up over coffee sometime?'

'Sorry,' she said. 'I've got research to do. You know, evidence.'

I moved to push in but a tall blonde woman was ahead of me, and I did not want to risk body contact. She spoke with a Norwegian accent.

'Professor Barrow?' she said, meaning Gene. 'With respect, I think you are oversimplifying the feminist position.'

'If we're going to talk philosophy, we should do it in a coffee shop,' Gene replied. 'I'll catch you at Barista's in five.'

The woman nodded and walked towards the door.

Finally, we had time to talk.

'What's her accent?' Gene asked me. 'Swedish?'

'Norwegian,' I said. 'I thought you had a Norwegian already.'

I told him that we had a discussion scheduled, but Gene was now focused on having coffee with the woman. Most male animals are programmed to give higher priority to sex than to assisting an unrelated individual, and Gene had the additional motivation of his research project. Arguing would be hopeless.

'Book the next slot in my diary,' he said.

The Beautiful Helena had presumably departed for the day, and I was again able to access Gene's diary. I amended my own schedule to accommodate the appointment. From now on, the Wife Project would have maximum priority.

I waited until exactly 7.30 a.m. the next day before knocking on Gene and Claudia's door. It had been necessary to shift my jog to the market for dinner purchases back to 5.45 a.m., which in turn had meant going to bed earlier the previous night, with a flow-on effect to a number of scheduled tasks.

I heard sounds of surprise through the door before their daughter Eugenie opened it. Eugenie was, as always, pleased to see me, and requested that I hoist her onto my shoulders and jump all the way to the kitchen. It was great fun. It occurred to me that I might be able to include Eugenie and her half-brother Carl as my friends, making a total of four.

Gene and Claudia were eating breakfast, and told me that they had not been expecting me. I advised Gene to put his diary online—he could remain up to date and I would avoid unpleasant encounters with The Beautiful Helena. He was not enthusiastic.

I had missed breakfast, so I took a tub of yoghurt from the refrigerator. Sweetened! No wonder Gene is overweight. Claudia is not yet overweight, but I had noticed some increase. I pointed out the problem, and identified the yoghurt as the possible culprit.

Claudia asked whether I had enjoyed the Asperger's lecture. She was under the impression that Gene had delivered the lecture and I had merely attended. I corrected her mistake and told her I had found the subject fascinating.

'Did the symptoms remind you of anyone?' she asked.

They certainly did. They were an almost perfect description of Laszlo Hevesi in the Physics Department.

I was about to relate the famous story of Laszlo and the pyjamas when Gene's son Carl, who is sixteen, arrived in his school uniform. He walked towards the refrigerator, as if to open it, then suddenly spun around and threw a full-blooded punch at my head. I caught the punch and pushed him gently but firmly to the floor, so he could see that I was achieving the result with leverage rather than strength. This is a game we always play, but he had not noticed the yoghurt, which was now on our clothes.

'Stay still,' said Claudia. 'I'll get a cloth.'

A cloth was not going to clean my shirt properly. Laundering a shirt requires a machine, detergent, fabric softener and considerable time.

'I'll borrow one of Gene's,' I said, and headed to their bedroom.

When I returned, wearing an uncomfortably large white shirt, with a decorative frill in the front, I tried to introduce the Wife Project, but Claudia was engaged in child-related activities. This was becoming frustrating. I booked dinner for Saturday night and asked them not to schedule any other conversation topics.

The delay was actually opportune, as it enabled me to undertake some research on questionnaire design, draw up a list of desirable attributes, and produce a draft proforma survey. All this, of course, had to be arranged around my teaching and research commitments and an appointment with the Dean.

On Friday morning we had yet another unpleasant interaction as a result of me reporting an honours-year student for academic dishonesty. I had already caught Kevin Yu cheating once. Then, marking his most recent assignment, I had recognised a sentence from another student's work of three years earlier.

Some investigation established that the past student was now Kevin's private tutor, and had written at least part of his essay for him. This had all happened some weeks ago. I had reported the matter and expected the disciplinary process to take its course. Apparently it was more complicated than this.

'The situation with Kevin is a little awkward,' said the Dean. We were in her corporate-style office and she was wearing her corporate-style costume of matching dark-blue skirt and jacket, which, according to Gene, is intended to make her appear more powerful. She is a short, slim person, aged approximately fifty, and it is possible that the costume makes her appear bigger, but I cannot see the relevance of physical dominance in an academic environment.

'This is Kevin's third offence, and university policy requires that he be expelled,' she said.

The facts seemed to be clear and the necessary action straightforward. I tried to identify the awkwardness that the Dean referred to. 'Is the evidence insufficient? Is he making a legal challenge?'

'No, that's all perfectly clear. But the first offence was very naive. He cut and pasted from the internet, and was picked up by the plagiarism software. He was in his first year and his English wasn't very good. And there are cultural differences.'

I had not known about this first offence.

'The second time, you reported him because he'd borrowed from an obscure paper that you were somehow familiar with.'

'Correct.'

'Don, none of the other lecturers are as…vigilant… as you.'

It was unusual for the Dean to compliment me on my wide reading and dedication.

'These kids pay a lot of money to study here. We rely on their fees. We don't want them stealing blatantly from the internet. But we have to recognise that they need assistance, and…Kevin has only a semester to go. We can't send him home after three and a half years without a qualification. It's not a good look.'

'What if he was a medical student? What if you went to the hospital and the doctor who operated on you had cheated in their exams?'

'Kevin's not a medical student. And he didn't cheat on his exams, he just got some help with an assignment.'

It seemed that the Dean had been flattering me only in order to procure unethical behaviour. But the solution to her dilemma was obvious. If she did not want to break the rules, then she should change the rules. I pointed this out.

I am not good at interpreting expressions, and was not familiar with the one that appeared on the Dean's face. 'We can't be seen to allow cheating.'

'Even though we do?'

The meeting left me confused and angry. There were serious matters at stake. What if our research was not accepted because we had a reputation for low academic standards? People could die while cures for diseases were delayed. What if a genetics laboratory hired a person whose qualification had been achieved through cheating, and that person made major errors?

The Dean seemed more concerned with perceptions than with these crucial matters.

I reflected on what it would be like to spend my life living with the Dean. It was a truly terrible thought. The underlying problem was the preoccupation with image. My questionnaire would be ruthless in filtering out women who were concerned with appearance.

4

Gene opened the door with a glass of red wine in his hand. I parked my bicycle in their hallway, took off my backpack and retrieved the Wife Project folder, pulling out Gene's copy of the draft. I had pruned it to sixteen double-sided pages.

'Relax, Don, plenty of time,' he said. 'We're going to have a civilised dinner, and then we'll do the questionnaire. If you're going to be dating, you need dinner practice.'

He was, of course, right. Claudia is an excellent cook and Gene has a vast collection of wines, organised by region, vintage and producer. We went to his 'cellar', which is not actually below ground, where he showed me his recent purchases and we selected a second bottle. We ate with Carl and Eugenie, and I was able to avoid small talk by playing a memory game with Eugenie. She noticed my folder marked 'Wife Project', which I put on the table as soon as I finished dessert.

'Are you getting married, Don?' she asked.

'Correct.'

'Who to?'

I was about to explain, but Claudia sent Eugenie and Carl to their rooms—a good decision, as they did not have the expertise to contribute.

I handed questionnaires to Claudia and Gene. Gene poured port for all of us. I explained that I had followed best practice in questionnaire design, including multiple-choice questions, Likert scales, cross-validation, dummy questions and surrogates. Claudia asked for an example of the last of these.

'Question 35: *Do you eat kidneys?* Correct answer is *(c) occasionally.* Testing for food problems. If you ask directly about food preferences, they say "I eat anything" and then you discover they're vegetarian.'

I am aware that there are many arguments in favour of vegetarianism. However, as I eat meat I considered it would be more convenient if my partner did so also. At this early stage, it seemed logical to specify the ideal solution and review the questionnaire later if necessary.

Claudia and Gene were reading.

Claudia said, 'For an appointment, I'm guessing *(b) a little early.*'

This was patently incorrect, demonstrating that even Claudia, who was a good friend, would be unsuitable as a partner.

'The correct answer is *(c) on time,*' I said. 'Habitual earliness is cumulatively a major waste of time.'

'I'd allow *a little early,*' said Claudia. 'She might be trying hard. That's not a bad thing.'

An interesting point. I made a note to consider it, but pointed out that *(d) a little late* and *(e) very late* were definitely unacceptable.

'I think if a woman describes herself as a brilliant cook she's a bit up herself,' said Claudia. 'Just ask her if she enjoys cooking. Mention that you do too.'

This was exactly the sort of input I was looking

for—subtle nuances of language that I am not conscious of. It struck me that if the respondent was someone like me she would not notice the difference, but it was unreasonable to require that my potential partner share my lack of subtlety.

'No jewellery, no make-up?' said Claudia, correctly predicting the answers to two questions that had been prompted by my recent interaction with the Dean.

'Jewellery isn't always about appearance,' she said. 'If you have to have a question, drop the jewellery one and keep the make-up. But just ask if she wears it daily.'

'Height, weight *and* body mass index.' Gene was skimming ahead. 'Can't you do the calculation yourself?'

'That's the purpose of the question,' I said. 'Checking they can do basic arithmetic. I don't want a partner who's mathematically illiterate.'

'I thought you might have wanted to get an idea of what they look like,' said Gene.

'There's a question on fitness,' I said.

'I was thinking about sex,' said Gene.

'Just for a change,' said Claudia, an odd statement as Gene talks constantly about sex. But he had made a good point.

'I'll add a question on HIV and herpes.'

'Stop,' said Claudia. 'You're being way too picky.'

I began to explain that an incurable sexually transmitted disease was a severe negative but Claudia interrupted.

'About everything.'

It was an understandable response. But my strategy was to minimise the chance of making a type-one error—wasting time on an unsuitable choice. Inevitably, that increased the risk of a type-two error—rejecting a suitable person. But this was an acceptable risk as I was dealing with a very large population.

Gene's turn: 'Non-smoking, fair enough. But what's the right answer on drinking?'

'Zero.'

'Hang on. You drink.' He pointed to my port glass, which he had topped up a few moments earlier. 'You drink quite a bit.'

I explained that I was expecting some improvement for myself from the project.

We continued in this manner and I received some excellent feedback. I did feel that the questionnaire was now less discriminating, but was still confident it would eliminate most if not all of the women who had given me problems in the past. Apricot Ice-cream Woman would have failed at least five questions.

My plan was to advertise on traditional dating sites, but to provide a link to the questionnaire in addition to posting the usual insufficiently discriminating information about height, profession and whether I enjoyed long walks on the beach.

Gene and Claudia suggested that I also undertake some face-to-face dating to practise my social skills. I could see the value of validating the questionnaires in the field, so, while I waited for online responses to arrive, I printed some questionnaires and returned to the dating process that I thought I had abandoned forever.

I began by registering with Table for Eight, run by a commercial matchmaking organisation. After an undoubtedly unsound preliminary matching process, based on manifestly inadequate data, four men and four women,

31

including me, were provided with details of a city restaurant at which a booking had been made. I packed four questionnaires and arrived precisely at 8.00 p.m. *Only one woman was there!* The other three were late. It was a stunning validation of the advantages of field work. These women may well have answered *(b) a little early* or *(c) on time*, but their actual behaviour demonstrated otherwise. I decided to temporarily allow *(d) a little late*, on the basis that a single occasion might not be representative of their overall performance. I could hear Claudia saying, 'Don, everyone's late occasionally.'

There were also two men seated at the table. We shook hands. It struck me that this was equivalent to bowing prior to a martial arts bout.

I assessed my competition. The man who had introduced himself as Craig was about my own age, but overweight, in a white business shirt that was too tight for him. He had a moustache, and his teeth were poorly maintained. The second, Danny, was probably a few years younger than me, and appeared to be in good health. He wore a white t-shirt. He had tattoos on his arms and his black hair contained some form of cosmetic additive.

The on-time woman's name was Olivia, and she initially (and logically) divided her attention among the three men. She told us she was an anthropologist. Danny confused it with an archaeologist and then Craig made a racist joke about pygmies. It was obvious, even to me, that Olivia was unimpressed by these responses, and I enjoyed a rare moment of not feeling like the least socially competent person in the room. Olivia turned to me, and I had just responded to her question about my job when we were interrupted by the arrival of the fourth man, who introduced himself as Gerry, a lawyer, and two women, Sharon and Maria, who were, respectively, an accountant and a nurse. It was a hot night, and Maria had chosen a dress with the twin advantages of coolness and overt sexual display. Sharon was wearing the conventional corporate uniform of trousers and jacket. I guessed that they were both about my age.

Olivia resumed talking to me while the others engaged in small talk—an extraordinary waste of time when a major life decision was at stake. On Claudia's advice, I had memorised the questionnaire. She thought that asking questions directly from the forms could create the wrong 'dynamic' and that I should attempt to incorporate them subtly into conversation. Subtlety, I had reminded her, is not my strength. She suggested that I not ask about sexually transmitted diseases and make my own estimates of weight, height and body mass index. I estimated Olivia's BMI at nineteen: slim, but no signs of anorexia. I estimated Sharon the Accountant's at twenty-three, and Maria the Nurse's at twenty-eight. The recommended healthy maximum is twenty-five.

Rather than ask about IQ, I decided to make an estimate based on Olivia's responses to questions about the historical impact of variations in susceptibility to syphilis across native South American populations. We had a fascinating conversation, and I felt that the topic might even allow me to slip in the sexually transmitted diseases question. Her IQ was definitely above the required minimum. Gerry the Lawyer offered a few comments that I think were meant to be jokes, but eventually left us to continue uninterrupted.

At this point, the missing woman arrived, *twenty-eight minutes late*. While Olivia was distracted, I took the opportunity to record the data I had acquired so far on three of the four questionnaires in my lap. I did not waste paper on the most recent arrival, as she announced that she was 'always late'. This did not seem to concern Gerry the Lawyer, who presumably billed by the six-minute interval, and should consequently have considered time to be of great value. He obviously valued sex more highly as his conversation began to resemble that of Gene.

With the arrival of Late Woman, the waiter appeared with menus. Olivia scanned hers then asked, 'The pumpkin soup, is it made with vegetable stock?'

I did not hear the answer. The question provided the critical information. Vegetarian.

She may have noted my expression of disappointment. 'I'm Hindu.'

I had previously deduced that Olivia was probably Indian from her sari and physical attributes. I was not sure whether the term 'Hindu' was being used as a genuine statement of religious belief or as an indicator of cultural heritage. I had been reprimanded for failing to make this distinction in the past.

'Do you eat ice-cream?' I asked. The question seemed appropriate after the vegetarian statement. Very neat.

'Oh yes, I am not vegan. As long as it is not made with eggs.'

This was not getting any better.

'Do you have a favourite flavour?'

'Pistachio. Very definitely pistachio.' She smiled.

Maria and Danny had stepped outside for a cigarette. With three women eliminated, including Late Woman, my task was almost complete.

My lambs' brains arrived, and I cut one in half, exposing the internal structure. I tapped Sharon, who was engaged in conversation with Craig the Racist, and pointed it out to her. 'Do you like brains?'

Four down, job complete. I continued my conversation with Olivia, who was excellent company, and even ordered an additional drink after the others had departed in the pairs that they had formed. We stayed, talking, until we were the last people in the restaurant. As I put the questionnaires in my backpack, Olivia gave me her contact information, which I wrote down in order not to be rude. Then we went our separate ways.

Cycling home, I reflected on the dinner. It had been a grossly inefficient method of selection, but the questionnaire had been of significant value. Without the questions it prompted, I would undoubtedly have attempted a second date with Olivia, who was an interesting and nice person. Perhaps we would have gone on a third and fourth and fifth date, then one day, when all of the desserts at the restaurant contained egg, we would have crossed the road to the ice-cream parlour, and discovered they had no egg-free pistachio. It was better to find out before we made an investment in the relationship.

5

I stood inside the entrance of a suburban house that reminded me of my parents' brick veneer residence in Shepparton. I had resolved never to attend another singles party, but the questionnaire allowed me to avoid the agony of unstructured social interaction with strangers.

As the female guests arrived, I gave each a questionnaire to complete at their convenience and return to me either at the party or by mail. The host, a woman, initially invited me to join the crowd in the living room, but I explained my strategy and she left me alone. After two hours, a woman of about thirty-five, estimated BMI twenty-one, returned from the living room, holding two glasses of sparkling wine. In her other hand was a questionnaire.

She passed me a glass. 'I thought you might be thirsty,' she said in an attractive French accent.

I was not thirsty, but I was pleased to be offered alcohol. I had decided that I would not give up drinking unless I found a non-drinking partner. And, after some self-analysis, I had concluded that *(c) moderately* was an acceptable answer to the drinking question and made a note to update the questionnaire.

'Thank you.' I hoped she would give me the questionnaire and that it might, improbably, signal the end of my quest. She was extremely attractive, and her gesture with the wine indicated a high level of consideration not exhibited by any of the other guests or the host.

'You are a researcher, am I right?' She tapped the questionnaire.

'Correct.'

'Me, also,' she said. 'There are not many academics here tonight.' Although it is dangerous to draw conclusions based on manner and conversation topics, my assessment of the guests was consistent with this observation.

'I'm Fabienne,' she said, and extended her free hand, which I shook, careful to apply the recommended level of firmness. 'This is terrible wine, no?'

I agreed. It was a carbonated sweet wine, acceptable only because of its alcohol content.

'You think we should go to a wine bar and get something better?' she asked.

I shook my head. The poor wine quality was annoying but not critical.

Fabienne took a deep breath. 'Listen. I have drunk two glasses of wine, I have not had sex for six weeks, and I would rather wait six more than try anyone else here. Now, can I buy you a drink?'

It was a very kind offer. But it was still early in the evening. I said, 'More guests are expected. You may find someone suitable if you wait.'

Fabienne gave me her questionnaire and said, 'I presume you will be notifying the winners in due course.' I told her that I would. When she had gone, I quickly checked her questionnaire. Predictably, she failed in a number of dimensions. It was disappointing.

* * *

My final non-internet option was speed dating, an approach I had not previously tried.

The venue was a function room in a hotel. At my insistence, the convenor disclosed the *actual* start time, and I waited in the bar to avoid aimless interaction until then. When I returned, I took the last remaining seat at a long table, opposite a person labelled Frances, aged approximately fifty, BMI approximately twenty-eight, not conventionally attractive.

The convenor rang a bell and my three minutes with Frances commenced.

I pulled out my questionnaire and scribbled her name on it—there was no time for subtlety under these circumstances.

'I've sequenced the questions for maximum speed of elimination,' I explained. 'I believe I can eliminate most women in less than forty seconds. Then you can choose the topic of discussion for the remaining time.'

'But then it won't matter,' said Frances. 'I'll have been eliminated.'

'Only as a potential partner. We may still be able to have an interesting discussion.'

'But I'll have been eliminated.'

I nodded. 'Do you smoke?'

'Occasionally,' she said.

I put the questionnaire away.

'Excellent.' I was pleased that my question sequencing was working so well. We could have wasted time talking about ice-cream flavours and make-up only to find that she smoked. Needless to say, smoking was not negotiable. 'No more questions. What would you like to discuss?'

Disappointingly, Frances was not interested in further conversation after I had determined that we were not compatible. This turned out to be the pattern for the remainder of the event.

These personal interactions were, of course, secondary. I was relying on the internet, and completed questionnaires began to flow in shortly after my initial postings. I scheduled a review meeting in my office with Gene.

'How many responses?' he asked.

'Two hundred and seventy-nine.'

He was clearly impressed. I did not tell him that the quality of responses varied widely, with many questionnaires only partially completed.

'No photos?'

Many women had included photos, but I had suppressed them in the database display to allow space for more important data.

'Let's see the photos,' Gene said.

I modified the settings to show photos, and Gene scanned a few before double-clicking on one. The resolution was impressive. It seemed that he approved, but a quick check of the data showed that the candidate was totally unsuitable. I took the mouse back and deleted her. Gene protested.

'Wha wha wha? What're you doing?'

'She believes in astrology and homeopathy. And she calculated her BMI incorrectly.'

'What was it?'

'Twenty-three point five.'

'Nice. Can you undelete her?'

'She's totally unsuitable.'

'How many *are* suitable?' asked Gene, finally getting to the point.

'So far, zero. The questionnaire is an excellent filter.'

'You don't think you're setting the bar just a tiny bit high?'

I pointed out that I was collecting data to support life's most critical decision. Compromise would be totally inappropriate.

'You always have to compromise,' Gene said. An incredible statement and totally untrue in his case.

'You found the perfect wife. Highly intelligent, extremely beautiful and she lets you have sex with other women.'

Gene suggested that I not congratulate Claudia in person for her tolerance, and asked me to repeat the number of questionnaires that had been completed. The actual total was greater than the number I had told him, as I had not included the paper questionnaires. Three hundred and four.

'Give me your list,' said Gene. 'I'll pick a few out for you.'

'None of them meet the criteria. They all have some fault.'

'Treat it as practice.'

He did have a point. I had thought a few times about Olivia the Indian Anthropologist, and considered the implications of living with a Hindu vegetarian with a strong ice-cream preference. Only reminding myself that I should wait until an exact match turned up had stopped me from contacting her. I had even rechecked the questionnaire from Fabienne the Sex-Deprived Researcher.

I emailed the spreadsheet to Gene.

'No smokers.'

'Okay,' said Gene, 'but you have to ask them out. To dinner. At a proper restaurant.'

Gene could probably tell that I was not excited by the prospect. He cleverly addressed the problem by proposing an even less acceptable alternative.

'There's always the faculty ball.'

'Restaurant.'

Gene smiled as if to compensate for my lack of enthusiasm. 'It's easy. "How about we do dinner tonight?" Say it after me.'

'How about we do dinner tonight?' I repeated.

'See, that wasn't so hard. Make only positive comments about their appearance. Pay for the meal. Do not mention sex.' Gene walked to the door, then turned back. 'What about the paper ones?'

I gave him my questionnaires from Table for Eight, the singles party and, at his insistence, even the partially completed ones from the speed dating. Now it was out of my hands.

6

Approximately two hours after Gene left my office with the completed Wife Project questionnaires, there was a knock on the door. I was weighing student essays, an activity that is not forbidden, but I suspect only because nobody is aware that I am doing it. It was part of a project to reduce the effort of assessment, by looking for easily measured parameters such as the inclusion of a table of contents, or a typed versus handwritten cover sheet, factors which might provide as good an indication of quality as the tedious process of reading the entire assignment.

I slipped the scales under my desk as the door opened and looked up to see a woman I did not recognise standing in the doorway. I estimated her age as thirty and her body mass index at twenty.

'Professor Tillman?'

As my name is on the door, this was not a particularly astute question.

'Correct.'

'Professor Barrow suggested I see you.'

I was amazed at Gene's efficiency, and looked at the woman more carefully as she approached my desk. There were no obvious signs of unsuitability. I did not detect any make-up. Her body shape and skin tone were consistent with health and fitness. She wore glasses with heavy frames that revived bad memories of Apricot Ice-cream Woman, a long black t-shirt that was torn in several places, and a black belt with metal chains. It was lucky that the jewellery question had been deleted because she was wearing big metal earrings and an interesting pendant around her neck.

Although I am usually oblivious to dress, hers seemed incompatible with my expectation of a highly qualified academic or professional and with the summer weather. I could only guess that she was self-employed or on holiday and, freed from workplace rules, had chosen her clothes randomly. I could relate to this.

There had been quite a long gap since either of us spoke and I realised it must be my turn. I looked up from the pendant and remembered Gene's instructions.

'How about we do dinner tonight?'

She seemed surprised at my question then replied, 'Yeah, right. How about we do dinner? How about Le Gavroche and you're paying?'

'Excellent. I'll make a reservation for 8.00 p.m.'

'You're kidding.'

It was an odd response. Why would I make a confusing joke with someone I barely knew?

'No. Is 8.00 p.m. tonight acceptable?'

'Let me get this straight. You're offering to buy me dinner at Le Gavroche tonight?'

Coming on top of the question about my name, I was beginning to think that this woman was what Gene would call 'not the sharpest tool in the shed'. I considered backing out, or at least employing some delaying tactic until I could check her questionnaire, but could not think of any socially acceptable way to do this, so

I just confirmed that she had interpreted my offer correctly. She turned and left and I realised that I did not even know her name.

I called Gene immediately. There seemed to be some confusion on his part at first, followed by mirth. Perhaps he had not expected me to handle the candidate so effectively.

'Her name's Rosie,' he said. 'And that's all I'm telling you. Have fun. And remember what I said about sex.'

Gene's failure to provide me with more details was unfortunate, because a problem arose. Le Gavroche did not have a table available at the agreed time. I tried to locate Rosie's profile on my computer, and for once the photos were useful. The woman who had come to my office did not look like any candidate whose name began with 'R'. She must have been one of the paper responses. Gene had left and his phone was off.

I was forced to take action that was not strictly illegal, but doubtless immoral. I justified it on the basis that it would be more immoral to fail to meet my commitment to Rosie. Le Gavroche's online reservation system had a facility for VIPs and I made a reservation under the name of the Dean after logging on using relatively unsophisticated hacking software.

I arrived at 7.59 p.m. The restaurant was located in a major hotel. I chained my bike in the foyer, as it was raining heavily outside. Fortunately it was not cold and my Gore-Tex jacket had done an excellent job of protecting me. My t-shirt was not even damp underneath.

A man in uniform approached me. He pointed towards the bike, but I spoke before he had a chance to complain.

'My name is Professor Lawrence and I interacted with your reservation system at 5.11 p.m.'

It appeared that the official did not know the Dean, or assumed that I was another Professor Lawrence, because he just checked a clipboard and nodded. I was impressed with the efficiency, though it was now 8.01 p.m. and Rosie was not there. Perhaps she was *(b) a little early* and already seated.

But then a problem arose.

'I'm sorry, sir, but we have a dress code,' said the official.

I knew about this. It was in bold type on the website: Gentlemen are required to wear a jacket.

'No jacket, no food, correct?'

'More or less, sir.'

What can I say about this sort of rule? I was prepared to keep my jacket on throughout the meal. The restaurant would presumably be air-conditioned to a temperature compatible with the requirement.

I continued towards the restaurant entrance, but the official blocked my path. 'I'm sorry. Perhaps I wasn't clear. You need to wear a jacket.'

'I'm wearing a jacket.'

'I'm afraid we require something a little more formal, sir.'

The hotel employee indicated his own jacket as an example. In defence of what followed, I submit the Oxford English Dictionary (Compact, 2nd Edition) definition of 'jacket': *1(a) An outer garment for the upper part of the body.*

I also note that the word 'jacket' appears on the care instructions for my relatively new and perfectly clean

Gore-Tex 'jacket'. But it seemed his definition of jacket was limited to 'conventional suit jacket'.

'We would be happy to lend you one, sir. In this style.'

'You have a supply of jackets? In every possible size?' I did not add that the need to maintain such an inventory was surely evidence of their failure to communicate the rule clearly, and that it would be more efficient to improve their wording or abandon the rule altogether. Nor did I mention that the cost of jacket purchase and cleaning must add to the price of their meals. Did their customers know that they were subsidising a jacket warehouse?

'I wouldn't know about that, sir,' he said. 'Let me organise a jacket.'

Needless to say I was uncomfortable at the idea of being re-dressed in an item of public clothing of dubious cleanliness. For a few moments, I was overwhelmed by the sheer unreasonableness of the situation. I was already under stress, preparing for the second encounter with a woman who might become my life partner. And now the institution that I was paying to supply us with a meal—the *service provider* who should surely be doing everything possible to make me comfortable—was putting arbitrary obstacles in my way. My Gore-Tex jacket, the high-technology garment that had protected me in rain and snowstorms, was being irrationally, unfairly and obstructively contrasted with the official's essentially decorative woollen equivalent. I had paid $1015 for it, including $120 extra for the customised reflective yellow. I outlined my argument.

'My jacket is superior to yours by all reasonable criteria: impermeability to water, visibility in low light, storage capacity.' I unzipped the jacket to display the internal pockets and continued, 'Speed of drying, resistance to food stains, hood…'

The official was still showing no interpretable reaction, although I had almost certainly raised my voice.

'Vastly superior tensile strength…'

To illustrate this last point, I took the lapel of the employee's jacket in my hands. I obviously had no intention of tearing it but I was suddenly grabbed from behind by an unknown person who attempted to throw me to the ground. I automatically responded with a safe, low-impact throw to disable him without dislodging my glasses. The term 'low impact' applies to a martial arts practitioner who knows how to fall. This person did not, and landed heavily.

I turned to see him—he was large and angry. In order to prevent further violence, I was forced to sit on him.

'Get the fuck off me. I'll fucking kill you,' he said.

On that basis, it seemed illogical to grant his request. At that point another man arrived and tried to drag me off. Concerned that Thug Number One would carry out his threat, I had no choice but to disable Thug Number Two as well. No one was seriously hurt, but it was a very awkward social situation, and I could feel my mind shutting down.

Fortunately, Rosie arrived.

Jacket Man said, apparently in surprise, 'Rosie!'

Obviously he knew her. She looked from him to me and said, 'Professor Tillman—Don—what's going on?'

'You're late,' I said. 'We have a social problem.'

'You know this man?' said Jacket Man to Rosie.

'What do you think, I guessed his name?' Rosie sounded belligerent and I thought this might not be the best approach. Surely we should seek to apologise and leave. I was assuming we would not now be eating in the restaurant.

A small crowd had gathered and it occurred to me that another thug might arrive, so I needed to work out a way of freeing up a hand without releasing the original two thugs. In the process one poked the other in the eye, and their anger levels increased noticeably. Jacket Man added, 'He assaulted Jason.'

Rosie replied, 'Right. Poor Jason. Always the victim.' I could now see her. She was wearing a black dress without decoration, thick-soled black boots and vast amounts of silver jewellery on her arms. Her red hair was spiky like some new species of cactus. I have heard the word 'stunning' used to describe women, but this was the first time I had actually been stunned by one. It was not just the costume or the jewellery or any individual characteristic of Rosie herself: it was their combined effect. I was not sure if her appearance would be regarded as conventionally beautiful or even acceptable to the restaurant that had rejected my jacket. 'Stunning' was the perfect word for it. But what she did was even more stunning. She took her phone from her bag and pointed it at us. It flashed twice. Jacket Man moved to take it from her.

'Don't you fucking think about it,' Rosie said. 'I'm going to have so much fun with these photos that these guys will never stand on a door again. *Professor teaches bouncers a lesson.*'

As Rosie was speaking, a man in a chef's hat arrived. He spoke briefly to Jacket Man and Rosie and, on the basis that we would be permitted to leave without further harassment, Rosie asked me to release my assailants. We all got to our feet, and, in keeping with tradition, I bowed, then extended my hand to the two men, who I had concluded must be security personnel. They had only been doing what they were paid for, and had risked injury in the course of their duties. It seemed that they were not expecting the formalities, but then one of them laughed and shook my hand, and the other followed his example. It was a good resolution, but I no longer felt like eating at the restaurant.

I collected my bike and we walked into the street. I expected Rosie to be angry about the incident, but she was smiling. I asked her how she knew Jacket Man.

'I used to work there.'

'You selected the restaurant because you were familiar with it?'

'You could say that. I wanted to stick it up them.' She began to laugh. 'Maybe not quite that much.'

I told her that her solution was brilliant.

'I work in a bar,' she said. 'Not just a bar—the Marquess of Queensbury. I deal with jerks for a living.'

I pointed out that if she had arrived on schedule she could have used her social skills and the violence would have been unnecessary.

'Glad I was late then. That was judo, right?'

'Aikido.' As we crossed the road, I switched my bike to my other side, between Rosie and me. 'I'm also proficient in karate, but aikido was more appropriate.'

'No way. It takes forever to learn that stuff, doesn't it?'

'I commenced at seven.'

'How often do you train?'

'Three times per week, except in the case of illness, public holidays and travel to overseas conferences.'

'What got you into it?' asked Rosie.

I pointed to my glasses.

'Revenge of the nerds,' she said.

'This is the first time I've required it for self-defence since I was at school. It's primarily for fitness.' I had relaxed a little, and Rosie had provided an opportunity to slip in a question from the Wife Project questionnaire. 'Do you exercise regularly?'

'Depends what you call regularly.' She laughed. 'I'm the unfittest person on the planet.'

'Exercise is extremely important for maintaining health.'

'So my dad tells me. He's a personal trainer. Constantly on my case. He gave me a gym membership for my birthday. At his gym. He has this idea we should train for a triathlon together.'

'Surely you should follow his advice,' I said.

'Fuck, I'm almost thirty. I don't need my dad telling me what to do.' She changed the subject. 'Listen, I'm starving. Let's get a pizza.'

I was not prepared to consider a restaurant after the preceding trauma. I told her that I intended to revert to my original plan for the evening, which was cooking at home.

'Got enough for two?' she asked. 'You still owe me dinner.'

This was true but there had been too many unscheduled events already in my day.

'Come on. I won't criticise your cooking. I can't cook to save my life.'

I was not concerned about my cooking being criticised. But the lack of cooking skills on her part was the third fault *so far* in terms of the Wife Project questionnaire, after the late arrival and the lack of fitness. There was almost certainly a fourth: it was unlikely that her profession as waitress and barmaid was consistent with the specified intellectual level. There was no point in continuing.

Before I could protest, Rosie had flagged down a minivan taxi with sufficient capacity for my bike.

'Where do you live?' she asked.

7

'Wow, Mr Neat. How come there are no pictures on the walls?'

I had not had visitors since Daphne moved out of the building. I knew that I only needed to put out an extra plate and cutlery. But it had already been a stressful evening, and the adrenaline-induced euphoria that had immediately followed the Jacket Incident had evaporated, at least on my part. Rosie seemed to be in a permanently manic state.

We were in the living area, which adjoins the kitchen.

'Because after a while I would stop noticing them. The human brain is wired to focus on differences in its environment—so it can rapidly discern a predator. If I installed pictures or other decorative objects, I would notice them for a few days and then my brain would ignore them. If I want to see art, I go to the gallery. The paintings there are of higher quality, and the total expenditure over time is less than the purchase price of cheap posters.' In fact, I had not been to an art gallery since the tenth of May, three years before. But this information would weaken my argument and I saw no reason to share it with Rosie and open up other aspects of my personal life to interrogation.

Rosie had moved on and was now examining my CD collection. The investigation was becoming annoying. Dinner was already late.

'You really love Bach,' she said. This was a reasonable deduction, as my CD collection consists only of the works of that composer. But it was not correct.

'I decided to focus on Bach after reading *Gödel, Escher, Bach* by Douglas Hofstadter. Unfortunately I haven't made much progress. I don't think my brain works fast enough to decode the patterns in the music.'

'You don't listen to it for fun?'

This was beginning to sound like the initial dinner conversations with Daphne and I didn't answer.

'You've got an iPhone?' she said.

'Of course, but I don't use it for music. I download podcasts.'

'Let me guess—on genetics.'

'Science in general.'

I moved to the kitchen to begin dinner preparation and Rosie followed me, stopping to look at my whiteboard schedule.

'Wow,' she said, again. This reaction was becoming predictable. I wondered what her response to DNA or evolution would be.

I commenced retrieval of vegetables and herbs from the refrigerator. 'Let me help,' she said. 'I can chop or something.' The implication was that chopping could be done by an inexperienced person unfamiliar with the recipe. After her comment that she was unable to cook even in a life-threatening situation, I had visions of huge chunks of leek and fragments of herbs too fine to sieve out.

'No assistance is required,' I said. 'I recommend reading a book.'

I watched Rosie walk to the bookshelf, briefly peruse the contents, then walk away. Perhaps she used IBM rather than Mac software, although many of the manuals applied to both.

The sound system has an iPod port that I use to play podcasts while I cook. Rosie plugged in her phone, and music emanated from the speakers. It was not loud, but I was certain that if I had put on a podcast without asking permission when visiting someone's house, I would have been accused of a social error. *Very* certain, as I had made this exact mistake at a dinner party four years and sixty-seven days ago.

Rosie continued her exploration, like an animal in a new environment, which of course was what she was. She opened the blinds and raised them, creating some dust. I consider myself fastidious in my cleaning, but I do not need to open the blinds and there must have been dust in places not reachable without doing so. Behind the blinds are doors, and Rosie released the bolts and opened them.

I was feeling very uncomfortable at this violation of my personal environment. I tried to concentrate on food preparation as Rosie stepped out of sight onto the balcony. I could hear her dragging the two big pot plants, which presumably were dead after all these years. I put the herb and vegetable mixture in the large saucepan with the water, salt, rice wine vinegar, mirin, orange peel and coriander seeds.

'I don't know what you're cooking,' Rosie called out, 'but I'm basically vegetarian.'

Vegetarian! I had already commenced cooking! Based on ingredients purchased on the assumption that I would be eating alone. And what did 'basically' mean—did it imply some limited level of flexibility, like my colleague Esther, who admitted, only under rigorous questioning, that she would eat pork if necessary to survive?

Vegetarians and vegans can be incredibly annoying. Gene has a joke: 'How can you tell if someone is a vegan? Just wait ten minutes and they'll tell you.' If this were so, it would not be so much of a problem. No! Vegetarians arrive for dinner and then say, 'I don't eat meat.' *This was the second time.* The Pig's Trotter Disaster happened six years ago, when Gene suggested that I invite a woman to dinner at my apartment. He argued that my cooking expertise would make me more desirable and I would not have to deal with the pressure of a restaurant environment. 'And you can drink as much as you like and stagger to the bedroom.'

The woman's name was Bethany, and her internet profile did *not* mention vegetarianism. Realising that the quality of the meal would be critical, I borrowed a recently published book of 'nose to tail' recipes from the library, and planned a multi-course meal featuring various parts of the animal: brains, tongue, mesentery, pancreas, kidneys, etc.

Bethany arrived on time and seemed very pleasant. We had a glass of wine, and then things went downhill. We started with fried pig's trotter, which had been quite complex to prepare, and Bethany ate very little of hers.

'I'm not big on pig's trotters,' she said. This was not entirely unreasonable: we all have preferences and perhaps she was concerned about fat and cholesterol. But when I outlined the courses to follow, she declared herself to be a vegetarian. Unbelievable!

She offered to buy dinner at a restaurant but, having spent so much time in preparation, I did not want to abandon the food. I ate alone and did not see Bethany again.

Now Rosie. In this case it might be a good thing. Rosie could leave and life would return to normal. She had obviously not filled in the questionnaire honestly, or Gene had made an error. Or possibly he had selected her for her high level of sexual attractiveness, imposing his own preferences on me.

Rosie came back inside, looking at me, as if expecting a response. 'Seafood is okay,' she said. 'If it's sustainable.'

I had mixed feelings. It is always satisfying to have the solution to a problem, but now Rosie would be staying for dinner. I walked to the bathroom, and Rosie followed. I picked up the lobster from the bath, where it had been crawling around.

'Oh shit,' said Rosie.

'You don't like lobster?' I carried it back to the kitchen.

'I love lobster but...'

The problem was now obvious and I could sympathise.

'You find the killing process unpleasant. Agreed.'

I put the lobster in the freezer, and explained to Rosie that I had researched lobster-execution methods, and the freezer method was considered the most humane. I gave her a website reference.

While the lobster died, Rosie continued her sniffing around. She opened the pantry and seemed impressed with its level of organisation: one shelf for each day of the week, plus storage spaces for common resources, alcohol, breakfast, etc, and stock data on the back of the door.

'You want to come and sort out my place?'

'You want to implement the Standardised Meal System?' Despite its substantial advantages, most people consider it odd.

'Just cleaning out the refrigerator would do,' she said. 'I'm guessing you want Tuesday ingredients?'

I informed her that, as today was Tuesday, no guessing was required.

She handed me the nori sheets and bonito flakes. I requested macadamia nut oil, sea salt and the pepper grinder from the common resources area.

'Chinese rice wine,' I added. 'Filed under alcohol.'

'Naturally,' said Rosie.

She passed me the wine, then began looking at the other bottles in the alcohol section. I purchase my wine in half-bottles.

'So, you cook this same meal every Tuesday, right?'

'Correct.' I listed the eight major advantages of the Standardised Meal System.

1. No need to accumulate recipe books.
2. Standard shopping list—hence very efficient shopping.
3. Almost zero waste—nothing in the refrigerator or pantry unless required for one of the recipes.
4. Diet planned and nutritionally balanced in advance.

5.   No time wasted wondering what to cook.
6.   No mistakes, no unpleasant surprises.
7.   Excellent food, superior to most restaurants at a much lower price (see point 3).
8.   Minimal cognitive load required.

'Cognitive load?'

'The cooking procedures are in my cerebellum—virtually no conscious effort is required.'

'Like riding a bike.'

'Correct.'

'You can make lobster whatever without thinking?'

'Lobster, mango and avocado salad with wasabi-coated flying fish roe and crispy seaweed and deep-fried leek garnish. Correct. My current project is quail-boning. It still requires conscious effort.'

Rosie was laughing. It brought back memories of school days. Good ones.

As I retrieved additional ingredients for the dressing from the refrigerator, Rosie brushed past me with two half-bottles of chablis and put them in the freezer with the lobster.

'Our dinner seems to have stopped moving.'

'Further time is required to be certain of death,' I said. 'Unfortunately, the Jacket Incident has disrupted the preparation schedule. All times will need to be recalculated.' I realised at this point that I should have put the lobster in the freezer as soon as we arrived home, but my brain had been overloaded by the problems created by Rosie's presence. I went to the whiteboard and started writing up revised preparation times. Rosie was examining the ingredients.

'You were going to eat all this by yourself?'

I had not revised the Standardised Meal System since Daphne's departure, and now ate the lobster salad by myself on Tuesdays, deleting the wine to compensate for the additional calorie intake.

'The quantity is sufficient for two,' I said. 'The recipe can't be scaled down. It's infeasible to purchase a fraction of a live lobster.' I had intended the last part as a mild joke, and Rosie reacted by laughing. I had another unexpected moment of feeling good as I continued recalculating times.

Rosie interrupted again. 'If you were on your usual schedule, what time would it be now?'

'6.38 p.m.'

The clock on the oven showed 9.09 p.m. Rosie located the controls and started adjusting the time. I realised what she was doing. A perfect solution. When she was finished, it showed 6.38 p.m. No recalculations required. I congratulated her on her thinking. 'You've created a new time zone. Dinner will be ready at 8.55 p.m.—Rosie time.'

'Beats doing the maths,' she said.

Her observation gave me an opportunity for another Wife Project question. 'Do you find mathematics difficult?'

She laughed. 'It's only the single hardest part of what I do. Drives me nuts.'

If the simple arithmetic of bar and restaurant bills was beyond her, it was hard to imagine how we could have meaningful discussions.

'Where do you hide the corkscrew?' she asked.

'Wine is not scheduled for Tuesdays.'

'Fuck that,' said Rosie.

There was a certain logic underlying Rosie's response. I would only be eating a single serve of dinner. It was the final step in the abandonment of the evening's schedule.

I announced the change. 'Time has been redefined. Previous rules no longer apply. Alcohol is hereby declared mandatory in the Rosie Time Zone.'

8

As I completed dinner preparation, Rosie set the table—
not the conventional dining table in the living room,
but a makeshift table on the balcony, created by taking a whiteboard from the kitchen wall and placing it
on top of the two big plant pots, from which the dead
plants had been removed. A white sheet from the linen
cupboard had been added in the role of tablecloth. Silver
cutlery—a housewarming gift from my parents that
had never been used—and the decorative wine glasses
were on the table. She was destroying my apartment!

It had never occurred to me to eat on the balcony.
The rain from early in the evening had cleared when
I came outside with the food, and I estimated the tem-
perature at twenty-two degrees.

'Do we have to eat right away?' asked Rosie, an odd
question, since she had claimed that she was starving
some hours ago.

'No, it won't get cold. It's already cold.' I was conscious of sounding awkward. 'Is there some reason to
delay?'

'The city lights. The view's amazing.'

'Unfortunately it's static. Once you've examined it,
there's no reason to look again. Like paintings.'

'But it changes all the time. What about in the early

morning? Or when it rains? What about coming up here just to sit?'

I had no answer that was likely to satisfy her. I had seen the view when I bought the apartment. It did not change much in different conditions. And the only times I just sat were when I was waiting for an appointment or if I was reflecting on a problem, in which case interesting surroundings would be a distraction.

I moved into the space beside Rosie and refilled her glass. She smiled. She was almost certainly wearing lipstick.

I attempt to produce a standard, repeatable meal, but obviously ingredients vary in their quality from week to week. Today's seemed to be of unusually high standard. The lobster salad had never tasted so good.

I remembered the basic rule of asking a woman to talk about herself. Rosie had already raised the topic of dealing with difficult customers in a bar, so I asked her to elaborate. This was an excellent move. She had a number of hilarious stories, and I noted some interpersonal techniques for possible future use.

We finished the lobster. Then Rosie opened her bag and pulled out a pack of cigarettes! How can I convey my horror? Smoking is not only unhealthy in itself, and dangerous to others in the vicinity. It is a clear indication of an irrational approach to life. There was a good reason for it being the first item on my questionnaire.

Rosie must have noticed my shock. 'Relax. We're outside.'

There was no point in arguing. I would not be seeing her again after tonight. The lighter flamed and she held it to the cigarette between her artificially red lips.

'Anyhow, I've got a genetics question,' she said.

'Proceed.' I was back in the world I knew.

'Someone told me you can tell if a person's monogamous by the size of their testicles.'

The sexual aspects of biology regularly feature in the popular press, so this was not as stupid a statement as it might appear, although it embodied a typical misconception. It occurred to me that it could be some sort of code for a sexual advance, but I decided to play safe and respond to the question literally.

'Ridiculous,' I said.

Rosie seemed very pleased with my answer.

'You're a star,' she said. 'I've just won a bet.'

I proceeded to elaborate and noted that Rosie's expression of satisfaction faded. I guessed that she had oversimplified her question and that my more detailed explanation was in fact what she had been told.

'There may be some correlation at the individual level, but the rule applies to species. Homo sapiens are basically monogamous, but tactically unfaithful. Males benefit from impregnating as many females as possible, but are able to support only one set of offspring. Females seek maximum-quality genes for their children plus a male to support them.'

I was just settling into the familiar role of lecturer when Rosie interrupted.

'What about the testicles?'

'Bigger testicles produce more semen. Monogamous species require only sufficient for their mate. Humans need extra to take advantage of random opportunities and to attack the sperm of recent intruders.'

'Nice,' said Rosie.

'Not really. The behaviour evolved in the ancestral environment. The modern world requires additional rules.'

'Yeah,' said Rosie. 'Like being there for your kids.'

'Correct. But instincts are incredibly powerful.'

'Tell me about it,' said Rosie.

I began to explain. 'Instinct is an expression of—'

'Rhetorical question,' said Rosie. 'I've lived it. My mother went gene shopping at her medical graduation party.'

'These behaviours are unconscious. People don't deliberately—'

'I get that.'

I doubted it. Non-professionals frequently misinterpret the findings of evolutionary psychology. But the story was interesting.

'You're saying your mother engaged in unprotected sex outside her primary relationship?'

'With some other student,' replied Rosie. 'While she was dating my'—at this point Rosie raised her hands and made a downwards movement, twice, with the index and middle fingers of both hands—'father. My real dad's a doctor. I just don't know which one. Really, really pisses me off.'

I was fascinated by the hand movements and silent for a while as I tried to work them out. Were they a sign of distress at not knowing who her father was? If so, it was not one I was familiar with. And why had she chosen to punctuate her speech at that point...of course! Punctuation!

'Quotation marks,' I said aloud as the idea hit me.

'What?'

'You made quotation marks around "father" to draw attention to the fact that the word should not be interpreted in the usual way. Very clever.'

'Well, there you go,' she said. 'And there I was thinking you were reflecting on my minor problem with my whole fucking life. And might have something intelligent to say.'

I corrected her. 'It's not a minor problem at all!' I pointed my finger in the air to indicate an exclamation mark. 'You should insist on being informed.' I stabbed the same finger to indicate a full stop. This was quite fun.

'My mother's dead. She died in a car accident when I was ten. She never told anyone who my father was—not even Phil.'

'Phil?' I couldn't think of how to indicate a question mark, and decided to drop the game temporarily. This was no time for experimentation.

'My'—hands up, fingers wiggled—'father. Who'd go ape-shit if I told him I wanted to know.'

Rosie drank the remaining wine in her glass and refilled it. The second half-bottle was now empty. Her story was sad, but not uncommon. Although my parents continued to make routine, ritual contact, it was my assessment that they had lost interest in me some years ago. Their duty had been completed when I was able to support myself. Her situation was somewhat different, however, as it involved a stepfather. I offered a genetic interpretation.

'His behaviour is completely predictable. You don't have his genes. Male lions kill the cubs from previous matings when they take over a pride.'

'Thanks for that information.'

'I can recommend some further reading if you are interested. You seem quite intelligent for a barmaid.'

'The compliments just keep on coming.'

It seemed I was doing well, and I allowed myself a moment of satisfaction, which I shared with Rosie.

'Excellent. I'm not proficient at dating. There are so many rules to remember.'

'You're doing okay,' she said. 'Except for staring at my boobs.'

This was disappointing feedback. Rosie's dress was quite revealing, but I had been working hard to maintain eye contact.

'I was just examining your pendant,' I said. 'It's extremely interesting.'

Rosie immediately covered it with her hand. 'What's on it?'

'An image of Isis with an inscription: *Sum omnia quae fuerunt suntque eruntque ego.* "I am all that has been, is and will be."' I hoped I had read the Latin correctly; the writing was very small.

Rosie seemed impressed. 'What about the pendant I had on this morning?'

'Dagger with three small red stones and four white ones.'

Rosie finished her wine. She seemed to be thinking about something. It turned out not to be anything profound.

'Want to get another bottle?'

I was a little stunned. We had already drunk the recommended maximum amount. On the other hand, she smoked, so obviously she had a careless attitude to health.

'You want more alcohol?'

'Correct,' she said, in an odd voice. She may have been mimicking me.

I went to the kitchen to select another bottle, deciding to reduce the next day's alcohol intake to compensate. Then I saw the clock: 11.40 p.m. I picked up the phone and ordered a taxi. With any luck it would arrive before the after-midnight tariff commenced. I opened a half-bottle of shiraz to drink while we waited.

Rosie wanted to continue the conversation about her biological father.

'Do you think there might be some sort of genetic motivation? That it's built into us to want to know who our parents are?'

'It's critical for parents to be able to recognise their own children. So they can protect the carriers of their genes. Small children need to be able to locate their parents to get that protection.'

'Maybe it's some sort of carry-over from that.'

'It seems unlikely. But possible. Our behaviour is strongly affected by instinct.'

'So you said. Whatever it is, it eats me up. Messes with my head.'

'Why don't you ask the candidates?'

'"Dear Doctor. Are you my father?" I don't think so.'

An obvious thought occurred to me, obvious because I am a geneticist.

'Your hair is a very unusual colour. Possibly—'

She laughed. 'There aren't any genes for this shade of red.'

She must have seen that I was confused.

'This colour only comes out of a bottle.'

I realised what she was saying. She had deliberately dyed her hair an unnaturally bright colour. Incredible. It hadn't even occurred to me to include hair dyeing on the questionnaire. I made a mental note to do so.

The doorbell buzzed. I had not mentioned the taxi to her, so brought her up to date with my plan. She quickly finished her wine, then stuck her hand out and it seemed to me that I was not the only one feeling awkward.

'Well,' she said, 'it's been an evening. Have a good life.'

It was a non-standard way of saying goodnight. I thought it safer to stick with convention.

'Goodnight. I've really enjoyed this evening.' I added, 'Good luck finding your father' to the formula.

'Thanks.'

Then she left.

I was agitated, but not in a bad way. It was more a case of sensory overload. I was pleased to find some wine left in the bottle. I poured it into my glass and phoned Gene. Claudia answered and I dispensed with pleasantries.

'I need to speak with Gene.'

'He's not home,' said Claudia. She sounded disoriented. Perhaps she had been drinking. 'I thought he was having lobster with you.'

'Gene sent me the world's most incompatible woman. A barmaid. Late, vegetarian, disorganised, irrational, unhealthy, smoker—smoker!—psychological problems, can't cook, mathematically incompetent, unnatural hair colour. I presume he was making a joke.'

Claudia must have interpreted this as a statement of distress because she said, 'Are you all right, Don?'

'Of course,' I said. 'She was highly entertaining. But

totally unsuitable for the Wife Project.' As I said these words, indisputably factual, I felt a twinge of regret at odds with my intellectual assessment. Claudia interrupted my attempt to reconcile the conflicting brain states.

'Don, do you know what time it is?'

I wasn't wearing a watch. And then I realised my error. I had used the kitchen clock as my reference when phoning the taxi. The clock that Rosie had reset. It must have been almost 2.30 a.m. How could I have lost track of time like that? It was a severe lesson in the dangers of messing with the schedule. Rosie would be paying the after-midnight tariff in the taxi.

I let Claudia return to sleep. As I picked up the two plates and two glasses to bring them inside, I looked again at the night-time view of the city—the view I had never seen before even though it had been there all the time.

I decided to skip my pre-bed aikido routine. And to leave the makeshift table in place.

9

'I threw her in as a wild card,' said Gene when I woke him up from the unscheduled sleep he was taking under his desk the next day.

Gene looked terrible and I told him he should refrain from staying up so late—although for once I had been guilty of the same error. It was important that he eat lunch at the correct time to get his circadian rhythm back on schedule. He had a packed lunch from home, and we headed for a grassy area in the university grounds. I collected seaweed salad, miso soup and an apple from the Japanese café on the way.

It was a fine day. Unfortunately this meant that there were a number of females in brief clothing sitting on the grass and walking by to distract Gene. Gene is fifty-six years old, although that information is not supposed to be disclosed. At that age, his testosterone should have fallen to a level where his sex drive was significantly reduced. It is my theory that his unusually high focus on sex is due to mental habit. But human physiology varies, and he may be an exception.

Conversely, I think Gene believes I have an abnormally low sex drive. This is not true—rather I am not as skilled as Gene in expressing it in a socially appropriate way. My occasional attempts to imitate Gene have been unsuccessful in the extreme.

We found a bench to sit on and Gene commenced his explanation.

'She's someone I know,' he said.

'No questionnaire?'

'No questionnaire.'

This explained the smoking. In fact, it explained everything. Gene had reverted to the inefficient practice of recommending acquaintances for dates. My expression must have conveyed my annoyance.

'You're wasting your time with the questionnaire. You'd be better off measuring the length of their earlobes.'

Sexual attraction is Gene's area of expertise. 'There's a correlation?' I asked.

'People with long earlobes are more likely to choose partners with long earlobes. It's a better predictor than IQ.'

This was incredible, but much behaviour that developed in the ancestral environment seems incredible when considered in the context of the current world. Evolution has not kept up. But earlobes! Could there be a more irrational basis for a relationship? No wonder marriages fail.

'So, did you have fun?' asked Gene.

I informed him that his question was irrelevant: my goal was to find a partner and Rosie was patently unsuitable. Gene had caused me to waste an evening.

'But did you have fun?' he repeated.

Did he expect a different answer to the same question? To be fair, I had not given him a proper answer, but for a good reason. I had not had time to reflect on the evening and determine a proper response. I guessed that 'fun' was going to be an over-simplification of a very complex experience.

I provided Gene with a summary of events. As I related the story of the dinner on the balcony, Gene interrupted. 'If you see her again—'

'There is zero reason for me to see her again.'

'*If you see her again,*' Gene continued, 'it's probably not a good idea to mention the Wife Project. Since she didn't measure up.'

Ignoring the incorrect assumption about seeing Rosie again, this seemed like good advice.

At that point, the conversation changed direction dramatically, and I did not have an opportunity to find out how Gene had met Rosie. The reason for the change was Gene's sandwich. He took a bite, then called out in pain and snatched my water bottle.

'Oh shit. Oh shit. Claudia put chillies in my sandwich.'

It was difficult to see how Claudia could make an error of this kind. But the priority was to reduce the pain. Chilli is insoluble in water, so drinking from my bottle would not be effective. I advised him to find some oil. We headed back to the Japanese café, and were not able to have any further conversation about Rosie. However, I had the basic information I needed. Gene had selected a woman without reference to the questionnaire. To see her again would be in total contradiction to the rationale for the Wife Project.

Riding home, I reconsidered. I could see three reasons that it might be necessary to see Rosie again.

1. Good experimental design requires the use of a control group. It would be interesting to use Rosie as a benchmark to compare with women selected by the questionnaire.
2. The questionnaire had not produced any matches to date. I could interact with Rosie in the meantime.
3. As a geneticist with access to DNA analysis, and the knowledge to interpret it, I was in a position to help Rosie find her biological father.

Reasons 1 and 2 were invalid. Rosie was clearly not a suitable life partner. There was no point in interaction with someone so patently inappropriate. But Reason 3 deserved consideration. Using my skills to assist her in a search for important knowledge aligned with my life purpose. I could do it in the time set aside for the Wife Project until a suitable candidate emerged.

In order to proceed, I needed to re-establish contact with Rosie. I did not want to tell Gene that I planned to see her again so soon after telling him that the probability of my doing so was zero. Fortunately, I recalled the name of the bar she worked at: the Marquess of Queensbury.

There was only one bar of that name, in a back street of an inner suburb. I had already modified the day's schedule, cancelling my market trip to catch up on the lost sleep. I would purchase a ready-made dinner instead. I am sometimes accused of being inflexible, but I think this demonstrates an ability to adapt to even the strangest of circumstances.

I arrived at 7.04 p.m. only to find that the bar did not open until 9.00 p.m. *Incredible*. No wonder people make mistakes at work. Would it be full of surgeons and flight controllers, drinking until after midnight then working the next day?

I ate dinner at a nearby Indian restaurant. By the time I had worked my way through the banquet, and returned to the bar, it was 9.27 p.m. There was a security official at the door, and I prepared myself for a repeat of the previous night. He examined me carefully, then asked, 'Do you know what sort of place this is?'

I am quite familiar with bars, perhaps even more familiar than most people. When I travel to conferences I generally find a pleasant bar near my hotel and eat and drink there every evening. I replied in the affirmative and entered.

I wondered if I had come to the right location. The most obvious characteristic of Rosie was that she was female, and the patrons at the Marquess of Queensbury were without exception male. Many were wearing unusual costumes, and I took a few minutes to examine the range. Two men noted me looking at them and one smiled broadly and nodded. I smiled back. It seemed to be a friendly place.

But I was there to find Rosie. I walked to the bar. The two men followed and sat on either side of me. The clean-shaven one was wearing a cut-off t-shirt and clearly spent time at the gym. Steroids could also have been involved. The one with the moustache wore a leather costume and a black cap.

'I haven't seen you here before,' said Black Cap.

I gave him the simple explanation. 'I haven't been here before.'

'Can I buy you a drink?'

'You're offering to buy my drink?' It was an unusual proposition from a stranger, and I guessed that I would be expected to reciprocate in some way.

'I think that's what I said,' said Black Cap. 'What can we tempt you with?'

I told him that the flavour didn't matter, as long as it contained alcohol. As in most social situations I was nervous.

Then Rosie appeared from the other side of the bar, dressed conventionally for her role in a collared black shirt. I was hugely relieved. I had come to the correct place and she was on duty. Black Cap waved to her. He ordered three Budweisers. Then Rosie saw me.

'Don.'

'Greetings.'

Rosie looked at us and asked, 'Are you guys together?'

'Give us a few minutes,' said Steroid Man.

Rosie said, 'I think Don's here to see me.'

'Correct.'

'Well, pardon us interrupting your social life with drinks orders,' Black Cap said to Rosie.

'You could use DNA,' I said.

Rosie clearly didn't follow, due to lack of context. 'What?'

'To identify your father. DNA is the obvious approach.'

'Sure,' said Rosie. 'Obvious. "Please send me your DNA so I can see if you're my father." Forget it, I was just mouthing off.'

'You could collect it.' I wasn't sure how Rosie would respond to the next part of my suggestion. 'Surreptitiously.'

Rosie went silent. She was at least considering the idea. Or perhaps wondering whether to report me. Her response supported the first possibility. 'And who's going to analyse it?'

'I'm a geneticist.'

'You're saying if I got a sample, you could analyse it for me?'

'Trivial,' I said. 'How many samples do we need to test?'

'Probably only one. I've got a pretty good idea. He's a family friend.'

Steroid Man coughed loudly, and Rosie fetched two beers from the refrigerator. Black Cap put a twenty-dollar note on the counter, but Rosie pushed it back and waved them away.

I tried the cough trick myself. Rosie took a moment to interpret the message this time, but then got me a beer.

'What do you need?' she asked. 'To test the DNA?'

I explained that normally we would use scrapings from the inner cheek, but that it would be impractical to obtain these without the subject's knowledge. 'Blood is excellent, but skin scrapings, mucus, urine—'

'Pass,' said Rosie.

'—faecal material, semen—'

'It keeps getting better,' said Rosie. 'I can screw a sixty-year-old family friend in the hope that he turns out to be my father.'

I was shocked. 'You'd have sex—'

Rosie explained that she was making a joke. On such a serious matter! It was getting busy around the bar, and there were a lot of cough signals happening. An effective way to spread disease. Rosie wrote a telephone number on a piece of paper.

'Call me.'

10

The next morning, I returned with some relief to the routine that had been so severely disrupted over the past two days. My Tuesday, Thursday and Saturday runs to the market are a feature of my schedule, combining exercise, meal-ingredients purchase and an opportunity for reflection. I was in great need of the last of these.

A woman had given me her phone number and told me to call her. More than the Jacket Incident, the Balcony Meal and even the excitement of the potential Father Project, this had disrupted my world. I knew that it happened regularly: people in books, films and TV shows do exactly what Rosie had done. But it had never happened to me. No woman had ever casually, unthinkingly, automatically, written down her phone number, given it to me and said, 'Call me.' I had temporarily been included in a culture that I considered closed to me. Although it was entirely logical that Rosie should provide me with a means of contacting her, I had an irrational feeling that, when I called, Rosie would realise that she had made some kind of error.

I arrived at the market and commenced purchasing. Because each day's ingredients are standard, I know which stalls to visit, and the vendors generally have my items pre-packaged in advance. I need only pay. The vendors know me well and are consistently friendly.

However, it is not possible to time-share major intellectual activity with the purchasing process, due to the quantity of human and inanimate obstacles: vegetable pieces on the ground, old ladies with shopping buggies, vendors still setting up stalls, Asian women comparing prices, goods being delivered, and tourists taking photos of each other in front of the produce. Fortunately I am usually the only jogger.

On the way home, I resumed my analysis of the Rosie situation. I realised that my actions had been driven more by instinct than logic. There were plenty of people in need of help, many in more distress than Rosie, and numerous worthy scientific projects that would represent better use of my time than a quest to find one individual's father. And, of course, I should be giving priority to the Wife Project. Better to push Gene to select more suitable women from the list, or to relax some of the less important selection criteria, as I had already done with the no-drinking rule.

The logical decision was to contact Rosie and explain that the Father Project was not a good idea. I phoned at 6.43 a.m. on returning from the run and left a message for her to call back. When I hung up, I was sweating despite the fact that the morning was still cool. I hoped I wasn't developing a fever.

Rosie called back while I was delivering a lecture. Normally, I turn my phone off at such times, but I was anxious to put this problem to bed. I was feeling stressed at the prospect of an interaction in which it was necessary for me to retract an offer. Speaking on the phone in front of a lecture theatre full of students was awkward, especially as I was wearing a lapel microphone.

They could hear my side of the conversation.

'Hi, Rosie.'

'Don, I just want to say thanks for doing this thing for me. I didn't realise how much it had been eating me up. Do you know that little coffee shop across from the Commerce Building—Barista's? How about two o'clock tomorrow?'

Now that Rosie had accepted my offer of help, it would have been immoral, and technically a breach of contract, to withdraw it.

'Barista's 2.00 p.m. tomorrow,' I confirmed, though I was temporarily unable to access the schedule in my brain due to overload.

'You're a star,' she said.

Her tone indicated that this was the end of her contribution to the conversation. It was my turn to use a standard platitude to reciprocate, and the obvious one was the simple reflection of 'You're a star'. But even I realised that made no sense. She was the beneficiary of my star-ness in the form of my genetics expertise. On reflection, I could have just said 'Goodbye' or 'See you', but I had no time for reflection. There was considerable pressure to make a timely response.

'I like you too.'

The entire lecture theatre exploded in applause.

A female student in the front row said, 'Smooth.' She was smiling.

Fortunately I am accustomed to creating amusement inadvertently.

I did not feel too unhappy at failing to terminate

the Father Project. The amount of work involved in one DNA test was trivial.

We met at Barista's the next day at 2.07 p.m. Needless to say, the delay was Rosie's fault. My students would be sitting in their 2.15 p.m. lecture waiting for my arrival. My intention had been only to advise her on the collection of a DNA sample, but she seemed unable to process the instructions. In retrospect, I was probably offering too many options and too much technical detail too rapidly. With only seven minutes to discuss the problem (allowing one minute for running to the lecture), we agreed that the simplest solution was to collect the sample together.

We arrived at the residence of Dr Eamonn Hughes, the suspected father, on the Saturday afternoon. Rosie had telephoned in advance.

Eamonn looked older than I had expected. I guessed sixty, BMI twenty-three. Eamonn's wife, whose name was Belinda (approximately fifty-five, BMI twenty-eight), made us coffee, as predicted by Rosie. This was critical, as we had decided that the coffee-cup rim would be an ideal source of saliva. I sat beside Rosie, pretending to be her friend. Eamonn and Belinda were opposite, and I was finding it hard to keep my eyes away from Eamonn's cup.

Fortunately, I was not required to make small talk. Eamonn was a cardiologist and we had a fascinating discussion about genetic markers for cardiac disease. Eamonn finally finished his coffee and Rosie stood up to take the cups to the kitchen. There, she would be able to swab the lip of the cup and we would have an excellent sample. When we discussed the plan, I suggested that this would be a breach of social convention, but Rosie assured me that she knew Eamonn and Belinda well as family friends, and, as a younger person, she would be allowed to perform this chore. For once, my understanding of social convention proved more accurate. Unfortunately.

As Rosie picked up Belinda's cup, Belinda said, 'Leave it, I'll do it later.'

Rosie responded, 'No, please,' and took Eamonn's cup.

Belinda picked up my cup and Rosie's and said, 'Okay, give me a hand.' They walked out to the kitchen together. It was obviously going to be difficult for Rosie to swab Eamonn's cup with Belinda present, but I could not think of a way of getting Belinda out of the kitchen.

'Did Rosie tell you I studied medicine with her mother?' asked Eamonn.

I nodded. Had I been a psychologist, I might have been able to infer from Eamonn's conversation and body language whether he was hiding the fact that he was Rosie's father. I might even have been able to lead the conversation in a direction to trap him. Fortunately we were not relying on my skills in this arena. If Rosie succeeded in collecting the sample, I would be able to provide a far more reliable answer than one derived from observations of behaviour.

'If I can offer you a little encouragement,' Eamonn said, 'Rosie's mother was a bit wild in her younger days. Very smart, good-looking, she could have had anyone. All the other women in medicine were going to marry doctors.' He smiled. 'But she surprised us all and picked the guy from left field who persisted and stuck around.'

It was lucky I wasn't looking for clues. My expression must have conveyed my total lack of comprehension.

'I suspect Rosie may follow in her mother's footsteps,' he said.

'In what component of her life?' It seemed safer to seek clarification than assume that he meant getting pregnant to an unknown fellow student or dying. These were the only facts I knew about Rosie's mother.

'I'm just saying I think you're probably good for her. And she's had a rough time. Tell me to mind my own business if you like. But she's a great kid.'

Now the intent of the conversation was clear, although Rosie was surely too old to be referred to as a kid. Eamonn thought I was Rosie's boyfriend. It was an understandable error. Correcting it would necessarily involve telling a lie, so I decided to remain silent. Then we heard the sound of breaking crockery.

Eamonn called out, 'Everything okay?'

'Just broke a cup,' said Belinda.

Breaking the cup was not part of the plan. Presumably, Rosie had dropped it in her nervousness or in trying to keep it from Belinda. I was annoyed at myself for not having a back-up plan. I had not treated this project as serious field work. It was embarrassingly unprofessional, and it was now my responsibility to find a solution. It would surely involve deception, and I am not skilled at deception.

My best approach was to source the DNA for a legitimate reason.

'Have you heard about the Genographic Project?'

'No,' said Eamonn.

I explained that with a sample of his DNA we could

trace his distant ancestry. He was fascinated. I offered to have his DNA processed if he organised a cheek scraping and sent it to me.

'Let's do it now, before I forget,' he said. 'Will blood do?'

'Blood is ideal for DNA testing, but—'

'I'm a doctor,' he said. 'Give me a minute.'

Eamonn left the room, and I could hear Belinda and Rosie speaking in the kitchen.

Belinda said, 'Seen your father at all?'

'Next question,' said Rosie.

Belinda instead responded with a statement. 'Don seems nice.'

Excellent. I was doing well.

'Just a friend,' said Rosie.

If she knew how many friends I had, she might have realised what a great compliment she had paid me.

'Oh well,' said Belinda.

Rosie and Belinda returned to the living room at the same time as Eamonn with his doctor's bag. Belinda reasonably deduced that there was some medical problem, but Eamonn explained about the Genographic Project. Belinda was a nurse and she took the blood with professional expertise.

As I handed the filled tube to Rosie to put in her handbag, I noticed her hands were shaking. I diagnosed anxiety, presumably related to the imminent confirmation of her paternity. I was not surprised when she asked, only seconds after leaving the Hughes's residence, if we could process the DNA sample immediately. It would require opening the lab on a Saturday evening but at least the project would be completed.

The laboratory was empty: throughout the university, the archaic idea of working Monday to Friday results in an incredible under-utilisation of expensive facilities. The university was trialling analysis equipment that could test for parent–child relationships very quickly. And we had an ideal DNA sample. It is possible to extract DNA from a wide variety of sources and only a few cells are needed for an analysis, but the preparatory work can be time consuming and complex. Blood was easy.

The new machine was located in a small room that had once been a tea-room with sink and refrigerator. For a moment I wished it had been more impressive—an unusual intrusion of ego into my thoughts. I unlocked the refrigerator and opened a beer. Rosie coughed loudly. I recognised the code and opened one for her also.

I tried to explain the process to Rosie as I set up, but she seemed unable to stop talking, even as she used the scraper on her inner cheek to provide me with her DNA sample.

'I can't believe it's this easy. This quick. I think I've always known at some level. He used to bring me stuff when I was a kid.'

'It's a vastly over-specified machine for such a trivial task.'

'One time he brought me a chess set. Phil gave me girly stuff—jewellery boxes and shit. Pretty weird for a personal trainer when you think about it.'

'You play chess?' I asked.

'Not really. That's not the point. He respected that

I have a brain. He and Belinda never had any kids of their own. I have a sense that he was always around. He might even have been my mum's best friend. But I've never consciously thought of him as my father.'

'He's not,' I said.

The result had come up on the computer screen. Job complete. I began packing up.

'Wow,' said Rosie. 'Ever thought of being a grief counsellor?'

'No. I considered a number of careers, but all in the sciences. My interpersonal skills are not strong.'

Rosie burst out laughing. 'You're about to get a crash course in advanced grief counselling.'

It turned out that Rosie was making a sort of joke, as her approach to grief counselling was based entirely on the administration of alcohol. We went to Jimmy Watson's on Lygon Street, a short walk away, and as usual, even on a weekend, it was full of academics. We sat at the bar, and I was surprised to find that Rosie, a professional server of drinks, had a very poor knowledge of wine. A few years ago Gene suggested that wine was the perfect topic for safe conversation and I did some research. I was familiar with the backgrounds of the wines offered regularly at this bar. We drank quite a lot.

Rosie had to go outside for a few minutes due to her nicotine addiction. The timing was fortunate, as a couple emerged from the courtyard and passed the bar. The man was Gene! The woman was not Claudia, but I recognised her. It was Olivia, the Indian Vegetarian from Table for Eight. Neither saw me, and they went past too quickly for me to say anything.

My confusion at seeing them together must have

contributed to my next decision. A waiter came up to me and said, 'There's a table for two that's just come free in the courtyard. Are you eating with us?'

I nodded. I would have to freeze the day's market purchases for the following Saturday, with the resulting loss of nutrients. Instinct had again displaced logic.

Rosie's reaction to finding a table being set for us on her return appeared to be positive. Doubtless she was hungry but it was reassuring to know that I had not committed a faux pas, always more likely when different genders are involved.

The food was excellent. We had freshly shucked oysters (sustainable), tuna sashimi (selected by Rosie and probably not sustainable), eggplant and mozzarella stack (Rosie), veal sweetbreads (me), cheese (shared) and a single serve of passionfruit mousse (divided and shared). I ordered a bottle of marsanne and it was an excellent accompaniment.

Rosie spent much of the meal trying to explain why she wanted to locate her biological father. I could see little reason for it. In the past, the knowledge might have been useful to determine the risk of genetically influenced diseases, but today Rosie could have her own DNA analysed directly. Practically, her stepfather Phil seemed to have executed the father role, although Rosie had numerous complaints about his performance. He was an egotist; he was inconsistent in his attitude towards her; he was subject to mood swings. He was also strongly opposed to alcohol. I considered this to be a thoroughly defensible position, but it was a cause of friction between them.

Rosie's motivation seemed to be emotional, and,

while I could not understand the psychology, it was clearly very important to her happiness.

After Rosie had finished her mousse, she left the table to 'go to the bathroom'. It gave me time to reflect and I realised that I was in the process of completing a non-eventful and in fact highly enjoyable dinner with a woman, a significant achievement that I was looking forward to sharing with Gene and Claudia.

I concluded that the lack of problems was due to three factors.

1. I was in a familiar restaurant. It had never occurred to me to take a woman— or indeed anyone—to Jimmy Watson's, which I had only previously used as a source of wine.
2. Rosie was not a date. I had rejected her, comprehensively, as a potential partner, and we were together because of a joint project. It was like a meeting.
3. I was somewhat intoxicated—hence relaxed. As a result, I may also have been unaware of any social errors.

At the end of the meal, I ordered two glasses of Sambuca and said, 'Who do we test next?'

11

Besides Eamonn Hughes, Rosie knew of only two other 'family friends' from her mother's medical graduation class. It struck me as unlikely that someone who had illicit sex with her mother would remain in contact, given the presence of Phil. But there was an evolutionary argument that he would wish to ensure that the carrier of his genes was receiving proper care. Essentially this was Rosie's argument also.

The first candidate was Dr Peter Enticott, who lived locally. The other, Alan McPhee, had died from prostate cancer, which was good news for Rosie, as, lacking a prostate gland, she could not inherit it. Apparently he had been an oncologist, but had not detected the cancer in himself, a not-uncommon scenario. Humans often fail to see what is close to them and obvious to others.

Fortunately, he had a daughter, with whom Rosie had socialised when she was younger. Rosie arranged a meeting with Natalie in three days' time, ostensibly to view Natalie's newborn baby.

I reverted to the normal schedule, but the Father Project kept intruding into my thoughts. I prepared for the DNA collection—I did not want a repeat of the broken cup problem. I also had another altercation with the Dean, as a result of the Flounder Incident.

One of my tasks is to teach genetics to medical students. In the first class of the previous semester, a student, who did not identify himself, had raised his hand shortly after I showed my first slide. The slide is a brilliant and beautiful diagrammatic summary of evolution from single-cell organisms to today's incredible variety of life. Only my colleagues in the Physics Department can match the extraordinary story that it tells. I cannot comprehend why some people are more interested in the outcome of a football match or the weight of an actress.

This student belonged to another category.

'Professor Tillman, you used the word "evolved".'

'Correct.'

'I think you should point out that evolution is just a theory.'

This was not the first time I had received a question—or statement—of this kind. I knew from experience that I would not sway the student's views, which would inevitably be based on religious dogma. I could only ensure that the student was not taken seriously by other trainee doctors.

'Correct,' I replied, 'but your use of the word "just" is misleading. Evolution is a theory supported by overwhelming evidence. Like the germ theory of disease, for example. As a doctor, you will be expected to rely on science. Unless you want to be a faith healer. In which case you are in the wrong course.'

There was some laughter. Faith Healer objected.

'I'm not talking about faith. I'm talking about creation *science*.'

There were only a few moans from the class. No doubt many of the students were from cultures where criticism of religion is not well tolerated. Such as ours. I had been forbidden to comment on religion after an earlier incident. But we were discussing science. I could have continued the argument, but I knew better than to be sidetracked by a student. My lectures are precisely timed to fit within fifty minutes.

'Evolution is a theory,' I said. 'There is no other theory of the origins of life with wide acceptance by scientists, or of any utility to medicine. Hence we will assume it in this class.' I believed I had handled the situation well, but I was annoyed that time had been insufficient to argue the case against the pseudo-science of creationism.

Some weeks later, eating in the University Club, I found a means of making the point succinctly. As I walked to the bar, I noticed one of the members eating a flounder, with its head still in place. After a slightly awkward conversation, I obtained the head and skeleton, which I wrapped and stored in my backpack.

Four days later, I had the class. I located Faith Healer, and asked him a preliminary question. 'Do you believe that fish were created in their current forms by an intelligent designer?'

He seemed surprised at the question, perhaps because it had been seven weeks since we had suspended the discussion. But he nodded in agreement.

I unwrapped the flounder. It had acquired a strong smell, but medical students should be prepared to deal with unpleasant organic objects in the interests of learning. I indicated the head: 'Observe that the eyes are not symmetrical.' In fact the eyes had decomposed, but the location of the eye sockets was quite clear. 'This is because the flounder evolved from a conventional fish with eyes on opposite sides of the head. One eye slowly migrated around, but just far enough to function effectively. Evolution did not bother to tidy up. But surely an intelligent designer would not have created a fish with this imperfection.' I gave Faith Healer the fish to enable him to examine it and continued the lecture.

He waited until the beginning of the new teaching year to lodge his complaint.

In my discussion with the Dean, she implied that I had tried to humiliate Faith Healer, whereas my intent had been to advance an argument. Since he had used the term 'creation *science*', with no mention of religion, I made the case that I was not guilty of denigrating religion. I was merely contrasting one theory with another. He was welcome to bring counter-examples to class.

'Don,' she said, 'as usual you haven't technically broken any rules. But—how can I put it?—if someone told me that a lecturer had brought a dead fish to class and given it to a student who had made a statement of religious faith, I would guess that the lecturer was you. Do you understand where I'm coming from?'

'You're saying that I am the person in the faculty most likely to act unconventionally. And you want me to act more conventionally. That seems an unreasonable request to make of a scientist.'

'I just don't want you to upset people.'

'Being upset and complaining because your theory is disproven is unscientific.'

The argument ended, once again, with the Dean being unhappy with me, though I had not broken any rules, and me being reminded that I needed to try harder to 'fit in'. As I left her office, her personal assistant, Regina, stopped me.

'I don't think I have you down for the faculty ball yet, Professor Tillman. I think you're the only professor who hasn't bought tickets.'

Riding home, I was aware of a tightness in my chest and realised it was a physical response to the Dean's advice. I knew that, if I could not 'fit in' in a science department of a university, I could not fit in anywhere.

Natalie McPhee, daughter of the late Dr Alan McPhee, potential biological father of Rosie, lived eighteen kilometres from the city, within riding distance, but Rosie decided we should travel by car. I was amazed to find that she drove a red Porsche convertible.

'It's Phil's.'

'Your "father's"?' I did the air quotes.

'Yeah, he's in Thailand.'

'I thought he didn't like you. But he lent you his car?'

'That's the sort of thing he does. No love, just stuff.'

The Porsche would be the perfect vehicle to lend to someone you did not like. It was seventeen years old (thus using old emissions technology), had appalling fuel economy, little leg room, high wind noise, and a non-functioning air-conditioning system. Rosie confirmed my guess that it was unreliable and expensive to maintain.

As we arrived at Natalie's I realised I had spent the entire journey listing and elaborating on the deficiencies of the vehicle. I had avoided small talk, but had not briefed Rosie on the DNA collection method.

'Your task is to occupy her in conversation while I collect DNA.' This would make best use of our respective skills.

It soon became clear that my back-up plan would be necessary. Natalie did not want to drink: she was abstaining from alcohol while breastfeeding her baby, and it was too late for coffee. These were responsible choices, but we would not be able to swab a cup or glass.

I deployed Plan B.

'Can I see the baby?'

'He's asleep,' she said, 'so you'll have to be quiet.'

I stood up and so did she.

'Just tell me where to go,' I said.

'I'll come with you.'

The more I insisted that I wanted to see the baby alone, the more she objected. We went to its room and, as she had predicted, it was sleeping. This was very annoying, as I had a number of plans that involved collecting DNA in a totally non-invasive way from the baby, who was, of course, also related to Alan McPhee. Unfortunately I had not factored in the mother's protective instinct. Every time I found a reason to leave the room, Natalie followed me. It was very awkward.

Finally, Rosie excused herself to go to the bathroom. Even if she had known what to do, she could not have visited the baby, as Natalie had positioned herself so that she could see the bedroom door and was checking frequently.

'Have you heard about the Genographic Project?' I asked.

She hadn't and was not interested. She changed the topic.

'You seem very interested in babies.'

There was surely an opportunity here if I could find a way to exploit it. 'I'm interested in their behaviour. Without the corrupting influence of a parent present.'

She looked at me strangely. 'Do you do any stuff with kids? I mean Scouts, church groups…'

'No,' I said. 'It's unlikely that I'd be suitable.'

Rosie returned and the baby started crying.

'Feeding time,' said Natalie.

'We should be going,' said Rosie.

Failure! Social skills had been the problem. With good social skills I could surely have got to the baby.

'I'm sorry,' I said as we walked to Phil's ridiculous vehicle.

'Don't be.' Rosie reached into her handbag and pulled out a wad of hair. 'I cleaned her hairbrush for her.'

'We need roots,' I said. But there was a lot of hair, so it was likely we would find a strand with its root attached.

She reached into her bag again and retrieved a toothbrush. It took me a few moments to realise what this meant.

'You stole her toothbrush!'

'There was a spare in the cupboard. It was time for a new one.'

I was shocked at the theft, but we would now almost certainly have a usable sample of DNA. It was difficult not to be impressed by Rosie's resourcefulness. And if Natalie was not replacing her toothbrush at regular intervals Rosie had done her a favour.

Rosie did not want to analyse the hair or toothbrush

immediately. She wanted to collect DNA from the final candidate and test the two samples together. This struck me as illogical. If Natalie's sample was a match we would not need to collect further DNA. However, Rosie did not seem to grasp the concept of sequencing tasks to minimise cost and risk.

After the problem with the baby access, we decided to collaborate on the most appropriate approach for Dr Peter Enticott.

'I'll tell him I'm thinking about studying medicine,' she said. Dr Enticott was now in the Medical Faculty at Deakin University.

She would arrange to meet him over coffee, which would provide an opportunity to use the coffee-cup swab procedure that currently had a one hundred per cent failure rate. I thought it unlikely that a barmaid could convince a professor that she had the credentials to study medicine. Rosie seemed insulted by this, and argued that it did not matter in any case. We only had to persuade him to have a drink with us.

A bigger problem was how to present me, as Rosie did not think she could do the job alone. 'You're my boyfriend,' she said. 'You'll be financing my studies, so you're a stakeholder.' She looked at me hard. 'You don't need to overplay it.'

On a Wednesday afternoon, with Gene covering a lecture for me in return for the Asperger's night, we travelled in Phil's toy car to Deakin University. I had been there many times before for guest lectures and collaborative research. I even knew some researchers in the Medical Faculty, though not Peter Enticott.

We met him at an outdoor café crowded with medical students back early from the summer break. Rosie was amazing! She spoke intelligently about medicine, and even psychiatry, in which she said she hoped to specialise. She claimed to have an honours degree in behavioural science and postgraduate research experience.

Peter seemed obsessed with the resemblance between Rosie and her mother, which was irrelevant for our purposes. Three times he interrupted Rosie to remind her of their physical similarity, and I wondered if this might indicate some particular bond between him and Rosie's mother—and hence be a predictor of paternity. I looked, as I had done in Eamonn Hughes's living room, for any physical similarities between Rosie and her potential father, but could see nothing obvious.

'That all sounds very positive, Rosie,' said Peter. 'I don't have anything to do with the selection process— at least officially.' His wording appeared to imply the possibility of unofficial, and hence unethical, assistance. Was this a sign of nepotism and thus a clue that he was Rosie's father?

'Your academic background is fine, but you'll have to do the GAMSAT.' Peter turned to me. 'The standard admission test for the MD program.'

'I did it last year,' said Rosie. 'I got seventy-four.'

Peter looked hugely impressed. 'You can walk into Harvard with that score. But we take other factors into account here, so if you do decide to apply, make sure you let me know.'

I hoped he never went for a drink at the Marquess of Queensbury.

A waiter brought the bill. As he went to take Peter's

cup, I automatically put my hand on it to stop him. The waiter looked at me extremely unpleasantly and snatched it away. I watched as he took it to a cart and added it to a tray of crockery.

Peter looked at his phone. 'I have to go,' he said. 'But now that you've made contact, stay in touch.'

As Peter left, I could see the waiter looking towards the cart.

'You need to distract him,' I said.

'Just get the cup,' said Rosie.

I walked towards the cart. The waiter was watching me but, just as I reached the tray, he snapped his head in Rosie's direction and began walking quickly towards her. I grabbed the cup.

We met at the car, which was parked some distance away. The walk gave me time to process the fact that I had, under pressure to achieve a goal, been guilty of theft. Should I send a cheque to the café? What was a cup worth? Cups were broken all the time, but by random events. If everyone stole cups, the café would probably become financially non-viable.

'Did you get the cup?'

I held it up.

'Is it the right one?' she said.

I am not good at non-verbal communication, but I believe I managed to convey the fact that while I might be a petty thief I do not make errors of observation.

'Did you pay the bill?' I asked.

'That's how I distracted him.'

'By paying the bill?'

'No, you pay at the counter. I just took off.'

'We have to go back.'

'Fuck 'em,' said Rosie, as we climbed into the Porsche and sped off.

What was happening to me?

12

We drove towards the university and the lab. The Father Project would soon be over. The weather was warm, though there were dark clouds on the horizon, and Rosie lowered the convertible roof. I was mulling over the theft.

'You still obsessing about the bill, Don?' Rosie shouted over the wind noise. 'You're hilarious. We're stealing DNA, and you're worried about a cup of coffee.'

'It's not illegal to take DNA samples,' I shouted back. This was true, although in the UK we would have been in violation of the Human Tissue Act of 2004. 'We should go back.'

'Highly inefficient use of time,' said Rosie in a strange voice, as we pulled up at traffic lights and were briefly able to communicate properly. She laughed and I realised she had been imitating me. Her statement was correct, but there was a moral question involved, and acting morally should override other issues.

'Relax,' she said. 'It's a beautiful day, we're going to find out who my father is, and I'll put a cheque in the mail for the coffee. *Promise*.' She looked at me. 'Do you know how to relax? How to just have fun?'

It was too complex a question to answer over the

wind noise as we pulled away from the lights. And the pursuit of fun does not lead to overall contentment. Studies have shown this consistently.

'You missed the exit,' I said.

'Correct,' she replied, in the joke voice. 'We're going to the beach.' She spoke right over the top of my protests. 'Can't hear you, can't hear you.'

Then she put on some music—very loud rock music. Now she really couldn't hear me. I was being kidnapped! We drove for ninety-four minutes. I could not see the speedometer, and was not accustomed to travelling in an open vehicle, but I estimated that we were consistently exceeding the speed limit.

Discordant sound, wind, risk of death—I tried to assume the mental state that I used at the dentist.

Finally, we stopped in a beachside car park. It was almost empty on a weekday afternoon.

Rosie looked at me. 'Smile. We're going for a walk, then we're going to the lab, and then I'm going to take you home. And you'll never see me again.'

'Can't we just go home now?' I said, and realised that I sounded like a child. I reminded myself that I was an adult male, ten years older and more experienced than the person with me, and that there must be a purpose for what she was doing. I asked what it was.

'I'm about to find out who my dad is. I need to clear my head. So can we walk for half an hour or so, and can you just pretend to be a regular human being and listen to me?'

I was not sure how well I could imitate a regular human being, but I agreed to the walk. It was obvious that Rosie was confused by emotions, and I respected her attempt to overcome them. As it turned out, she hardly spoke at all. This made the walk quite pleasant—it was virtually the same as walking alone.

As we approached the car on our return, Rosie asked, 'What music *do* you like?'

'Why?'

'You didn't like what I was playing on the drive down, did you?'

'Correct.'

'So, your turn going back. But I don't have any Bach.'

'I don't really listen to music,' I said. 'The Bach was an experiment that didn't work.'

'You can't go through life not listening to music.'

'I just don't pay it any attention. I prefer to listen to information.'

There was a long silence. We had reached the car.

'Did your parents listen to music? Brothers and sisters?'

'My parents listened to rock music. Primarily my father. From the era in which he was young.'

We got in the car and Rosie lowered the roof again. She played with her iPhone, which she was using as the music source.

'Blast from the past,' she said, and activated the music.

I was just settling into the dentist's chair again when I realised the accuracy of Rosie's words. I knew this music. It had been in the background when I was growing up. I was suddenly taken back to my room, door closed, writing in BASIC on my early-generation computer, the song in the background.

'I know this song!'

Rosie laughed. 'If you didn't, that'd be the final proof that you're from Mars.'

Hurtling back to town, in a red Porsche driven by a beautiful woman, with the song playing, I had the sense of standing on the brink of another world. I recognised the feeling, which, if anything, became stronger as the rain started falling and the convertible roof malfunctioned so we were unable to raise it. It was the same feeling that I had experienced looking over the city after the Balcony Meal, and again after Rosie had written down her phone number. Another world, another life, proximate but inaccessible.

The elusive...*Sat-is-fac-tion*.

It was dark when we arrived back at the university. We were both wet. With the aid of the instruction manual, I was able to close the car roof manually.

In the lab, I opened two beers (no cough-signal required) and Rosie tapped her bottle against mine.

'Cheers,' she said. 'Well done.'

'You promise to send a cheque to the café?'

'Whatever. Promise.' Good.

'You were brilliant,' I said. I had been meaning to convey this for some time. Rosie's performance as an aspiring medical student had been very impressive. 'But why did you claim such a high score on the medical admission test?'

'Why do you think?'

I explained that if I could have deduced the answer, I would not have asked.

'Because I didn't want to look stupid.'

'To your potential father?'

'Yeah. To him. To anybody. I'm getting a bit sick of certain people thinking I'm stupid.'

'I consider you remarkably intelligent—'

'Don't say it.'

'Say what?'

'For a barmaid. You were going to say that, weren't you?'

Rosie had predicted correctly.

'My mother was a doctor. So is my father, if you're talking about genes. And you don't have to be a professor to be smart. I saw your face when I said I got seventy-four on the GAMSAT. You were thinking, "He won't believe this woman is that smart." But he did. So, put your prejudices away.'

It was a reasonable criticism. I had little contact with people outside academia, and had formed my assumptions about the rest of the world primarily from watching films and television as a child. I recognised that the characters in *Lost in Space* and *Star Trek* were probably not representative of humans in general. Certainly, Rosie did not conform to my barmaid stereotype. It was quite likely that many of my other assumptions about people were wrong. This was no surprise.

The DNA analyser was ready.

'Do you have a preference?' I asked.

'Whichever. I don't want to make any decisions.'

I realised that she was referring to the sequence of testing rather than the choice of father. I clarified the question.

'I don't know,' she said. 'I've been thinking about it all afternoon. Alan's dead, which would suck. And Natalie would be my sister, which I've got to tell you is pretty weird. But it's a sort of closure if that makes sense. I like Peter, but I don't really know anything about him. He's probably got a family.'

It struck me once again that this Father Project had not been well thought through. Rosie had spent the afternoon trying to subdue unwanted emotions, yet the motivation for the project seemed to be entirely emotional.

I tested Peter Enticott first, as the hair from Natalie's brush required more time for pre-processing. No match.

I had found several roots in the wad of hair, so there was no need to have stolen the toothbrush. As I processed them, I reflected that Rosie's first two candidates, including the one she had felt was a high probability, Eamonn Hughes, had not matched. It was my prediction that Alan's daughter would not match either.

I was right. I remembered to look at Rosie for her reaction. She looked very sad. It seemed we would have to get drunk again.

'Remember,' she said, 'the sample's not from him; it's his daughter's.'

'I've already factored it in.'

'Naturally. So that's it.'

'But we haven't solved the problem.' As a scientist I am not accustomed to abandoning difficult problems.

'We're not going to,' said Rosie. 'We've tested everyone I ever heard of.'

'Difficulties are inevitable,' I said. 'Major projects require persistence.'

'Save it for something that matters to you.'

***

Why do we focus on certain things at the expense of others? We will risk our lives to save a person from drowning, yet not make a donation that could save dozens of children from starvation. We install solar panels when their impact on CO_2 emissions is minimal—and indeed may have a net negative effect if manufacturing and installation are taken into account—rather than contributing to more efficient infrastructure projects.

I consider my own decision-making in these areas to be more rational than that of most people but I also make errors of the same kind. We are genetically programmed to react to stimuli in our immediate vicinity. Responding to complex issues that we cannot perceive directly requires the application of reasoning, which is less powerful than instinct.

This seemed to be the most likely explanation for my continued interest in the Father Project. Rationally, there were more important uses for my research capabilities, but instinctively I was driven to assist Rosie with her more immediate problem. As we drank a glass of Muddy Water pinot noir at Jimmy Watson's before Rosie had to go to work, I tried to persuade her to continue with the project but she argued, rationally enough, that there was now no reason to consider any member of her mother's graduation class more likely than any other. She guessed that there would be a hundred or more students, and pointed out that thirty years ago, as a result of entrenched gender bias, the majority would be male. The logistics of finding and testing fifty doctors, many of whom would be living in other cities or countries, would be prohibitive. Rosie said she didn't care *that* much.

Rosie offered me a lift home, but I decided to stay and drink.

13

Before abandoning the Father Project, I decided to check Rosie's estimate of the number of father candidates. It occurred to me that some possibilities could be easily eliminated. The medical classes I teach contain numerous foreign students. Given Rosie's distinctly pale skin, I considered it unlikely that her father was Chinese, Vietnamese, black or Indian.

I began with some basic research—an internet search for information about the medical graduation class, based on the three names I knew.

The results exceeded my expectations, but problem-solving often requires an element of luck. It was no surprise that Rosie's mother had graduated from my current university. At the time, there were only two medical courses in Melbourne.

I found two relevant photos. One was a formal photo of the entire graduation class, with the names of the one hundred and forty-six students. The other was taken at the graduation party, also with names. There were only one hundred and twenty-four faces, presumably because some students did not attend. Since the gene-shopping had occurred at the party, or after, we would not have to worry about the non-attendees. I verified that the one hundred and twenty-four were a subset of the one hundred and forty-six.

I had expected that my search would produce a list of graduates and probably a photo. An unexpected bonus was a 'Where are they now?' discussion board. But the major stroke of luck was the information that a thirtieth anniversary reunion had been scheduled. The date was only three weeks away. We would need to act quickly.

I ate dinner at home and rode to the Marquess of Queensbury. Disaster! Rosie wasn't working. The barman informed me that Rosie worked only three nights per week, which struck me as insufficient to provide an adequate income. Perhaps she had a day job as well. I knew very little about her, beyond her job, her interest in finding her father and her age, which, based on her mother's graduation party being thirty years earlier, must be twenty-nine. I had not asked Gene how he had met her. I did not even know her mother's name to identify her in the photo.

The barman was friendly, so I ordered a beer and some nuts and reviewed the notes I had brought.

There were sixty-three males in the graduation party photo, a margin of only two over the females, insufficient to support Rosie's claim of discrimination. Some were unambiguously non-Caucasian, though not as many as I expected. It was thirty years ago, and the influx of Chinese students had not yet commenced. There was still a large number of candidates, but the reunion offered an opportunity for batch processing.

I had by now deduced that the Marquess of Queensbury was a gay bar. On the first visit, I had not observed the social interactions, as I was too focused on finding Rosie and initiating the Father Project, but this time I was able to analyse my surroundings in more detail. I was reminded of the chess club that I belonged to when I was at school. People drawn together by a common interest. It was the only club I had ever joined, excluding the University Club which was more of a dining facility.

I did not have any gay friends, but this was related to my overall small number of friends rather than to any prejudice. Perhaps Rosie was gay? She worked in a gay bar, although the clients were all males. I asked the barman. He laughed.

'Good luck with that one,' he said. It didn't answer the question, but he had moved on to serve another customer.

As I finished lunch at the University Club the following day, Gene walked in, accompanied by a woman I recognised from the singles party—Fabienne the Sex-Deprived Researcher. It appeared that she had found a solution to her problem. We passed each other at the dining room entrance.

Gene winked at me, and said, 'Don, this is Fabienne. She's visiting from Belgium and we're going to discuss some options for collaboration.' He winked again, and quickly moved past.

Belgium. I had assumed Fabienne was French. Belgian explained it. Gene already had France.

I was waiting outside the Marquess of Queensbury when Rosie opened the doors at 9.00 p.m.

'Don.' Rosie looked surprised. 'Is everything okay?'

'I have some information.'

'Better be quick.'

'It's not quick, there's quite a lot of detail.'

'I'm sorry, Don, my boss is here. I'll get into trouble. I need this job.'

'What time do you finish?'

'Three a.m.'

I couldn't believe it! What sort of jobs did Rosie's patrons have? Maybe they all worked in bars that opened at 9.00 p.m. and had four nights a week off. A whole invisible nocturnal subculture, using resources that would otherwise stand idle. I took a huge breath and a huge decision.

'I'll meet you then.'

I rode home, went to bed, and set the alarm for 2.30 a.m. I cancelled the run I had scheduled with Gene for the following morning to retrieve an hour. I would also skip karate.

At 2.50 a.m. I was riding through the inner suburbs. It was not a totally unpleasant experience. In fact, I could see major advantages for myself in working at night. Empty laboratories. No students. Faster response times on the network. No contact with the Dean. If I could find a pure research position, with no teaching, it would be entirely feasible. Perhaps I could teach via video-link at a university in another time zone.

I arrived at Rosie's workplace at exactly 3.00 a.m. The door was locked and a 'Closed' sign was up. I knocked hard. Rosie came to the door.

'I'm stuffed,' she said. This was hardly surprising. 'Come in—I'm almost done.'

Apparently the bar closed at 2.30 a.m. but Rosie had to clean up.

'You want a beer?' she said. A beer! At 3 a.m. Ridiculous.

'Yes, please.'

I sat at the bar watching her clean up. The question I had asked sitting in the same place the previous day popped into my mind.

'Are you gay?' I asked.

'You came here to ask me that?'

'No, the question is unrelated to the main purpose of my visit.'

'Pleased to hear it, alone at three in the morning in a bar with a strange man.'

'I'm not strange.'

'Not much,' she said, but she was laughing, presumably making a joke to herself based on the two meanings of *strange*. I still didn't have an answer to the gay question. She opened a beer for herself. I pulled out my folder and extracted the party photo.

'Is this the party where your mother was impregnated?'

'Shit. Where did this come from?'

I explained about my research and showed her my spreadsheet. 'All names are listed. Sixty-three males, nineteen obviously non-Caucasian, as determined by visual assessment and supported by names, three already eliminated.'

'You've got to be kidding. We're not testing…thirty-one people.'

'Forty-one.'

'Whatever. I don't have an excuse to meet any of them.'

I told her about the reunion.

'Minor problem,' said Rosie. 'We're not invited.'

'Correct,' I said. 'The problem is minor and already solved. There will be alcohol.'

'So?'

I indicated the bar, and the collection of bottles on shelves behind it. 'Your skills will be required.'

'You're kidding me.'

'Can you secure employment at the event?'

'Hang on, hang on. This is getting seriously crazy. You think we're going to turn up at this party and start swabbing people's glasses. Oh man.'

'Not us. You. I don't have the skills. But otherwise, correct.'

'Forget it.'

'I thought you wanted to know who your father was.'

'I told you,' she said. 'Not that much.'

Two days later, Rosie appeared at my apartment. It was 8.47 p.m., and I was cleaning the bathroom, as Eva the short-skirted cleaner had cancelled due to illness. I buzzed her upstairs. I was wearing my bathroom-cleaning costume of shorts, surgical boots and gloves but no shirt.

'Wow.' She stared at me for a few moments. 'This is what martial arts training does, is it?' She appeared to be referring to my pectoral muscles. Then suddenly she jumped up and down like a child.

'We got the gig! I found the agency and I offered them shit rates and they went yeah, yeah, yeah, don't tell anyone. I'll report them to the union when it's over.'

'I thought you didn't want to do this.'

'Changed my mind.' She gave me a stained paperback. 'Memorise this. I've got to get to work.' She turned and left.

I looked at the book—*The Bartender's Companion: A Complete Guide to Making and Serving Drinks*. It appeared to specify the duties of the role I was to perform. I memorised the first few recipes before finishing the bathroom. As I prepared for sleep, having skipped the aikido routine to spend further time studying the book, it occurred to me that things *were* getting crazy. It was not the first time that my life had become chaotic and I had established a protocol for dealing with the problem and the consequent disturbance to rational thinking. I called Claudia.

She was able to see me the next day. Because I am not officially one of her clients, we have to have our discussions over coffee rather than in her office. And I am the one accused of rigidity!

I outlined the situation, omitting the Father Project component, as I did not want to admit to the surreptitious collection of DNA, which Claudia was likely to consider unethical. Instead I suggested that Rosie and I had a common interest in movies.

'Have you talked to Gene about her?' asked Claudia.

I told her that Gene had introduced Rosie as a candidate for the Wife Project, and that he would only encourage me to have sex with her. I explained that Rosie was totally unsuitable as a partner, but was presumably under the illusion that I was interested in her on that basis. Perhaps she thought that our common interest was an excuse for pursuing her. I had made a major social error in asking her about her sexual orientation—it would only reinforce that impression.

Yet Rosie had never mentioned the Wife Project.

We had been sidetracked so quickly by the Jacket Incident, and after that things had unfolded in a totally unplanned way. But I saw a risk that at some point I would hurt her feelings by telling her that she had been eliminated from consideration for the Wife Project after the first date.

'So that's what you're worried about,' said Claudia. 'Hurting her feelings?'

'Correct.'

'That's excellent, Don.'

'Incorrect. It's a major problem.'

'I mean that you're concerned about her feelings. And you're enjoying time together?'

'Immensely,' I said, realising it for the first time.

'And is she enjoying herself?'

'Presumably. But she applied for the Wife Project.'

'Don't worry about it,' said Claudia. 'She sounds pretty resilient. Just have some fun.'

A strange thing happened the next day. For the first time ever, Gene made an appointment to see me in his office. I had always been the one to organise conversations, but there had been an unusually long gap as a result of the Father Project.

Gene's office is larger than mine, due to his higher status rather than any actual requirement for space. The Beautiful Helena let me in, as Gene was late in returning from a meeting. I took the opportunity to check his world map for pins in India and Belgium. I was fairly certain that the Indian one had been there before, but it was possible that Olivia was not actually Indian. She had said she was Hindu, so she could have been

Balinese or Fijian or indeed from any country with a Hindu population. Gene worked on nationalities rather than ethnicities, in the same way that travellers count the countries they have visited. North Korea predictably remained without a pin.

Gene arrived, and commanded The Beautiful Helena to fetch us coffees. We sat at his table, as if in a meeting.

'So,' said Gene, 'you've been talking to Claudia.' This was one of the negatives of not being an official client of Claudia: I did not have the protection of confidentiality. 'I gather you've been seeing Rosie. As the expert predicted.'

'Yes,' I said, 'but not for the Wife Project.' Gene is my best friend, but I still felt uncomfortable about sharing information about the Father Project. Fortunately he did not pursue it, probably because he assumed I had sexual intentions towards Rosie. In fact I was amazed that he didn't immediately raise the topic.

'What do you know about Rosie?' he asked.

'Not very much,' I said honestly. 'We haven't talked much about her. Our discussion has focused on external issues.'

'Give me a break,' he said. 'You know what she does, where she spends her time.'

'She's a barmaid.'

'Okay,' said Gene. 'That's all you know?'

'And she doesn't like her father.'

Gene laughed for no obvious reason. 'I don't think he's Robinson Crusoe.' This seemed a ludicrous statement about Rosie's paternity until I recalled that the reference to the fictional shipwreck survivor could be used as a metaphorical phrase meaning 'not alone' or in this context 'not alone in not being liked by Rosie'. Gene must have noticed my puzzled expression as I worked it out, and elaborated: 'The list of men that Rosie likes is not a long one.'

'She's gay?'

'Might as well be,' said Gene. 'Look at the way she dresses.'

Gene's comment seemed to refer to the type of costume she was wearing when she first appeared in my office. But she dressed conventionally for her bar work and on our visits to collect DNA had worn unexceptional jeans and tops. On the night of the Jacket Incident she had been unconventional but extremely attractive.

Perhaps she did not want to send out mating signals in the environment in which Gene had encountered her, presumably a bar or restaurant. Much of women's clothing is designed to enhance their sexual attraction in order to secure a mate. If Rosie was not looking for a mate, it seemed perfectly rational for her to dress otherwise. There were many things that I wanted to ask Gene about Rosie, but I suspected that asking would imply a level of interest that Gene would misinterpret. But there was one critical question.

'Why was she prepared to participate in the Wife Project?'

Gene hesitated a while. 'Who knows?' he said. 'I don't think she's a lost cause, but just don't expect too much. She's got a lot of issues. Don't forget the rest of your life.'

Gene's advice was surprisingly perceptive. Did he know how much time I was spending with the cocktail book?

14

My name is Don Tillman and I am an alcoholic. I formed these words in my head but I did not say them out loud, not because I was drunk (which I was) but because it seemed that if I said them they would be true, and I would have no choice but to follow the rational path which was to stop drinking permanently.

My intoxication was a result of the Father Project—specifically the need to gain competence as a drinks waiter. I had purchased a cocktail shaker, glasses, olives, lemons, a zester and a substantial stock of liquor as recommended in *The Bartender's Companion* in order to master the mechanical component of cocktail making. It was surprisingly complex, and I am not naturally a dextrous person. In fact, with the exception of rock-climbing, which I have not practised since I was a student, and martial arts, I am clumsy and incompetent at most forms of sport. The expertise in karate and aikido is the result of considerable practice over a long period.

I practised first for accuracy, then speed. At 11.07 p.m., I was exhausted, and decided that it would be interesting to test the cocktails for quality. I made a classic martini, a vodka martini, a margarita and a cock-sucking cowboy—cocktails noted by the book as being among the most popular. They were all excellent, and tasted far more different from one another than ice-cream varieties. I had squeezed more lime juice than was required for the margarita, and made a second so as not to waste it.

Research consistently shows that the risks to health outweigh the benefits of drinking alcohol. My argument is that the benefits to my *mental* health justify the risks. Alcohol seems to both calm me down and elevate my mood, a paradoxical but pleasant combination. And it reduces my discomfort in social situations.

I generally manage my consumption carefully, scheduling two days abstinence per week, although the Father Project had caused this rule to be broken a number of times. My level of consumption does not of itself qualify me as an alcoholic. However, I suspect that my strong antipathy towards discontinuing it might do so.

The Mass DNA Collection Subproject was proceeding satisfactorily, and I was working my way through the cocktail book at the required rate. Contrary to popular belief, alcohol does not destroy brain cells.

As I prepared for bed, I felt a strong desire to telephone Rosie and report on progress. Logically it was not necessary, and it is a waste of effort to report that a project is proceeding to plan, which should be the default assumption. Rationality prevailed. Just.

Rosie and I met for coffee twenty-eight minutes before the reunion function. To my first-class honours degree and PhD, I could now add a Responsible Service of Alcohol certificate. The exam had not been difficult.

Rosie was already in server uniform, and had brought a male equivalent for me.

'I picked it up early and washed it,' she said. 'I didn't want a karate exhibition.'

She was obviously referring to the Jacket Incident, even though the martial art I had employed was aikido.

I had prepared carefully for the DNA collection—zip-lock bags, tissues, and pre-printed adhesive labels with the names from the graduation photo. Rosie insisted that we did not need to collect samples from those who had not attended the graduation party, so I crossed out their names. She seemed surprised that I had memorised them, but I was determined not to cause errors due to lack of knowledge.

The reunion was held at a golf club, which seemed odd to me, but I discovered that the facilities were largely for eating and drinking rather than supporting the playing of golf. I also discovered that we were vastly overqualified. There were regular bar personnel who were responsible for preparing the drinks. Our job was merely to take orders, deliver drinks and, most importantly, collect the empty glasses. The hours spent in developing my drink-making skills had apparently been wasted.

The guests began arriving, and I was given a tray of drinks to distribute. I immediately perceived a problem. No name tags! How would we identify the DNA sources? I managed to find Rosie, who had also realised the problem but had a solution, based on her knowledge of social behaviour.

'Say to them, "Hi, I'm Don and I'll be looking after you this evening, Doctor—"' She demonstrated how to give the impression that the sentence was incomplete, encouraging them to contribute their name.

Extraordinarily, it turned out to work 72.5 per cent of the time. I realised that I needed to do this with the women as well, to avoid appearing sexist.

Eamonn Hughes and Peter Enticott, the candidates we had eliminated, arrived. As a family friend, Eamonn must have known Rosie's profession, and she explained to him that I worked evenings to supplement my academic income. Rosie told Peter Enticott that she did bar work part-time to finance her PhD. Perhaps they both assumed that we had met through working together.

Actually swabbing the glasses discreetly proved the most difficult problem and I was able to get at most one sample from each tray that I returned to the bar. Rosie was having even more problems.

'I can't keep track of all the names,' she said, frantically, as we passed each other with drinks trays in our hands. It was getting busy and she seemed a little emotional. I sometimes forget that many people are not familiar with basic techniques for remembering data. The success of the subproject would be in my hands.

'There will be adequate opportunity when they sit down,' I said. 'There is no reason for concern.'

I surveyed the tables set for dinner, ten seats per table, plus two with eleven seats, and calculated the attendance at ninety-two. This of course included female doctors. Partners had not been invited. There was a small risk that Rosie's father was a transsexual. I made a mental note to check the women for signs of male features, and test any that appeared doubtful. Overall, however, the numbers looked promising.

When the guests sat down, the mode of service moved from provision of a limited selection of drinks to taking orders. Apparently, this arrangement was unusual. Normally, we would just bring bottles of wine, beer and water to the table, but as this was an upmarket function, the club was taking orders and we had been told to 'push the top shelf stuff', apparently to increase the club's profits. It occurred to me that if I did this well, I might be forgiven for any other errors.

I approached one of the tables of eleven. I had already introduced myself to seven of the guests, and obtained six names.

I commenced with a woman whose name I already knew.

'Greetings, Dr Collie. What can I get you to drink?'

She looked at me strangely and for a moment I thought I had made an error with the word-association method I was using and that her name was perhaps Doberman or Poodle. But she did not correct me.

'Just a white wine, thanks.'

'I recommend a margarita. World's most popular cocktail.'

'You're doing cocktails?'

'Correct.'

'In that case,' she said, 'I'll have a martini.'

'Standard?'

'Yes, thanks.' Easy.

I turned to the unidentified man beside her and tried the Rosie name-extraction trick. 'Greetings, my name is Don and I'll be looking after you this evening, Doctor—'

'You said you're doing cocktails?'

'Correct.'

'Have you heard of a Rob Roy?'

'Of course.'

'Well, put me down for one.'

'Sweet, dry or perfect?' I asked.

One of the men opposite my customer laughed. 'Cop that, Brian.'

'Perfect,' said the man I now knew as Dr Brian Joyce. There were two Brians but I had already identified the first.

Dr Walsh (female, no transsexual characteristics) ordered a margarita.

'Standard, premium, strawberry, mango, melon or sage and pineapple?' I asked.

'Sage and pineapple? Why not?'

My next customer was the only remaining unidentified man, the one who had laughed at Brian's order. He had previously failed to respond to the name-extraction trick. I decided not to repeat it.

'What would you like?' I asked.

'I'll have a double-coddled Kurdistani sailmaker with a reverse twist,' he said. 'Shaken, not stirred.'

I was unfamiliar with this drink, but assumed the professionals behind the bar would know it.

'Your name, please?'

'Sorry?'

'I require your name. To avoid errors.'

There was a silence. Dr Jenny Broadhurst, beside him, said, 'His name's Rod.'

'Dr Roderick Broadhurst, correct?' I said by way of confirmation. The rule against partners did not apply, of course, to people who were in a relationship with someone from the same class. There were seven such couples and Jenny was predictably sitting beside her husband.

'What—' started Rod, but Jenny interrupted.

'Quite correct. I'm Jenny and I'll have a sage and pineapple margarita too, please.' She turned to Rod. 'Are you being a jerk? About the sailmaker? Pick on someone with your own complement of synapses.'

Rod looked at her, then at me. 'Sorry, mate, just taking the piss. I'll have a martini. Standard.'

I collected the remainder of the names and orders without difficulty. I understood that Jenny had been trying to tell Rod discreetly that I was unintelligent, presumably because of my waiter role. She had used a neat social trick, which I noted for future use, but had made a factual error which Rod had not corrected. Perhaps one day he or she would make a clinical or research mistake as a result of this misunderstanding.

Before I returned to the bar, I spoke to them again.

'There is no experimental evidence of a correlation between synapse numbers and intelligence level within primate populations. I recommend reading Williams and Herrup, *Annual Review of Neuroscience*.' I hoped this would be helpful.

Back at the bar, the cocktail orders caused some confusion. Only one of the three bar persons knew how to make a Rob Roy, and then only a conventional one. I gave her the instructions for the perfect version. Then there was an ingredient problem with the sage and pineapple margarita. The bar had pineapple (tinned— the book had said 'fresh if possible' so I decided that this would be acceptable) but no sage. I headed for the kitchen where they could not even offer me dried sage. Obviously this was not what *The Bartender's Companion* had called a 'well-stocked bar, ready for any occasion'.

The kitchen staff were also busy, but we settled on coriander leaves and I took a quick mental inventory of the bar's ingredients to avoid further problems of this kind.

Rosie was also taking orders. We had not yet progressed to the stage of collecting glasses, and some people seemed to be drinking quite slowly. I realised that our chances would be improved if there was a high turnover of drinks. Unfortunately, I was unable to encourage faster consumption, as I would be violating my duty as the holder of a Responsible Service of Alcohol certificate. I decided to take a middle ground by reminding them of some of the delicious cocktails available.

As I took orders, I observed a change in the dynamic of the ecosystem, evidenced by Rosie looking annoyed as she came past me.

'Table Five won't let me take their order. They want to wait for you.' It appeared that almost everyone wanted cocktails rather than wine. No doubt the proprietors would be pleased with the profit results. Unfortunately it appeared that staff numbers had been calculated on the basis that most orders would be for beer or wine, and the bar personnel were having trouble keeping up. Their knowledge of cocktails was surprisingly poor, and I was having to dictate recipes along with the orders.

The solution to both problems was simple. Rosie went behind the bar to assist while I took all the orders myself. A good memory was a huge asset, as I did not need to write anything down, or process just one table at a time. I took orders for the whole room, then relayed them back to the bar at consistent intervals. If people needed 'time to think', I left them and returned rather than waiting. I was actually running rather than walk-ing, and increased my word rate to the maximum that I considered comprehensible. The process was very effi-cient, and seemed to be appreciated by the diners, who would occasionally applaud when I was able to propose a drink to meet a particular requirement or replayed a table's orders when they were concerned that I might have misheard.

People were finishing their drinks, and I found that I could swab three glasses between the dining room and the bar. The remainder I grouped together and indi-cated to Rosie as I left the tray on the bar, rapidly advis-ing her of the owners' names.

She seemed a little pressured. I was enjoying myself immensely. I had the presence of mind to check the cream supplies before dessert was served. Predictably the quantity was insufficient for the number of cocktails I expected to sell to complement the mango mousse and sticky date pudding. Rosie headed for the kitchen to find more. When I returned to the bar, one of the barmen called out to me, 'I've got the boss on the phone. He's bringing cream. Do you need anything else?' I surveyed the shelves and made some predictions based on the 'ten most popular dessert cocktails'.

'Brandy, Galliano, crème de menthe, Cointreau, advocaat, dark rum, light rum.'

'Slow down, slow down,' he said.

I wasn't slowing down now. I was, as they say, on a roll.

15

The boss, a middle-aged man (estimated BMI twenty-seven), arrived with the additional supplies just in time for dessert, and did some reorganisation of the process behind the bar. Dessert was great fun, although it was hard to hear orders over the volume of conversation. I sold primarily the cream-based cocktails, which most of the diners were unfamiliar with, but responded to enthusiastically.

As the food waiters cleared the dessert dishes, I made a rough mental calculation of our coverage. It depended a great deal on Rosie, but I believed we had samples from at least eighty-five per cent of the males. Good, but not optimum use of our opportunity. Having ascertained the names of the guests, I had determined that all but twelve of the Caucasian males from the graduation party were present. The missing twelve included Alan McPhee, unable to attend due to death, but already eliminated by means of his daughter's hairbrush.

I headed for the bar, and Dr Ralph Browning followed me. 'Can I bother you for another Cadillac? That was maybe the best drink I've ever had.'

The bar staff were packing up, but the boss said to Rosie, 'Make the man a Cadillac.'

Jenny and Rod Broadhurst appeared from the dining room. 'Make that three,' said Rod.

The other bar personnel surrounded the owner, and there was a conversation.

'These guys have to go,' said the boss to me, shrugging his shoulders. He turned to Rosie. 'Double time?'

Meanwhile, the diners were forming a throng around the bar, raising their hands for attention.

Rosie handed a Cadillac to Dr Browning then turned to the boss. 'Sorry, I need at least two to stay. I can't run a bar for a hundred people by myself.'

'Me and him,' said the boss, pointing to me.

Finally, I had a chance to use my expertise. Rosie lifted the hinged part of the bar and let me through.

Dr Miranda Ball raised her hand. 'Same again, please.'

I called to Rosie, loudly, as the bar area was now very noisy. 'Miranda Ball. Alabama Slammer. One part each sloe gin, whisky, Galliano, triple sec, orange juice, orange slice and a cherry.'

'We're out of triple sec,' yelled Rosie.

'Substitute Cointreau. Reduce the quantity by twenty per cent.'

Dr Lucas put his finished drink on the bar, and raised his finger. One more.

'Gerry Lucas. Empty glass,' I called.

Rosie took the glass: I hoped she realised that we didn't have a sample for him yet.

'Another Anal Probe for Dr Lucas.'

'Got that,' she called from the kitchen. Excellent, she had remembered to swab.

Dr Martin van Krieger called out, loudly, 'Is there a cocktail with Galliano and tequila?'

The crowd quietened. This sort of question had

become common during dinner, and the guests had seemed impressed with my responses. I took a few moments to think.

Martin called out again, 'Don't worry if there isn't.'

'I'm re-indexing my internal database,' I said to explain the delay. It took a few moments. 'Mexican Gold or Freddy Fudpucker.' The crowd applauded.

'One of each,' he said.

Rosie knew how to make a Freddy Fudpucker. I gave the boss the Mexican Gold recipe.

We continued in this mode, with great success. I decided to take advantage of the opportunity to test all male doctors present, including those I had previously filtered out because of incompatible ethnic appearance. At 1.22 a.m. I was confident that we had tested all but one person. It was time to be proactive.

'Dr Anwar Khan. Approach the bar please.' It was an expression I had heard used on television. I hoped it carried the required authority.

Dr Khan had drunk only from his water glass, and carried it with him to the bar. 'You haven't ordered a drink all night,' I said.

'Is that a problem? I don't drink alcohol.'

'Very wise,' I said, although I was providing a bad example, with a beer open beside me. 'I recommend a Virgin Colada. Virgin Mary. Virgin—'

At this moment, Dr Eva Gold put her arm around Dr Khan. She was obviously affected by alcohol. 'Loosen up, Anwar.'

Dr Khan looked back at her, and then at the crowd, who were, in my assessment, also exhibiting the effects of intoxication.

'What the hell,' he said. 'Line up the virgins.'

He put his empty glass on the bar.

I did not leave the golf club until very late. The last guests departed at 2.32 a.m., two hours and two minutes after the scheduled completion time. Rosie, the boss and I had made one hundred and forty-three cocktails. Rosie and the boss also sold some beer which I did not keep track of.

'You guys can go,' said the boss. 'We'll clean up in the morning.' He extended his hand to me and I shook it according to custom, although it seemed very late for introductions. 'Amghad,' he said. 'Nice work, guys.'

He didn't shake Rosie's hand but looked at her and smiled. I noticed that she was looking a little tired. I was still full of energy.

'Got time for a drink?' said Amghad.

'Excellent idea.'

'You've got to be kidding,' said Rosie. 'I'm going. All the stuff's in your bag. You don't want a lift, Don?'

I had my cycle, and had only drunk three beers over the course of a long evening. I estimated that my blood alcohol would be well below the legal limit, even after a drink with Amghad. Rosie departed.

'What's your poison?' said Amghad.

'Poison?'

'What do you want to drink?'

Of course. But why, why, why can't people just say what they mean?

'Beer, please.'

Amghad opened two pale ales and we clicked bottles.

'How long have you been doing this?' he asked.

Though some deception had been necessary for the purposes of the Father Project, I was not comfortable with it.

'This is my first work in the field,' I said. 'Did I make some error?'

Amghad laughed. 'Funny guy. Listen,' he said. 'This place here is okay, but it's mostly steak and beer and mid-range wine. Tonight was a one-off, and mainly because of you.' He drank some beer, and looked at me without speaking for a while. 'I've been thinking of opening in the inner west—a little cocktail bar with a bit of flair. New York feel, but something a bit extra behind the bar, if you know what I mean. If you're interested—'

He was offering me a job! This was flattering, considering my limited experience, and my immediate irrational thought was that I wished Rosie had been present to witness it.

'I already have a job. Thank you.'

'I'm not talking about a job. I'm talking about a share in a business.'

'No, thank you,' I said. 'I'm sorry. But I think you would find me unsatisfactory.'

'Maybe, but I'm a pretty good judge. Give me a call if you change your mind. I'm in no hurry.'

The following day was Sunday.

Rosie and I arranged to meet at the lab at 3.00 p.m. She was predictably late, and I was already at work. I confirmed that we had obtained samples from all attendees at the reunion, meaning we had now tested all but eleven of the Caucasian males in the class.

Rosie arrived in tight blue jeans and a white shirt

and headed for the refrigerator. 'No beer until all samples are tested,' I said.

The work took some time, and I needed to source additional chemicals from the main laboratory.

At 7.06 p.m. Rosie went out for pizza, an unhealthy choice, but I had missed dinner the previous night and calculated that my body would be able to process the extra kilojoules. When she returned, I was testing the fourth-to-last candidate. As we were opening the pizza, my mobile phone rang. I realised immediately who it was.

'You didn't answer at home,' said my mother. 'I was worried.' This was a reasonable reaction on her part, as her Sunday phone call is part of my weekly schedule. 'Where are you?'

'At work.'

'Are you all right?'

'I'm fine.'

It was embarrassing to have Rosie listen to a personal conversation, and I did everything I could to terminate it quickly, keeping my responses as brief as possible. Rosie started laughing—fortunately not loudly enough for my mother to hear—and making funny faces.

'Your mother?' she said when I was finally able to hang up.

'Correct. How did you guess?'

'You sound like any sixteen-year-old boy talking to his mum in front of—' She stopped. My annoyance must have been obvious. 'Or me talking to Phil.'

It was interesting that Rosie also found conversation with a parent difficult. My mother is a good person, but very focused on sharing personal information. Rosie picked up a slice of pizza and looked at the computer screen.

'I'm guessing no news.'

'Plenty of news. Five more eliminated, only four to go. Including this one.' The result had come up while I was on the phone. 'Delete Anwar Khan.'

Rosie updated the spreadsheet. 'Allah be praised.'

'World's most complicated drink order,' I reminded her. Dr Khan had ordered five different drinks, compensating for his abstinence earlier in the evening. At the end of the night, he had left with his arm around Dr Gold.

'Yeah and I messed it up too. Put rum in the Virgin Colada.'

'You gave him alcohol?' I presumed this was in violation of his personal or religious standards.

'Maybe he'll miss out on his seventy-two virgins.'

I was familiar with this religious theory. My public position, as negotiated with the Dean, is that I regard all non-science based beliefs as having equal merit. But I found this one curious.

'Seems irrational,' I said. 'Wanting virgins. Surely a woman with sexual experience would be preferable to a novice.'

Rosie laughed and opened two beers. Then she stared at me, in the way that I am not supposed to do to others. 'Amazing. You. You're the most amazing person I've ever met. I don't know why you're doing this, but thanks.' She tapped her bottle against mine and drank.

It was enjoyable to be appreciated, but this was exactly what I had been worried about when I spoke to Claudia. Now Rosie was asking about my motives. She had applied for the Wife Project and presumably had expectations on that basis. It was time to be honest.

'Presumably you think it's in order to initiate a romantic relationship.'

'The thought had crossed my mind,' said Rosie.

Assumption confirmed.

'I'm extremely sorry if I've created an incorrect impression.'

'What do you mean?' said Rosie.

'I'm not interested in you as a partner. I should have told you earlier, but you're totally unsuitable.' I tried to gauge Rosie's reaction, but the interpretation of facial expressions is not one of my strengths.

'Well, you'll be pleased to know I can cope. I think you're pretty unsuitable too,' she said.

This was a relief. I hadn't hurt her feelings. But it did leave a question unanswered.

'Then why did you apply for the Wife Project?' I was using the word 'apply' loosely, as Gene had not required Rosie to complete the questionnaire. But her answer suggested a more serious level of miscommunication.

'*Wife Project*?' she said, as if she had never heard of it.

'Gene sent you to me as a candidate for the Wife Project. A wild card.'

'He did what?'

'You haven't heard of the Wife Project?' I asked, trying to establish the correct starting point.

'No,' she said, speaking in the tone that is traditionally used for giving instructions to a child. 'I have never heard of the Wife Project. But I'm about to. In detail.'

'Of course,' I said. 'But we should time-share it with pizza-consumption and beer-drinking.'

'Of course,' said Rosie.

I explained in some detail about the Wife Project, including the review with Gene and field visits to dating establishments. I finished as we consumed the final slices of pizza. Rosie had not really asked any questions except to make exclamations such as 'Jesus' and 'Fuck'.

'So,' said Rosie. 'Are you still doing it? The Wife Project?'

I explained that the project was still technically active, but in the absence of any qualified candidates there had been no progress.

'What a shame,' said Rosie. 'The perfect woman hasn't checked in yet.'

'I would assume that there is more than one candidate who meets the criteria,' I said, 'but it's like finding a bone-marrow donor. Not enough registrations.'

'I can only hope that enough women realise their civic duty and take the test.'

It was an interesting comment. I didn't really feel it was a duty. In the last few weeks, reflecting on the Wife Project and its lack of success, I had felt sad that there were so many women who were looking for partners, and desperate enough to register, even though there was only a low probability that they would meet the criteria.

'It's entirely optional,' I said.

'How nice for them. Here's a thought for you. Any woman who takes that test is happy to be treated as an object. You can say that's their choice. But if you spent two minutes looking at how much society forces women to think of themselves as objects, you might not think so. What I want to know is, do you want a woman who thinks like that? Is that the sort of wife you want?'

Rosie was sounding angry. 'You know why I dress the way I do? Why these glasses? Because I *don't* want to be treated as an object. If you knew how insulted I am that you think I was an applicant, a *candidate*—'

'Then why did you come to see me that day?' I asked. 'The day of the Jacket Incident?'

She shook her head. 'Remember at your apartment, on your balcony, I asked you a question about the size of testicles?'

I nodded.

'It didn't strike you as odd that here I was, on a first date, asking about testicles?'

'Not really. On a date I'm too focused on not saying odd things myself.'

'Okay, strike that.' She seemed a little calmer. 'The reason I asked the question was that I had a bet with Gene. Gene, who is a sexist pig, bet me that humans were naturally non-monogamous, and that the evidence was the size of their testicles. He sent me to a genetics expert to settle the bet.'

It took me a few moments to process fully the implications of what Rosie was saying. Gene had not prepared her for the dinner invitation. A woman—Rosie—had accepted an offer of a date with me without being pre-warned, set up. I was suffused with an irrationally disproportionate sense of satisfaction. But Gene had misled me. And it seemed he had taken advantage of Rosie financially.

'Did you lose much money?' I asked. 'It seems exploitative for a professor of psychology to make a bet with a barmaid.'

'I'm not a fucking barmaid.'

I could tell by the use of the obscenity that Rosie was getting angry again. But she could hardly contradict the evidence. I realised my error—one that would have caused trouble if I had made it in front of a class.

'Bar-*person*.'

'*Bartender* is the established non-sexist term,' she said. 'That's not the point. It's my part-time job. I'm doing my PhD in psychology, okay? In Gene's department. Does that make sense now?'

Of course! I suddenly remembered where I had seen her before—arguing with Gene after his public lecture. I recalled that Gene had asked her to have coffee with him—as he habitually did with attractive women—but that she had refused. For some reason I felt pleased about this. But if I had recognised her when she first came to my office, the whole misunderstanding could have been avoided. Everything now made sense, including the performance she had given in her medical-school enquiry. Except for two things.

'Why didn't you tell me?'

'Because I *am* a barmaid, and I'm not ashamed of it. You can take me or leave me as a barmaid.' I assumed she was speaking metaphorically.

'Excellent,' I said. 'That explains almost everything.'

'Oh, that's fine then. Why the "almost"? Don't feel you have to leave anything hanging.'

'Why Gene didn't tell me.'

'Because he's an arsehole.'

'Gene is my best friend.'

'God help you,' she said.

With matters clarified, it was time to finish the project, although our chances of finding the father tonight were looking poor. Fourteen candidates remained and we had only three samples left. I got up and walked to the machine.

'Listen,' said Rosie. 'I'm going to ask you again. Why are you doing this?'

I remembered my reflection on this question, and the answer I had reached involving scientific challenge and altruism to adjacent humans. But as I began my explanation, I realised that it was not true. Tonight we had corrected numerous invalid assumptions and errors in communication. I should not create a new one.

'I don't know,' I said.

I turned back to the machine and began to load the sample. My work was interrupted by a sudden smashing of glass. Rosie had thrown a beaker, fortunately not one containing an untested sample, against the wall.

'I am so *so* over this.' She walked out.

The next morning there was a knock at my office door. Rosie.

'Enter,' I said. 'I assume you want to know the final three results.'

Rosie walked unnaturally slowly to my desk where I was reviewing some potentially life-changing data. 'No,' she said. 'I figured they were negative. Even you would have phoned if you'd got a match.'

'Correct.'

She stood and looked at me without saying anything. I am aware that such silences are provided as opportunities for me to speak further, but I could think of nothing useful to say. Finally, she filled the gap.

'Hey—sorry I blew up last night.'

'Totally understandable. It's incredibly frustrating to work so hard for no result. But very common in science.' I remembered that she was a science graduate, as well as a barmaid. 'As you know.'

'I meant your Wife Project. I think it's wrong, but you're no different from every other man I know in objectifying women—just more honest about it. Anyway, you've done so much for me—'

'A communication error. Fortunately now rectified. We can proceed with the Father Project without the personal aspect.'

'Not till I understand why you're doing it.'

That difficult question again. But she had been happy to proceed when she thought that my motivation was romantic interest even though she did not reciprocate that interest.

'There has been no change in my motivation,' I said, truthfully. 'It was your motivation that was a concern. I thought you were interested in me as a partner. Fortunately, that assumption was based on false information.'

'Shouldn't you be spending the time on your objectification project?'

The question was perfectly timed. The data I was looking at on my screen indicated a major breakthrough.

'Good news. I have an applicant who satisfies all requirements.'

'Well,' said Rosie, 'you won't be needing me.'

This was a truly strange response. I hadn't needed Rosie for anything other than her own project.

16

The candidate's name was Bianca Rivera and she met all criteria. There was one obstacle, which I would need to devote time to. She noted that she had twice won the state ballroom dancing championship, and required her partner to be an accomplished dancer. It seemed perfectly reasonable for her to have some criteria of her own, and this one was easy to satisfy. And I had the perfect place to take her.

I called Regina, the Dean's assistant, and confirmed that she was still selling tickets for the faculty ball. Then I emailed Bianca and invited her as my partner. She accepted! I had a date—the perfect date. Now I had ten days to learn to dance.

Gene entered my office as I was practising my dance steps.

'I think the longevity statistics were based on marriages to live women, Don.'

He was referring to the skeleton I was using for practice. I had obtained it on loan from the Anatomy Department, and no one had asked what I required it for. Judging from the pelvis size, it was almost certainly a male skeleton, but this was irrelevant for dancing practice. I explained its purpose to Gene, pointing out the scene from the film *Grease* that was showing on the wall of my office.

'So,' said Gene, 'Ms Right—sorry, Dr Right, PhD, just popped into your inbox.'

'Her name's not Wright,' I said, 'it's Rivera.'

'Photo?'

'Not necessary. The meeting arrangements are quite precise. She's coming to the faculty ball.'

'Oh shit.' Gene went silent for a while and I resumed dancing practice. 'Don, the faculty ball is Friday after next.'

'Correct.'

'You can't learn to dance in nine days.'

'Ten. I started yesterday. The steps are trivial to remember. I just need to practise the mechanics. They're considerably less demanding than martial arts.'

I demonstrated a sequence.

'Very impressive,' said Gene. 'Sit down, Don.'

I sat.

'I hope you're not too pissed off at me about Rosie,' he said.

I had almost forgotten. 'Why didn't you tell me she was a psychology student? And about the bet?'

'From what Claudia said, you guys seemed to be having a good time. I thought if she wasn't telling you it was for a reason. She may be a bit twisted but she's not stupid.'

'Perfectly reasonable,' I said. On matters of human interaction, why argue with a professor of psychology?

'I'm glad one of you is all right with it,' said Gene. 'I have to tell you, Rosie was a little unhappy with me. A little unhappy with life. Listen, Don, I persuaded her to go to the ball. Alone. If you knew how often Rosie takes my advice, you'd realise what a big deal that was. I was going to suggest you do the same.'

'Take your advice?'

'No, go to the ball—alone. Or invite Rosie as your partner.'

I now saw what Gene was suggesting. Gene is so focused on attraction and sex that he sees it everywhere. This time he was totally in error.

'Rosie and I discussed the question of a relationship explicitly. Neither of us is interested.'

'Since when do women discuss anything explicitly?' said Gene.

I visited Claudia for some advice on my crucial date with Bianca. I assumed that she would be there in her role as Gene's wife, and I advised her that I might require assistance on the night. It turned out she wasn't even aware of the ball.

'Just be yourself, Don. If she doesn't want you for yourself, then she's not the right person for you.'

'I think it's unlikely that any woman would accept me for myself.'

'What about Daphne?' asked Claudia.

It was true—Daphne was unlike the women I had dated. This was excellent therapy; refutation by counter-example. Perhaps Bianca would be a younger, dancing, version of Daphne.

'And what about Rosie?' asked Claudia.

'Rosie is totally unsuitable.'

'I wasn't asking that,' said Claudia. 'Just whether she accepts you for yourself.'

I thought about it for a few moments. It was a difficult question.

'I think so. Because she isn't evaluating me as a partner.'

'It's probably good that you feel like that,' said Claudia.

Feel! Feel, feel, feel! Feelings were disrupting my sense of well-being. In addition to a nagging desire to be working on the Father Project rather than the Wife Project, I now had a high level of anxiety related to Bianca.

Throughout my life I have been criticised for a perceived lack of emotion, as if this were some absolute fault. Interactions with psychiatrists and psychologists—even including Claudia—start from the premise that I should be more 'in touch' with my emotions. What they really mean is that I should give in to them. I am perfectly happy to detect, recognise and analyse emotions. This is a useful skill and I would like to be better at it. Occasionally an emotion can be enjoyed—the gratitude I felt for my sister who visited me even during the bad times, the primitive feeling of well-being after a glass of wine—but we need to be vigilant that emotions do not cripple us.

I diagnosed brain overload and set up a spreadsheet to analyse the situation.

I began by listing the recent disturbances to my schedule. Two were unquestionably positive. Eva, the short-skirted cleaner, was doing an excellent job and had freed up considerable time. Without her, most of the recent additional activities would not have been possible. And, anxiety notwithstanding, I had my first fully qualified applicant for the Wife Project. I had made a decision that I wanted a partner and for the first time I had a viable candidate. Logic dictated that the Wife Project, to which I had planned to allocate most of my free time, should now receive maximum attention. Here, I identified Problem Number One. My emotions were not aligned with logic. I was reluctant to pursue the opportunity.

I did not know whether to list the Father Project as positive or negative but it had consumed enormous time for zero outcome. My arguments for pursuing it had always been weak, and I had done far more than could reasonably be expected of me. If Rosie wanted to locate and obtain DNA from the remaining candidates, she could do so herself. She now had substantial practical experience with the collection procedure. I could offer to perform the actual tests. Once again, logic and emotion were not in step. I wanted to continue the Father Project. Why?

It is virtually impossible to make useful comparisons of levels of happiness, especially across long periods of time. But if I had been asked to choose the happiest day of my life, I would have nominated, without hesitation, the first day I spent at the American Museum of Natural History in New York when I travelled there for a conference during my PhD studies. The second-best day was the second day there, and the third-best the third day there. But after recent events, it was not so clear. It was difficult to choose between the Natural History Museum and the night of cocktail-making at the golf club. Should I therefore consider resigning my job and accepting Amghad's offer of a partnership in a cocktail bar? Would I be permanently happier? The idea seemed ludicrous.

The cause of my confusion was that I was dealing with an equation which contained large negative values—most seriously the disruption to my schedule—and large positive values—the consequential enjoyable experiences. My inability to quantify these factors accurately meant that I could not determine the net result—negative or positive. And the margin of error was huge. I marked the Father Project as being of undetermined net value, and ranked it the most serious disturbance.

The last item on my spreadsheet was the immediate risk that my nervousness and ambivalence about the Wife Project would impede my social interaction with Bianca. I was not concerned about the dancing—I was confident that I could draw on my experience of preparing for martial arts competitions, with the supplementary advantage of an optimum intake of alcohol, which for martial arts is not permitted. My concern was more with social faux pas. It would be terrible to lose the perfect relationship because I failed to detect sarcasm or looked into her eyes for greater or less than the conventional period of time. I reassured myself that Claudia was essentially correct: if these things concerned Bianca excessively, she was not the perfect match, and I would at least be in a position to refine the questionnaire for future use.

I visited a formal costume hire establishment as recommended by Gene and specified maximum formality. I did not want a repeat of the Jacket Incident.

17

The ball was on a Friday evening at a reception centre on the river. For efficiency, I had brought my costume to work, and practised the cha-cha and rhumba with my skeleton while I waited to leave. When I went to the lab to get a beer I felt a strong twinge of emotion. I was missing the stimulation of the Father Project.

The morning suit, with its tails and tall hat, was totally impractical for cycling, so I took a taxi and arrived at exactly 7.55 p.m., as planned. Behind me, another taxi pulled up and a tall, dark-haired woman stepped out. She was wearing the world's most amazing dress: multiple bright colours—red, blue, yellow, green—with a complex structure including a split up one side. I had never seen anyone so spectacular. Estimated age thirty-five, BMI twenty-two, consistent with the questionnaire responses. Neither a little early nor a little late. Was I looking at my future wife? It was almost unbelievable.

As I stepped out of the taxi, she looked at me for a moment then turned and walked towards the door. I took a deep breath and followed. She stepped inside and looked around. She saw me again, and looked more carefully this time. I approached her, close enough to speak, being careful not to invade her personal space. I looked into her eyes. I counted one, two. Then I lowered my eyes a little, downwards, but only a tiny distance.

'Hi,' I said. 'I'm Don.'

She looked at me for a while before extending her hand to shake with low pressure.

'I'm Bianca. You've...really dressed up.'

'Of course, the invitation specified formal.'

After approximately two seconds she burst into laughter. 'You had me for a minute there. So deadpan. You know, you write "good sense of humour" on the list of things you're looking for, but you never expect to get a real comedian. I think you and I are going to have fun.'

Things were going extremely well.

The ballroom was huge—dozens of tables with formally dressed academics. *Everyone* turned to look at us, and it was obvious that we had made an impression. At first I thought it must be Bianca's spectacular dress, but there were numerous other interestingly dressed women. Then I noticed that the men were almost without exception dressed in black suits with white shirts and bowties. None wore tails or a hat. It accounted for Bianca's initial reaction. It was annoying, but not a situation I was unfamiliar with. I doffed my hat to the crowd and they shouted greetings. Bianca seemed to enjoy the attention.

We were at table twelve, according to the seating index, right on the edge of the dance floor. A band was tuning up. Observing their instruments, it seemed that my skills at cha-cha, samba, rhumba, foxtrot, waltz, tango and lambada would not be required. I would need to draw on the work of the second day of the dancing project—rock 'n' roll.

Gene's recommendation to arrive thirty minutes after the official start time meant that all but three of the seats at the table were already occupied. One of these belonged to Gene, who was walking around, pouring champagne. Claudia was not present.

I identified Laszlo Hevesi from Physics, who was dressed totally inappropriately in combat trousers and a hiking shirt, sitting next to a woman whom I recognised with surprise as Frances from the speed-dating night. On Laszlo's other side was The Beautiful Helena. There was also a dark-haired man of about thirty (BMI approximately twenty) who appeared not to have shaved for several days, and, beside him, the most beautiful woman I had ever seen. In contrast to the complexity of Bianca's costume, she was wearing a green dress with zero decoration, so minimal that it did not even have straps to hold it in place. It took me a moment to realise that its wearer was Rosie.

Bianca and I took the two vacant seats between Stubble Man and Frances, following the alternating male-female pattern that had been established. Rosie began the introductions, and I recognised the protocol that I had learned for conferences and never actually used.

'Don, this is Stefan.' She was referring to Stubble Man. I extended my hand, and shook, matching his pressure, which I judged as excessive. I had an immediate negative reaction to him. I am generally not competent at assessing other humans, except through the content of their conversation or written communication. But I am reasonably astute at identifying students who are likely to be disruptive.

'Your reputation precedes you,' Stefan said.

Perhaps my assessment was too hasty.

'You're familiar with my work?'

'You might say that.' He laughed.

I realised that I could not pursue the conversation until I introduced Bianca.

'Rosie, Stefan, allow me to present Bianca Rivera.'

Rosie extended her hand and said, 'Delighted to meet you.'

They smiled hard at each other and Stefan shook Bianca's hand also.

My duty done, I turned to Laszlo, whom I had not spoken to for some time. Laszlo is the only person I know with poorer social skills than mine, and it was reassuring to have him nearby for contrast.

'Greetings, Laszlo,' I said, assessing that formality would not be appropriate in his case. 'Greetings, Frances. You found a partner. How many encounters were required?'

'Gene introduced us,' said Laszlo. He was staring inappropriately at Rosie. Gene gave a 'thumbs up' signal to Laszlo, then moved between Bianca and me with the champagne bottle. Bianca immediately upended her glass. 'Don and I don't drink,' she said, turning mine down as well. Gene gave me a huge smile. It was an odd response to an annoying version-control oversight on my part—Bianca had apparently responded to the original questionnaire.

Rosie asked Bianca, 'How do you and Don know each other?'

'We share an interest in dancing,' Bianca said.

I thought this was an excellent reply, not referring to the Wife Project, but Rosie gave me a strange look.

'How nice,' she said. 'I'm a bit too busy with my PhD to have time for dancing.'

'You have to be organised,' said Bianca. 'I believe in being *very* organised.'

'Yes,' said Rosie, 'I—'

'The first time I made the final of the nationals was in the middle of my PhD. I thought about dropping the triathlon or the Japanese cookery course, but...'

Rosie smiled, but not in the way she usually did. 'No, that would have been silly. Men love a woman who can cook.'

'I like to think we've moved beyond that sort of stereo-typing,' said Bianca. 'Don's quite a cook himself.'

Claudia's suggestion that I mention my competence in cooking on the questionnaire had obviously been effective. Rosie provided some evidence.

'He's fabulous. We had the most amazing lobster on his balcony.'

'Oh, really?'

It was helpful that Rosie was recommending me to Bianca, but Stefan was displaying the disruptive-student expression again. I applied my lecture technique of asking him a question first.

'Are you Rosie's boyfriend?'

Stefan did not have a ready answer, and in a lecture that would have been my cue to continue, with the student now healthily wary of me. But Rosie answered for him.

'Stefan is doing his PhD with me.'

'I believe the term is *partner*,' said Stefan.

'For this evening,' said Rosie.

Stefan smiled. 'First date.'

It was odd that they did not seem to have agreed on the nature of their relationship. Rosie turned back to Bianca.

'And yours and Don's first date too?'

'That's right, Rosie.'

'How did you find the questionnaire?'

Bianca looked quickly at me, then turned back to Rosie. 'Wonderful. Most men only want to talk about themselves. It was so nice to have someone focusing on me.'

'I can see how that would work for you,' said Rosie.

'And a dancer,' Bianca said. 'I couldn't believe my luck. But you know what they say: the harder I work, the luckier I get.'

Rosie picked up her champagne glass, and Stefan said, 'How long have *you* been dancing, Don? Won any prizes?'

I was saved from answering by the arrival of the Dean.

She was wearing a complex pink dress, the lower part of which spread out widely, and was accompanied by a woman of approximately the same age dressed in the standard male ball costume of black suit and bowtie. The reaction of the ball-goers was similar to that at my entrance, without the friendly greetings at the end.

'Oh dear,' said Bianca. I had a low opinion of the Dean, but the comment made me uncomfortable.

'You have a problem with gay women?' said Rosie, slightly aggressively.

'Not at all,' said Bianca. 'My problem's with her dress sense.'

'You'll have fun with Don, then,' said Rosie.

'I think Don looks *fabulous*,' said Bianca. 'It takes flair to pull off something a little different. Anyone can wear a dinner suit or a plain frock. Don't you think so, Don?'

I nodded in polite agreement. Bianca was exhibiting exactly the characteristics I was looking for. There was every chance she would be perfect. But for some reason, my instincts were rebelling. Perhaps it was the no-drinking rule. My underlying addiction to alcohol was causing my subconscious to send a signal to reject someone who stopped me drinking. I needed to overcome it.

We finished our entrées and the band played a few loud chords. Stefan walked over to them and took the microphone from the singer.

'Good evening, everyone,' he said. 'I thought you should know that we have a former finalist in the national dancing championships with us this evening. You may have seen her on television. Bianca Rivera. Let's give Bianca and her partner Don a few minutes to entertain us.'

I had not expected my first performance to be so public, but there was the advantage of an unobstructed dance floor. I have given lectures to larger audiences, and participated in martial arts bouts in front of crowds. There was no reason to be nervous. Bianca and I stepped onto the dance floor.

I took her in the standard jive hold that I had practised on the skeleton, and immediately felt the awkwardness, approaching revulsion, that I feel when forced into intimate contact with another human. I had mentally prepared for this, but not for a more serious problem. I had not practised with music. I am sure I executed the steps accurately, but not at precisely the correct speed, and not at the same time as the beat. We were immediately tripping over each other and the net effect was a *disaster*. Bianca tried to lead, but I had no experience with a living partner, let alone one who was trying to be in control.

People began laughing. I am an expert at being laughed at and, as Bianca pulled away from me, I scanned the audience to see who was not laughing, an excellent means of identifying friends. Gene and Rosie and, surprisingly, the Dean and her partner were my friends tonight. Stefan was definitely not.

Something major was required to save the situation. In my dancing research, I had noted some specialised moves that I had not intended to use but remembered because they were so interesting. They had the advantage of not being highly dependent on synchronised timing or body contact. Now was the time to deploy them.

I performed the running man, milking the cow, and the fishing imitation, reeling Bianca in, though she did not actually move as required. In fact she was standing totally still. Finally, I attempted a body-contact manoeuvre, traditionally used for a spectacular finish, in which the male swings the female on either side, over his back and between his legs. Unfortunately this requires cooperation on the part of the partner, particularly if she is heavier than a skeleton. Bianca offered no such cooperation and the effect was as if I had attacked her. Unlike aikido, dancing training apparently does not include practice in falling safely.

I offered to help her up, but she ignored my hand and walked towards the bathroom, apparently uninjured.

I went back to the table and sat down. Stefan was still laughing.

'You bastard,' Rosie said to him.

Gene said something to Rosie, presumably to prevent inappropriate public anger, and she seemed to calm down.

Bianca returned to her seat, but only to collect her bag.

'The problem was synchronisation,' I tried to tell her. 'The metronome in my head is not set to the same frequency as the band.'

Bianca turned away, but Rosie seemed prepared to listen to my explanation. 'I turned off the sound during practice so I could focus on learning the steps.'

Rosie did not reply and I heard Bianca speaking to Stefan. 'It happens. This isn't the first time, just the worst. Men say they can dance...' She walked towards the exit without saying goodnight to me, but Gene followed and intercepted her.

This gave me an opportunity. I righted my glass, and filled it with wine. It was a poorly made gordo blanco with excessive residual sugar. I drank it and poured another. Rosie got up from her seat and walked over to the band. She spoke to the singer, then the drummer.

She returned and pointed at me in a stylised manner. I recognised the action—I had seen it twelve times. It was the signal that Olivia Newton-John gave to John Travolta in *Grease* to commence the dance sequence that I had been practising when Gene interrupted me nine days earlier. Rosie pulled me towards the dance floor.

'Dance,' she said. 'Just fucking dance.'

I started dancing without music. This was what I had practised. Rosie followed according to my tempo. Then she raised her arm and started waving it in time with our movements. I heard the drummer start playing and could tell in my body that he was in time with us. I barely noticed the rest of the band start up.

Rosie was a good dancer and considerably easier to manipulate than the skeleton. I led her through the more difficult moves, totally focused on the mechanics and on not making errors. The *Grease* song finished and everyone clapped. But before we could return to the table, the band started again and the audience clapped in time: *Satisfaction*. It may have been due to the effect of the gordo blanco on my cognitive functions, but I was suddenly overwhelmed by an extraordinary feeling— not of satisfaction but of absolute joy. It was the feeling I had in the Museum of Natural History and when I was making cocktails. We started dancing again, and this time I allowed myself to focus on the sensations of my body moving to the beat of the song from my childhood and of Rosie moving to the same rhythm.

The music finished and everyone clapped again.

I looked for Bianca, my date, and located her near the exit with Gene. I had presumed she would be impressed that the problem was solved, but even from a distance and with my limited ability to interpret expressions, I could see that she was furious. She turned and left.

The rest of the evening was incredible, changed totally by one dance. *Everyone* came up to Rosie and me to offer compliments. The photographer gave us each a photo without charging us. Stefan left early. Gene obtained some high-quality champagne from the bar, and we drank several glasses with him and a Hungarian postdoc named Klara from Physics. Rosie and I danced again, and then I danced with almost every woman at the ball. I asked Gene if I should invite the Dean or her partner, but he considered this to be a question beyond even his social expertise. In the end I did not, as the Dean was visibly in a bad mood. The crowd had made it clear that they would rather dance than listen to her scheduled speech.

At the end of the night, the band played a waltz, and when it was finished I looked around and it was just Rosie and me on the dance floor. And everyone applauded again. It was only later that I realised that I had experienced extended close contact with another human without feeling uncomfortable. I attributed it to my concentration on correctly executing the dance steps.

'You want to share a taxi?' asked Rosie.

It seemed a sensible use of fossil fuel.

In the taxi, Rosie said to me, 'You should have practised with different beats. You're not as smart as I thought you were.'

I just looked out the window of the taxi.

Then she said, 'No way. No *fucking* way. You did, didn't you? That's worse. You'd rather make a fool of yourself in front of everyone than tell her she didn't float your boat.'

'It would have been extremely awkward. I had no reason to reject her.'

'Besides not wanting to marry a parakeet,' said Rosie.

I found this incredibly funny, no doubt as a result of alcohol and decompensation after the stress. We both laughed for several minutes, and Rosie even touched me a few times on the shoulder. I didn't mind, but when we stopped laughing I felt awkward again and averted my gaze.

'You're unbelievable,' said Rosie. 'Look at me when I'm talking.'

I kept looking out the window. I was already over-stimulated. 'I know what you look like.'

'What colour eyes do I have?'

'Brown.'

'When I was born, I had blue eyes,' she said. 'Baby blues. Like my mother. She was Irish but she had blue eyes. Then they turned brown.'

I looked at Rosie. This was incredible.

'Your mother's eyes changed colour?'

'*My* eyes. It happens with babies. That was when my mother realised that Phil wasn't my father. She had blue eyes and so does Phil. And she decided to tell him. I suppose I should be grateful he wasn't a lion.'

I was having trouble making sense of all that Rosie was saying, doubtless due to the effects of the alcohol and her perfume. However, she had given me an opportunity to keep the conversation on safe ground. The inheritance of common genetically influenced traits such as eye colour is more complex than is generally understood, and I was confident that I could speak on the topic for long enough to occupy the remainder of our journey. But I realised that this was a defensive action and impolite to Rosie who had risked considerable embarrassment and damage to her relationship with Stefan for my benefit.

I rolled back my thoughts and re-parsed her

statement: 'I suppose I should be grateful he wasn't a lion.' I assumed she was referring to our conversation on the night of the Balcony Meal when I informed her that lions kill the offspring of previous matings. Perhaps she wanted to talk about Phil. This was interesting to me too. The entire motivation for the Father Project was Phil's failure in that role. But Rosie had offered no real evidence beyond his opposition to alcohol, ownership of an impractical vehicle and selection of a jewellery box as a gift.

'Was he violent?' I asked.

'No.' She paused for a while. 'He was just—all over the place. One day I'd be the most special kid in the world, next day he didn't want me there.'

This seemed very general, and hardly a justification for a major DNA-investigation project. 'Can you provide an example?'

'Where do I start? Okay, the first time was when I was ten. He promised to take me to Disneyland. I told everyone at school. And I waited and waited and waited and it never happened.'

The taxi stopped outside a block of flats. Rosie kept talking, looking at the back of the driver's seat. 'So I have this whole thing about rejection.' She turned to me. 'How do *you* deal with it?'

'The problem has never occurred,' I told her. It was not the time to begin a new conversation.

'Bullshit,' said Rosie. It appeared that I would need to answer honestly. I was in the presence of a psychology graduate.

'There were some problems at school,' I said. 'Hence the martial arts. But I developed some nonviolent techniques for dealing with difficult social situations.'

'Like tonight.'

'I emphasised the things that people found amusing.'

Rosie didn't respond. I recognised the therapy technique, but could not think of anything to do but elaborate.

'I didn't have many friends. Basically zero, except my sister. Unfortunately she died two years ago due to medical incompetence.'

'What happened?' said Rosie, quietly.

'An undiagnosed ectopic pregnancy.'

'Oh, Don,' said Rosie, very sympathetically. I sensed that I had chosen an appropriate person to confide in.

'Was she…in a relationship?'

'No.' I anticipated her next question. 'We never found out the source.'

'What was her name?'

This was, on the surface, an innocuous question, though I could see no purpose in Rosie knowing my sister's name. The indirect reference was unambiguous, as I had only one sister. But I felt very uncomfortable. It took me a few moments to realise why. Although there had been no deliberate decision on my part, I had not said her name since her death.

'Michelle,' I said to Rosie. After that, neither of us spoke for a while.

The taxi driver coughed artificially. I presumed he wasn't asking for a beer.

'You want to come up?' said Rosie.

I was feeling overwhelmed. Meeting Bianca, dancing, rejection by Bianca, social overload, discussion of personal matters—now, just when I thought the ordeal was over, Rosie seemed to be proposing more conversation. I was not sure I could cope.

'It's extremely late,' I said. I was sure this was a socially acceptable way of saying that I wanted to go home.

'The taxi fares go down again in the morning.'

If I understood correctly, I was now definitely far out of my depth. I needed to be sure that I wasn't misinterpreting her.

'Are you suggesting I stay the night?'

'Maybe. First you have to listen to the story of my life.'

Warning! Danger, Will Robinson. Unidentified alien approaching! I could feel myself slipping into the emotional abyss. I managed to stay calm enough to respond.

'Unfortunately I have a number of activities scheduled for the morning.' Routine, normality.

Rosie opened the taxi door. I willed her to go. But she had more to say.

'Don, can I ask you something?'

'One question.'

'Do you find me attractive?'

Gene told me the next day that I got it wrong. But he was not in a taxi, after an evening of total sensory overload, with the most beautiful woman in the world. I believed I did well. I detected the trick question. I wanted Rosie to like me, and I remembered her passionate statement about men treating women as objects. She was testing to see if I saw her as an object or as a person. Obviously the correct answer was the latter.

'I haven't really noticed,' I told the most beautiful woman in the world.

18

I texted Gene from the taxi. It was 1.08 a.m. but he had left the ball at the same time as I did, and had further to travel. *Urgent: Run tomorrow 6 a.m.* Gene texted back: *Sunday at 8: Bring Bianca's contact info.* I was about to insist on the earlier date when I realised that I could profitably use the time to organise my thoughts.

It seemed obvious that Rosie had invited me to have sex with her. I was right to have avoided the situation. We had both drunk a substantial quantity of champagne, and alcohol is notorious for encouraging unwise decisions about sex. Rosie had the perfect example. Her mother's decision, doubtless prompted by alcohol, was still causing Rosie significant distress.

My own sexual experience was limited. Gene had advised that it was conventional to wait until the third date, and my relationships had never progressed beyond the first. In fact, Rosie and I had technically had only one date—the night of the Jacket Incident and the Balcony Meal.

I did not use the services of brothels, not for any moral reason, but because I found the idea distasteful. This was not a rational reason, but since the benefits I was seeking were only primitive, a primitive reason was sufficient.

But I now seemed to have an opportunity for what Gene would call 'no-strings-attached sex'. The required conditions were in place: Rosie and I had clearly agreed that neither of us had an interest in a romantic relationship, then Rosie had indicated that she wanted to have sex with me. Did I want to have sex with Rosie? There seemed no logical reason not to, leaving me free to obey the dictates of my primitive desires. The answer was an extremely clear yes. Having made this completely rational decision, I could think of nothing else.

On Sunday morning, Gene met me outside his house. I had brought Bianca's contact details and checked her nationality—Panamanian. Gene was very pleased about the latter.

Gene wanted full details of my encounter with Rosie, but I had decided it was a waste of effort to explain it twice: I would tell him and Claudia together. As I had no other subject to discuss and Gene had difficulty in running and speaking concurrently, we spent the next forty-seven minutes in silence.

When we returned to Gene's house, Claudia and Eugenie were having breakfast.

I sat down and said, 'I require some advice.'

'Can it wait?' said Claudia. 'We have to take Eugenie to horseriding and then we're meeting people for brunch.'

'No. I may have made a social error. I broke one of Gene's rules.'

Gene said, 'Don, I think the Panamanian bird has flown. Put that one down to experience.'

'The rule applies to Rosie, not Bianca. Never pass up a chance to have sex with a woman under thirty.'

'Gene told you that?' said Claudia.

Carl had entered the room and I prepared to defend myself against his ritual attack, but he stopped to look at his father.

'I thought I should consult with you because you're a psychologist and with Gene because of his extensive practical experience,' I said.

Gene looked at Claudia, then at Carl.

'In my misspent youth,' he said. '*Not* my teens.' He turned back to me. 'I think this can wait till lunch tomorrow.'

'What about Claudia?' I asked.

Claudia got up from the table. 'I'm sure there's nothing Gene doesn't know.'

This was encouraging, especially coming from his wife.

'You said what?' said Gene. We were having lunch in the University Club as scheduled.

'I said that I hadn't noticed her appearance. I didn't want her to think I saw her as a sexual object.'

'Jesus,' said Gene. 'The one time you think before you speak is the one time you shouldn't have.'

'I should have said she was beautiful?' I was incredulous.

'Got it in one,' said Gene, incorrectly, as the problem was that I hadn't got it right the first time. 'That'll explain the cake.'

I must have looked blank. For obvious reasons.

'She's been eating chocolate cake. At her desk. For breakfast.'

This seemed to me to be an unhealthy choice,

consistent with smoking, but not an indicator of distress. But Gene assured me that it was to make herself feel better.

Having supplied Gene with the necessary background information, I presented my problem.

'You're saying she's not The One,' said Gene. 'Not a life partner.'

'Totally unsuitable. But she's extremely attractive. If I'm going to have uncommitted sex with anyone, she's the perfect candidate. She has no emotional attachment to me either.'

'So why the stress?' said Gene. 'You have had sex before?'

'Of course,' I said. 'My doctor is strongly in favour.'

'Frontiers of medical science,' said Gene.

He was probably making a joke. I think the value of regular sex has been known for some time.

I explained further. 'It's just that adding a second person makes it more complicated.'

'Naturally,' said Gene. 'I should have thought of that. Why not get a book?'

The information was available on the internet, but a few minutes of examining the search results on 'sexual positions' convinced me that the book option would provide a more relevant tutorial with less extraneous information.

I had no difficulty finding a suitable book and, back in my office, selected a random position. It was called the Reverse Cowboy Position (Variant 2). I tried it— simple. But, as I had pointed out to Gene, the problem was the involvement of the second person. I got the skeleton from the closet and arranged it on top of me, following the diagram in the book.

There is a rule at the university that no one opens a door without knocking first. Gene violates it in my case but we are good friends. I do not consider the Dean my friend. It was an embarrassing moment, especially as the Dean was accompanied by another person, but entirely her fault. It was fortunate that I had kept my clothes on.

'Don,' she said, 'if you can leave off repairing that skeleton for a moment, I'd like you to meet Dr Peter Enticott from the Medical Research Council. I mentioned your work in cirrhosis and he was keen to meet you. To consider a *funding package*.' She emphasised the last two words as though I was so unconnected with university politics that I might forget that funding was the centre of her world. She was right to do so.

I recognised Peter instantly. He was the former father candidate who worked at Deakin University, and who had prompted the cup-stealing incident. He also recognised me.

'Don and I have met,' he said. 'His partner is considering applying for the MD program. And we met recently at a social occasion.' He winked at me. 'I don't think you're paying your academic staff enough.'

We had an excellent discussion about my work with alcoholic mice. Peter seemed highly interested and I had to reassure him repeatedly that I had designed the research so there was no need for external grants. The Dean was making hand signals and contorting her face, and I guessed that she wanted me to misrepresent my study as requiring funding, so that she could divert the money to some project that would not be funded on its merits. I chose to feign a lack of comprehension, but this had the effect of increasing the intensity of the Dean's signalling. It was only afterwards that I realised that I should not have left the sexual positions book open on the floor.

I decided that ten positions would be sufficient initially. More could be learned if the initial encounter was successful. It did not take long—less time than learning the cha-cha. In terms of reward for effort, it seemed strongly preferable to dancing and I was greatly looking forward to it.

I went to visit Rosie in her workplace. The PhD students' area was a windowless space with desks along the walls. I counted eight students, including Rosie and Stefan, whose desk was beside Rosie's.

Stefan gave me an odd smile. I was still suspicious of him.

'You're all over Facebook, Don.' He turned to Rosie. 'You'll have to update your relationship status.'

On his screen was a spectacular photo of Rosie and me dancing, similar to the one that the photographer had given me and which now sat by my computer at home. I was spinning Rosie, and her facial expression indicated extreme happiness. I had not technically been 'tagged' as I was not registered on Facebook (social networking not being an interest of mine) but our names had been added to the photo: *A/Prof Don Tillman of Genetics and Rosie Jarman, PhD Candidate, Psychology.*

'Don't talk to me about it,' said Rosie.

'You don't like the photo?' This seemed a bad sign.

'It's Phil. I don't want him seeing this.'

Stefan said, 'You think your father spends his life looking at Facebook?'

'Wait till he calls,' said Rosie. '"How much does he earn?" "Are you screwing him?" "What can he bench press?"'

'Hardly unusual questions for a father to ask about a man who's dating his daughter,' said Stefan.

'I'm not dating Don. We shared a taxi. That's all. Right, Don?'

'Correct.'

Rosie turned back to Stefan. 'So you can stick your little theory where it fits. Permanently.'

'I need to talk to you in private,' I said to Rosie.

She looked at me very directly. 'I don't think there's anything we need to say in private.'

This seemed odd. But presumably she and Stefan shared information in the same way that Gene and I did. He had accompanied her to the ball.

'I was reconsidering your offer of sex,' I said.

Stefan put his hand over his mouth. There was quite a long silence—I would estimate six seconds.

Then Rosie said, 'Don, it was a joke. A joke.'

I could make no sense of this. I could understand that she might have changed her mind. Perhaps the problem around the sexual objectification response had been fatal. But a joke? Surely I could not be so insensitive to social cues to have missed the fact that she was joking. Yes, I could be. I had failed to detect jokes in the past. Frequently. A joke. I had been obsessing about a joke.

'Oh. When should we meet about the other project?'

Rosie looked down at her desk. 'There is no other project.'

19

For a week, I did my best to return to my regular schedule, using the time freed up by Eva's cleaning and the cancellation of the Father Project to catch up on the karate and aikido training that I had been missing.

Sensei, fifth dan, a man who says very little, especially to the black belts, pulled me aside as I was working the punching bag in the dojo.

'Something has made you very angry,' he said. That was all.

He knew me well enough to know that once an emotion was identified I would not let it defeat me. But he was right to speak to me, because I had not realised that I was angry.

I was briefly angry with Rosie because she unexpectedly refused me something I wanted. But then I became angry with myself over the social incompetence that had doubtless caused Rosie embarrassment.

I made several attempts to contact Rosie and got her answering service. Finally I left a message: 'What if you get leukaemia and don't know where to source a bone-marrow transplant? Your biological father would be an excellent candidate with a strong motivation to assist. Failure to complete the project could result in death. There are only eleven candidates remaining.'

She did not return my call.

'These things happen,' said Claudia over the third coffee meeting in four weeks. 'You get involved with a woman, it doesn't work out...'

So that was it. I had, in my own way, become 'involved' with Rosie.

'What should I do?'

'It's not easy,' said Claudia, 'but anyone will give you the same advice. Move on. Something else will turn up.'

Claudia's logic, built on sound theoretical foundations and drawing on substantial professional experience, was obviously superior to my own irrational feelings. But as I reflected on it, I realised that her advice, and indeed the discipline of psychology itself, embodied the results of research on normal humans. I am well aware that I have some unusual characteristics. Was it possible that Claudia's advice was not appropriate for me?

I decided on a compromise course of action. I would continue the Wife Project. If (and *only* if) there was further time available, I would use it for the Father Project, proceeding alone. If I could present Rosie with the solution, perhaps we could become friends again.

Based on the Bianca Disaster I revised the questionnaire, adding more stringent criteria. I included questions on dancing, racquet sports and bridge to eliminate candidates who would require me to gain competence in useless activities, and increased the difficulty of the mathematics, physics and genetics problems. Option *(c) moderately* would be the *only* acceptable answer to the alcohol question. I organised for the responses to go directly to Gene, who was obviously engaging in the well-established research practice of making secondary use of the data. He could advise me if anyone met my criteria. Exactly.

In the absence of Wife Project candidates, I thought hard about the best way to get DNA samples for the Father Project.

The answer came to me as I was boning a quail. The candidates were doctors who would presumably be willing to contribute to genetics research. I just needed a plausible excuse to ask for their DNA. Thanks to the preparation I had done for the Asperger's lecture, I had one.

I pulled out my list of eleven names. Two were confirmed dead, leaving nine, seven of whom were living overseas, which explained their absence at the reunion. But two had local phone numbers. One was the head of the Medical Research Institute at my own university. I rang it first.

'Professor Lefebvre's office,' said a woman's voice.

'It's Professor Tillman from the Department of Genetics. I'd like to invite Professor Lefebvre to participate in a research project.'

'Professor Lefebvre is on sabbatical in the US. He'll be back in two weeks.'

'Excellent. The project is *Presence of Genetic Markers for Autism in High-Achieving Individuals*. I require him to complete a questionnaire and provide a DNA sample.'

Two days later, I had succeeded in locating all nine living candidates and posted them questionnaires, created from the Asperger's research papers, and cheek scrapers. The questionnaires were irrelevant, but were needed to make the research appear legitimate. My covering letter made clear my credentials as a professor of genetics at a prestigious university. In the meantime, I needed to find relatives of the two dead doctors.

I found an obituary for Dr Gerhard von Deyn, a victim of a heart attack, on the internet. It mentioned his daughter, a medical student at the time of his death. I had no trouble tracking down Dr Brigitte von Deyn and she was happy to participate in the survey. Simple.

Geoffrey Case was a much more difficult challenge. He had died a year after graduating. I had long ago noted his basic details from the reunion website. He had not married and had no (known) children.

Meanwhile the DNA samples trickled back. Two doctors, both in New York, declined to participate. Why would medical practitioners not participate in an important study? Did they have something to hide? Such as an illegitimate daughter in the same city that the request came from? It occurred to me that, if they suspected my motives, they could send a friend's DNA. At least refusal was better than cheating.

Seven candidates, including Dr von Deyn, Jr, returned samples. None of them was Rosie's father or half-sister. Professor Simon Lefebvre returned from his sabbatical and wanted to meet me in person.

'I'm here to collect a package from Professor Lefebvre,' I said to the receptionist at the city hospital where he was based, hoping to avoid an actual meeting and interrogation. I was unsuccessful. She buzzed the phone, announced my name, and Professor Lefebvre appeared. He was, I assumed, approximately fifty-four years old. I had met many fifty-four-year-olds in the past thirteen weeks. He was carrying a large envelope, presumably containing the questionnaire, which was destined for the recycling bin, and his DNA.

As he reached me, I tried to take the envelope, but he extended his other hand to shake mine. It was awkward, but the net result was that we shook hands and he retained the envelope.

'Simon Lefebvre,' he said. 'So, what are you really after?'

This was totally unexpected. Why should he question my motives?

'Your DNA,' I said. 'And the questionnaire. For a major research study. Critical.' I was feeling stressed and my voice doubtless reflected it.

'I'm sure it is.' Simon laughed. 'And you randomly select the head of medical research as a subject?'

'We were looking for high achievers.'

'What's Charlie after this time?'

'Charlie?' I didn't know anyone called Charlie.

'All right,' he said. 'Dumb question. How much do you want me to put in?'

'No putting in is required. There is no Charlie involved. I just require the DNA…and the questionnaire.'

Simon laughed, again. 'You've got my attention. You can tell Charlie that. Shoot me through the project description. And the ethics approval. The whole catastrophe.'

'Then I can have my sample?' I said. 'A high response rate is critical for the statistical analysis.'

'Just send me the paperwork.'

Simon Lefebvre's request was entirely reasonable. Unfortunately I did not have the required paperwork, because the project was fictitious. To develop a plausible project proposal would potentially require hundreds of hours of work.

I attempted an estimate of the probability that Simon Lefebvre was Rosie's father. There were now four untested candidates: Lefebvre, Geoffrey Case (dead), and the two New Yorkers, Isaac Esler and Solomon Freyberg. On the basis of Rosie's information, any one of them had a twenty-five per cent probability of being her father. But having proceeded so far without a positive result, I had to consider other possibilities. Two of our results relied on relatives rather than direct testing. It was possible that one or both of these daughters were, like Rosie, the result of extra-relationship sex, which, as Gene points out, is a more common phenomenon than popularly believed. And there was the possibility that one or more of my respondents to the fictitious research project might have deliberately sent a false sample.

I also had to consider that Rosie's mother might not have told the truth. It took me a long time to think of this, as my default assumption is that people will be honest. But perhaps Rosie's mother wanted Rosie to believe that her father was a doctor, as she was, rather than a less prestigious person. On balance, I estimated the chance that Simon Lefebvre was Rosie's father was sixteen per cent. In developing documentation for the Asperger's research project I would be doing an enormous amount of work with a low probability that it would provide the answer.

I chose to proceed. The decision was barely rational.

In the midst of this work, I received a phone call from a solicitor to advise me that Daphne had died. Despite the fact that she had been effectively dead for some time, I detected in myself an unexpected feeling of loneliness.

Our friendship had been simple. Everything was so much more complicated now.

The reason for the call was that Daphne had left me what the solicitor referred to as a 'small sum' in her will. Ten thousand dollars. And she had also left a letter, written before she had gone to live in the nursing home. It was handwritten on decorative paper.

Dear Don,
Thank you for making the final years of my life so stimulating. After Edward was admitted to the nursing home, I did not believe that there was much left for me. I'm sure you know how much you have taught me, and how interesting our conversations have been, but you may not realise what a wonderful companion and support you have been to me.

I once told you that you would make someone a wonderful husband, and, in case you have forgotten, I am telling you again. I'm sure if you look hard enough, you will find the right person. Do not give up, Don.

I know you don't need my money, and my children do, but I have left you a small sum. I would be pleased if you would use it for something irrational.
Much love,
Your friend,
Daphne Speldewind

It took me less than ten seconds to think of an irrational purchase: in fact I allowed myself only that amount of time to ensure that the decision was not affected by any logical thought process.

The Asperger's research project was fascinating but very time-consuming. The final proposal was impressive and I was confident it would have passed the peer-review process if it had been submitted to a funding organisation. I was implying it had been, though I stopped short of forging an approval letter. I called Lefebvre's personal assistant and explained that I had forgotten to send him the documents, but would now bring them personally. I was becoming more competent at deception.

I arrived at reception, and the process of summoning Lefebvre was repeated. This time he was not holding an envelope. I tried to give him the documents and he tried to shake my hand, and we had a repeat of the confusion that had occurred the previous time. Lefebvre seemed to find this funny. I was conscious of being tense. After all this work, I wanted the DNA.

'Greetings,' I said. 'Documentation as requested. All requirements have been fulfilled. I now need the DNA sample and questionnaire.'

Lefebvre laughed again, and looked me up and down. Was there something odd about my appearance? My t-shirt was the one I wear on alternate days, featuring the periodic table, a birthday gift from the year after my graduation, and my trousers were the serviceable pair that are equally suitable for walking, lecturing, research and physical tasks. Plus high-quality running shoes. The only error was that my socks, which would have been visible below my trousers, were of slightly different colours, a common error when dressing in poor light. But Simon Lefebvre seemed to find everything amusing.

'Beautiful,' he said. Then he repeated my words in

what seemed to be an attempt to imitate my intonation: 'All requirements have been fulfilled.' He added, in his normal voice, 'Tell Charlie I promise I'll read the proposal.'

Charlie again! This was ridiculous.

'The DNA,' I said, forcefully. 'I need the sample.'

Lefebvre laughed as though I had made the biggest joke of all time. There were tears running down his face. Actual tears.

'You've made my day.'

He grabbed a tissue from a box on the reception desk, wiped his face, blew his nose and tossed the used tissue in the bin as he left with my proposal.

I walked to the bin and retrieved the tissue.

20

I sat with a newspaper in the University Club reading room for the third day in succession. I wanted this to look accidental. From my position, I could observe the queue at the counter where Rosie sometimes purchased her lunch, even though she was not qualified to be a member. Gene had given me this information, reluctantly.

'Don, I think it's time to leave this one alone. You're going to get hurt.'

I disagreed. I am very good at dealing with emotions. I was prepared for rejection.

Rosie walked in and joined the queue. I got up and slipped in behind her.

'Don,' she said. 'What a coincidence.'

'I have news on the project.'

'There's no project. I'm sorry about…last time you saw me. Shit! You embarrass me and I say sorry.'

'Apology accepted,' I said. 'I need you to come to New York with me.'

'What? No. No, Don. Absolutely not.'

We had reached the cash register and failed to select any food and had to return to the tail of the queue. By the time we sat down, I had explained the Asperger's research project. 'I had to invent an entire proposal—three hundred and seventy-one pages—for this one professor. I'm now an expert on the Savant syndrome.'

It was difficult to decode Rosie's reaction but she appeared to be more amazed than impressed.

'An unemployed expert if you get caught,' she said. 'I gather he's not my father.'

'Correct.' I had been relieved when Lefebvre's sample had tested negative, even after the considerable effort that had been required to obtain it. I had already made plans, and a positive test would have disrupted them.

'There are now only three possibilities left. Two are in New York, and both refused to participate in the study. Hence, I have categorised them as difficult, and hence I need you to come to New York with me.'

'New York! Don, no. No, no, no, no. You're not going to New York and neither am I.'

I had considered the possibility that Rosie would refuse. But Daphne's legacy had been sufficient to purchase two tickets.

'If necessary I will go alone. But I'm not confident I can handle the social aspects of the collection.'

Rosie shook her head. 'This is seriously crazy.'

'You don't want to know who they are?' I said. 'Two of the three men who may be your father?'

'Go on.'

'Isaac Esler. Psychiatrist.'

I could see Rosie digging deep into her memory.

'Maybe. Isaac. I think so. Maybe a friend of someone. Shit, it's so long ago.' She paused. 'And?'

'Solomon Freyberg. Surgeon.'

'No relation to Max Freyberg?'

'Maxwell is his middle name.'

'Shit. Max Freyberg. He's gone to New York now? No way. You're saying I've got one chance in three of being his daughter. And two chances in three of being Jewish.'

'Assuming your mother told the truth.'

'My mother wouldn't have lied.'

'How old were you when she died?'

'Ten. I know what you're thinking. But I know I'm right.'

It was obviously not possible to discuss this issue rationally. I moved to her other statement.

'Is there a problem with being Jewish?'

'Jewish is fine. Freyberg is not fine. But if it's Freyberg it would explain why my mother kept mum. No pun intended. You've never heard of him?'

'Only as a result of this project.'

'If you followed football you would have.'

'He was a footballer?'

'A club president. And well-known jerk. What about the third person?'

'Geoffrey Case.'

'Oh my God.' Rosie went white. 'He died.'

'Correct.'

'Mum talked about him a lot. He had an accident. Or some illness—maybe cancer. Something bad, obviously. But I didn't think he was in her year.'

It struck me now that we had been extremely careless in the way we had addressed the project, primarily because of the misunderstandings that had led to temporary abandonments followed by restarts. If we had worked through the names at the outset such obvious possibilities would not have been overlooked.

'Do you know any more about him?'

'No. Mum was really sad about what happened to him. Shit. It makes total sense, doesn't it? Why she wouldn't tell me.'

It made no sense to me.

'He was from the country,' Rosie said. 'I think his father had a practice out in the sticks.'

The website had provided the information that Geoffrey Case was from Moree in northern New South Wales, but this hardly explained why Rosie's mother would have hidden his identity if he was the father. His only other distinguishing feature was that he was dead, so perhaps this was what Rosie was referring to—her mother not wanting to tell her that her father had died. But surely Phil could have been given this information to pass on when Rosie was old enough to deal with it.

While we were talking, Gene entered. With Bianca! They waved to us then went upstairs to the private dining section. Incredible.

'Gross,' said Rosie.

'He's researching attraction to different nationalities.'

'Right. I just pity his wife.'

I told Rosie that Gene and Claudia had an open marriage.

'Lucky her,' said Rosie. 'Are you planning to offer the same deal to the winner of the Wife Project?'

'Of course,' I said.

'Of course,' said Rosie.

'If that was what she wanted,' I added in case Rosie had misinterpreted.

'You think that's likely?'

'If I find a partner, which seems increasingly *unlikely*,

I wouldn't want a sexual relationship with anyone else. But I'm not good at understanding what other people want.'

'Tell me something I don't know,' said Rosie for no obvious reason.

I quickly searched my mind for an interesting fact. 'Ahhh…The testicles of drone bees and wasp spiders explode during sex.'

It was annoying that the first thing that occurred to me was related to sex. As a psychology graduate, Rosie may have made some sort of Freudian interpretation. But she looked at me and shook her head. Then she laughed. 'I can't afford to go to New York. But you're not safe by yourself.'

There was a phone number listed for an M. Case in Moree. The woman who answered told me that Dr Case, Sr, whose name was confusingly also Geoffrey, had passed away some years ago and that his widow Margaret had been in the local nursing home with Alzheimer's disease for the past two years. This was good news. Better that the mother was alive than the father—there is seldom any doubt about the identity of the biological mother.

I could have asked Rosie to come with me, but she had already agreed to the New York visit and I did not want to create an opportunity for a social error that might jeopardise the trip. I knew from my experience with Daphne that it would be easy to collect a DNA sample from a person with Alzheimer's disease. I hired a car and packed swabs, cheek-scraper, zip-lock bags and tweezers. I also took a university business card from before I was promoted to associate professor. *Doctor* Don Tillman receives superior service in medical facilities.

Moree is one thousand two hundred and thirty kilometres from Melbourne. I collected the hire car at 3.43 p.m. after my last lecture on the Friday. The internet route-planner estimated fourteen hours and thirty-four minutes of driving each way.

When I was a university student, I had regularly driven to and from my parents' home in Shepparton, and found that the long journeys had a similar effect to my market jogs. Research has shown that creativity is enhanced when performing straightforward mechanical tasks such as jogging, cooking and driving. Unobstructed thinking time is always useful.

I took the Hume Highway north, and used the precise speed indication on the GPS to set the cruise control to the exact speed limit, rather than relying on the artificially inflated figure provided by the speedometer. This would save me some minutes without the risk of law-breaking. Alone in the car, I had the feeling that my whole life had been transformed into an adventure, which would culminate in the trip to New York.

I had decided not to play podcasts on the journey in order to reduce cognitive load and encourage my subconscious to process its recent inputs. But after three hours, I found myself becoming bored. I take little notice of my surroundings beyond the need to avoid accidents, and in any case the freeway was largely devoid of interest. The radio would be as distracting as podcasts, so I decided to purchase my first CD since the Bach experiment. The service station just short of the

New South Wales border had a limited selection but I recognised a few albums from my father's collection. I settled on Jackson Browne's *Running on Empty*. With the repeat button on, it became the soundtrack to my driving and reflections over three days. Unlike many people, I am very comfortable with repetition. It was probably fortunate that I was driving alone.

With my unconscious failing to deliver anything, I attempted an objective analysis of the state of the Father Project.

What did I know?

1. I had tested forty-one of forty-four candidates. (And also several of those of incompatible ethnic appearance.) None had matched. There was the possibility that one of the seven Asperger's survey respondents who had returned samples had sent someone else's cheek scraping. I considered it unlikely. It would be easier simply not to participate, as Isaac Esler and Max Freyberg had done.

2. Rosie had identified four candidates as being known to her mother—Eamonn Hughes, Peter Enticott, Alan McPhee and, recently, Geoffrey Case. She had considered the first three as high probability, and this would also apply to Geoffrey Case. He was now clearly the most likely candidate.

3. The entire project was reliant on Rosie's mother's testimony that she had

performed the critical sexual act at the graduation party. It was possible that she had lied because the biological father was someone less prestigious. This would explain her failure to reveal his identity.

4. Rosie's mother had chosen to remain with Phil. This was my first new thought. It supported the idea that the biological father was less appealing or perhaps unavailable for marriage. It would be interesting to know whether Esler or Freyberg were already married or with partners at that time.

5. Geoffrey Case's death occurred within months of Rosie's birth and presumably the realisation that Phil was not the father. It might have taken some time for Rosie's mother to organise a confirmatory DNA test, by which time Geoffrey Case might have been dead and hence unavailable as an alternative partner.

This was a useful exercise. The project status was clearer in my mind, I had added some minor insights and I was certain that my journey was justified by the probability that Geoffrey Case was Rosie's father.

I decided to drive until I was tired—a radical decision, as I would normally have scheduled my driving time according to published studies on fatigue and booked accommodation accordingly. But I had been too busy to plan. Nevertheless, I stopped for rest breaks every two hours and found myself able to maintain concentration.

At 11.43 p.m., I detected tiredness, but rather than sleep I stopped at a service station, refuelled, and ordered four double espressos. I opened the sunroof and turned up the CD player volume to combat fatigue, and at 7.19 a.m. on Saturday, with the caffeine still running all around my brain, Jackson Browne and I pulled into Moree.

21

I had set the GPS to take me to the nursing home, where I introduced myself as a family friend.

'I'm afraid she won't know you,' said the nurse. This was the assumption I had made, although I was prepared with a plausible story if necessary. The nurse took me to a single room with its own bathroom. Mrs Case was asleep.

'Shall I wake her?' asked the nurse.

'No, I'll just sit here.'

'I'll leave you to it. Call if you need anything.'

I thought it would look odd if I left too quickly so I sat beside the bed for a while. I guessed Margaret Case was about eighty, much the same age as Daphne had been when she moved to the nursing home. Given the story Rosie had told me, it was very possible that I was looking at her grandmother.

As Margaret Case remained still and silent in her single bed, I thought about the Father Project. It was only possible because of technology. For all but the last few years of human existence, the secret would have died with Rosie's mother.

I believe it is the duty of science, of humanity, to discover as much as we can. But I am a physical scientist, not a psychologist.

The woman in front of me was not a fifty-four-year-old male medical practitioner who might have run from his parental responsibilities. She was totally helpless. It would be easy to take a hair sample, or to swab her toothbrush, but it felt wrong.

For these reasons, and for others that I did not fully grasp at the time, I decided not to collect a sample.

Then Margaret Case woke up. She opened her eyes and looked directly at me.

'Geoffrey?' she said, quietly but very clearly. Was she asking for her husband or for her long-dead son? There was a time when I would have replied without thinking, 'They're dead,' not out of malice but because I am wired to respond to the facts before others' feelings. But something had changed in me, and I managed to suppress the statement.

She must have realised that I was not the person she had hoped to see, and began crying. She was not making any noise, but there were tears on her cheeks. Automatically, because I had experienced this situation with Daphne, I pulled out my handkerchief and wiped away the tears. She closed her eyes again. But fate had delivered me my sample.

I was exhausted, and by the time I walked out of the nursing home there were tears in my own eyes from lack of sleep. It was early autumn, and this far north the day was already warm. I lay under a tree and fell asleep.

I woke to see a male doctor in a white coat standing over me and for a frightening moment I was taken back to the bad times of twenty years ago. It was only momentary; I quickly remembered where I was and he was only checking to see that I was not ill or dead. I was not breaking any rules. It was four hours and eight minutes since I had left Margaret Case's room.

The incident was a timely reminder of the dangers of fatigue and I planned the return trip more carefully. I scheduled a five-minute break every hour and at 7.06 p.m. I stopped at a motel, ate an overcooked steak and went to bed. The early night enabled a 5.00 a.m. start on the Sunday.

The highway bypasses Shepparton, but I took the turnoff and went to the city centre. I decided not to visit my parents. The extra sixteen kilometres involved in driving the full distance to their house and back to the highway would add a dangerous unplanned increment to what was already a demanding journey, but I did want to see the town.

I drove past Tillman Hardware. It was closed on Sunday, and my father and brother would be at home with my mother. My father was probably straightening pictures, and my mother asking my brother to clear his construction project from the dining table so she could set it for Sunday dinner. I had not been back since my sister's funeral.

The service station was open and I filled the tank. A man of about forty-five, BMI about thirty, was behind the counter. As I approached, I recognised him, and revised his age to thirty-nine. He had lost hair, grown a beard and gained weight, but he was obviously Gary Parkinson, who had been at high school with me. He had wanted to join the army and travel. He had apparently not realised this ambition. I was reminded how lucky I was to have been able to leave and reinvent my life.

'Hey, Don,' he said, obviously also recognising me.

'Greetings, GP.'

He laughed. 'You haven't changed.'

It was getting dark on Sunday evening when I arrived back in Melbourne and returned the rental car. I left the Jackson Browne CD in the player.

Two thousand four hundred and seventy-two kilometres according to the GPS. The handkerchief was safe in a zip-lock bag, but its existence did not change my decision not to test Margaret Case.

We would still have to go to New York.

I met Rosie at the airport. She remained uncomfortable about me purchasing her ticket, so I told her she could pay me back by selecting some Wife Project applicants for me to date.

'Fuck you,' she said.

It seemed we were friends again.

I could not believe how much baggage Rosie had brought. I had told her to pack as lightly as possible but she exceeded the seven kilogram limit for carry-on luggage. Fortunately I was able to transfer some of her excess equipment to my bag. I had packed my ultra-light PC, toothbrush, razor, spare shirt, gym shorts, change of underwear and (annoyingly) bulky parting gifts from Gene and Claudia. I had only been allowed a week's leave and, even then, the Dean had made it difficult. It was increasingly obvious that she was looking for a reason to get rid of me.

Rosie had never been to the United States, but was familiar with international airport procedures. She was highly impressed by the special treatment that I received. We checked in at the service desk, where there was no queue, and were accompanied through security to the business-class lounge, despite travelling in economy class.

As we drank champagne in the lounge, I explained that I had earned special privileges by being particularly vigilant and observant of rules and procedures on previous flights, and by making a substantial number of helpful suggestions regarding check-in procedures, flight scheduling, pilot training and ways in which security systems might be subverted. I was no longer expected to offer advice, having contributed 'enough for a lifetime of flying'.

'Here's to being special,' said Rosie. 'So, what's the plan?'

Organisation is obviously critical when travelling, and I had an hour-by-hour plan (with hours subdivided as necessary) replacing my usual weekly schedule. It incorporated the appointments that Rosie had made to meet the two father candidates—Esler the psychiatrist and Freyberg the cosmetic surgeon. Amazingly, she had made no other plans beyond arriving at the airport to meet me. At least it meant that there were no incompatible schedules to reconcile.

I opened the schedule on my laptop and began outlining it to Rosie. I had not even completed my list of activities for the flight when she interrupted.

'Fast forward, Don. What are we doing in New York? Between Saturday dinner at the Eslers and Freyberg on Wednesday—which is evening, right? We have four whole days of New York City in between.'

'Saturday, after dinner, walk to the Marcy Avenue subway station and take the J, M or Z train to Delancey Street, change to the F train—'

'Overview, overview. Sunday to Wednesday. One sentence per day. Leave out eating, sleeping and travel.'

That made it easy. 'Sunday, Museum of Natural History; Monday, Museum of Natural History; Tuesday, Museum of Natural History; Wednesday—'

'Stop, wait! Don't tell me Wednesday. Keep it as a surprise.'

'You'll probably guess.'

'Probably,' said Rosie. 'How many times have you been to New York?'

'This is my third.'

'And I'm guessing this is not going to be your first visit to the museum.'

'No.'

'What did you think I was going to do while you were at the museum?'

'I hadn't considered it. I presume you've made independent plans for your time in New York.'

'You presume wrong,' said Rosie. 'We are going to see New York. Sunday and Monday, I'm in charge. Tuesday and Wednesday it's your turn. If you want me to spend two days at the museum, I'll spend two days at the museum. With you. But Sunday and Monday, I'm the tour guide.'

'But you don't know New York.'

'Nor do you.' Rosie took our champagne glasses to the bar to top them up. It was only 9.42 a.m. in Melbourne, but I was already on New York time. While she was gone, I flipped open my computer again and connected

191

to the Museum of Natural History site. I would have to replan my visits.

Rosie returned and immediately invaded my personal space. She shut the lid of the computer! Incredible. If I had done that to a *student* playing Angry Birds, I would have been in the Dean's office the next day. In the university hierarchy, I am an associate professor and Rosie is a PhD student. I was entitled to some respect.

'Talk to me,' she said. 'We've had no time to talk about anything except DNA. Now we've got a week, and I want to know who you are. And if you're going to be the guy who tells me who my father is, you should know who I am.'

In less than fifteen minutes, my entire schedule had been torn apart, shattered, rendered redundant. Rosie had taken over.

An escort from the lounge took us to the plane for the fourteen-and-a-half-hour flight to Los Angeles. As a result of my special status, Rosie and I had two seats in a row of three. I am only placed next to other passengers when flights are full.

'Start with your childhood,' said Rosie.

All it needed was for her to turn on the overhead light for the scenario of interrogation to be complete. I was a prisoner, so I negotiated—and made escape plans.

'We have to get some sleep. It's evening in New York.'

'It's seven o'clock. Who goes to bed at seven? Anyway, I won't be able to sleep.'

'I've brought sleeping pills.'

Rosie was amazed that I would use sleeping pills. She thought I would have some objection to chemicals.

She was right about not knowing much about me. We agreed that I would summarise my childhood experiences, which, given her background in psychology, she would doubtless consider hugely significant, eat dinner, take the sleeping pills and sleep. On the pretext of visiting the bathroom, I asked the cabin manager to bring our dinner as quickly as possible.

22

Telling Rosie my life story was not difficult. Every psychologist and psychiatrist I have seen has asked for a summary, so I have the essential facts clear in my mind.

My father owns a hardware store in a regional city. He lives there with my mother and my younger brother, who will probably take over when my father retires or dies. My older sister died at the age of forty as a result of medical incompetence. When it happened my mother did not get out of bed for two weeks, except to attend the funeral. I was very sad about my sister's death. Yes, I was angry too.

My father and I have an effective but not emotional relationship. This is satisfactory to both of us. My mother is very caring but I find her stifling. My brother does not like me. I believe this is because he saw me as a threat to his dream of inheriting the hardware store and now does not respect my alternative choice. The hardware store may well have been a metaphor for the affection of our father. If so, my brother won, but I am not unhappy about losing. I do not see my family very often. My mother calls me on Sundays.

I had an uneventful time at school. I enjoyed the science subjects. I did not have many friends and was briefly the object of bullying. I was the top student in the school in all subjects except English, where I was the top boy. At the end of my schooling I left home to attend university. I originally enrolled in computer science, but on my twenty-first birthday made a decision to change to genetics. This may have been the result of a subconscious desire to remain a student, but it was a logical choice. Genetics was a burgeoning field. There is no family history of mental illness.

I turned towards Rosie and smiled. I had already told her about my sister and the bullying. The statement about mental illness was correct, unless I included myself in the definition of 'family'. Somewhere in a medical archive is a twenty-year-old file with my name and the words 'depression, bipolar disorder? OCD?' and 'schizophrenia?' The question marks are important—beyond the obvious observation that I was depressed, no definitive diagnosis was ever made, despite attempts by the psychiatric profession to fit me into a simplistic category. I now believe that virtually all my problems could be attributed to my brain being configured differently from those of the majority of humans. All the psychiatric symptoms were a result of this, not of any underlying disease. Of course I was depressed: I lacked friends, sex and a social life, due to being incompatible with other people. My intensity and focus were misinterpreted as mania. And my concern with organisation was labelled as obsessive-compulsive disorder. Julie's Asperger's kids might well face similar problems in their lives. However, they had been labelled with an underlying syndrome, and perhaps the psychiatric profession would be intelligent enough to apply Occam's razor and see that the problems they might face would be largely due to their Asperger's brain configuration.

'What happened on your twenty-first birthday?' asked Rosie.

Had Rosie read my thoughts? What happened on my twenty-first birthday was that I decided that I needed to take a new direction in my life, because any change was better than staying in the pit of depression. I actually visualised it as a pit.

I told Rosie part of the truth. I don't generally celebrate birthdays, but my family had insisted in this case and had invited numerous friends and relatives to compensate for my own lack of friends.

My uncle made a speech. I understood that it was traditional to make fun of the guest of honour, but my uncle became so encouraged by his ability to provoke laughter that he kept going, telling story after story. I was shocked to discover that he knew some extremely personal facts, and realised that my mother must have shared them with him. She was pulling at his arm, trying to get him to stop, but he ignored her, and did not stop until he noticed that she was crying by which time he had completed a detailed exposition of my faults and of the embarrassment and pain that they had caused. The core of the problem, it seemed, was that I was a stereotypical computer geek. So I decided to change.

'To a genetics geek,' said Rosie.

'That wasn't exactly my goal.' But it was obviously the outcome. And I got out of the pit to work hard in a new discipline. Where was dinner?

'Tell me more about your father.'

'Why?' I wasn't actually interested in why. I was doing the social equivalent of saying 'over' to put the responsibility back on Rosie. It was a trick suggested by

Claudia for dealing with difficult personal questions. I recalled her advice not to overuse it. But this was the first occasion.

'I guess because I want to see if your dad is the reason you're fucked-up.'

'I'm not fucked-up.'

'Okay, not fucked-up. Sorry, I didn't mean to be judgmental. But you're not exactly average,' said Rosie, psychology PhD candidate.

'Agreed. Does "fucked-up" mean "not exactly average"?'

'Bad choice of words. Start again. I guess I'm asking because my father is the reason that *I'm* fucked-up.'

An extraordinary statement. With the exception of her careless attitude to health, Rosie had never exhibited any sign of brain malfunction.

'What are the symptoms of being fucked-up?'

'I've got crap in my life that I wish I hadn't. And I'm not good at dealing with it. Am I making sense?'

'Of course,' I said. 'Unwanted events occur and you lack certain skills for minimising the personal impact. I thought when you said "fucked-up" that there was some problem with your personality that you wanted to rectify.'

'No, I'm okay with being me.'

'So what is the nature of the damage caused by Phil?'

Rosie did not have an instant reply to this critical question. Perhaps this was a symptom of being fucked-up. Finally she spoke. 'Jesus, what's taking them so long with dinner?'

Rosie went to the bathroom, and I took the opportunity to unwrap the presents that Gene and Claudia had given me. They had driven me to the airport, so it was impossible not to accept the packages. It was fortunate that Rosie was not watching when I opened them. Gene's present was a new book of sexual positions and he had inscribed it: 'In case you run out of ideas.' He had drawn the gene symbol that he uses as his signature underneath. Claudia's present was not embarrassing, but was irrelevant to the trip—a pair of jeans and a shirt. Clothes are always useful, but I had already packed a spare shirt, and did not see a need for additional pants in only eight days.

Gene had again misconstrued the current nature of my relationship with Rosie, but this was understandable. I could not explain the real purpose for taking Rosie to New York and Gene had made an assumption consistent with his world view. On the way to the airport, I had asked Claudia for advice on dealing with so much time in the company of one person.

'Remember to listen,' said Claudia. 'If she asks you an awkward question, ask her why she's asking. Turn it back to her. If she's a psychology student, she'll love talking about herself. Take notice of your emotions as well as logic. Emotions have their own logic. And try to go with the flow.'

In fact, Rosie spent most of the remainder of the flight to Los Angeles either sleeping or watching films, but confirmed—twice—that I had not offended her and she just needed time out.

I did not complain.

23

We survived US Immigration. Previous experience had taught me not to offer observations or suggestions, and I did not need to use my letter of recommendation from David Borenstein at Columbia University characterising me as a sane and competent person. Rosie seemed extremely nervous, even to someone who is poor at judging emotional states, and I was worried that she would cause suspicion and that we would be refused entry *for no justifiable reason*, as had happened to me on a previous occasion.

The official asked, 'What do you do?' and I said, 'Genetics researcher,' and he said, 'Best in the world?' and I said, 'Yes.' We were through. Rosie almost ran towards Customs and then to the exit. I was several metres behind, carrying both bags. Something was obviously wrong.

I caught up to her outside the automatic doors, reaching into her handbag.

'Cigarette,' she said. She lit a cigarette and took a long drag. 'Just don't say anything, okay? If I ever needed a reason to give up, I've got one now. Eighteen and a half hours. Fuck.'

It was fortunate that Rosie had told me not to say anything. I remained silent but shocked at the impact of addiction on her life.

She finished her cigarette and we headed to the bar. It was only 7.48 a.m. in Los Angeles, but we could be on Melbourne time until our arrival in New York.

'What was the deal about "best geneticist on the planet"?'

I explained that I had a special O-1 Visa for Aliens of Extraordinary Ability. I had needed a visa after the occasion when I was refused entry and this was deemed the safest choice. O-1 visas were quite rare and 'yes' was the correct answer to any question about the extraordinariness of my abilities. Rosie found the word 'alien' amusing. Correction, hilarious.

Since we did not have bags checked, and the immigration process had proceeded smoothly, I was able to implement my best-case alternative and we caught an earlier flight to New York. I had made plans for the time gained through this manoeuvre.

At JFK, I steered Rosie towards the AirTrain. 'We have two subway options.'

'I supposed you've memorised the timetable,' said Rosie.

'Not worth the effort. I just know the lines and stations we need for our journeys.' I love New York. The layout is so logical, at least uptown from 14th Street.

When Rosie had telephoned Isaac Esler's wife she was very positive about some contact from Australia and news from the reunion. On the subway, Rosie said, 'You'll need an alias. In case Esler recognises your name from the Asperger's survey.'

I had already considered this. 'Austin,' I said. 'From *Austin Powers*. International Man of Mystery.' Rosie thought this was hilarious. I had made a successful, deliberate joke that was not related to exhibiting some quirk in my personality. A memorable moment.

'Profession?' she asked.

'Hardware-store owner.' The idea appeared in my brain spontaneously.

'Okaaaaaay,' said Rosie. 'Right.'

We took the E train to Lexington Avenue and 53rd Street and headed uptown.

'Where's the hotel?' Rosie asked as I steered us towards Madison Avenue.

'Lower East Side. But we have to shop first.'

'Fuck, Don, it's after 5.30. We're due at the Eslers' at 7.30. We don't have time for shopping. I need time to change.'

I looked at Rosie. She was wearing jeans and shirt—conventional attire. I could not see the problem, but we had time. 'I hadn't planned to go to the hotel before dinner, but since we arrived early—'

'Don, I've been flying for twenty-four hours. We are doing nothing more with your schedule until I've checked it for craziness.'

'I've scheduled four minutes for the transaction,' I said. We were already outside the Hermès store, which my research had identified as the world's best scarf shop. I walked in and Rosie followed.

The shop was empty except for us. Perfect.

'Don, you're not exactly dressed for this.'

Dressed for shopping! I was dressed for travelling, eating, socialising, museum-visiting—and shopping: runners, cargo pants, t-shirt and the jumper knitted by my mother. This was not Le Gavroche. It seemed highly unlikely that they would refuse to participate in a commercial exchange on the basis of my costume. I was right.

Two women stood behind the counter, one (age approximately fifty-five, BMI approximately nineteen) wearing rings on all eight fingers, and the other (age approximately twenty, BMI approximately twenty-two) wearing huge purple glasses creating the impression of a human ant. They were very formally dressed. I initiated the transaction.

'I require a high-quality scarf.'

Ring Woman smiled. 'I can help you with that. It's for the lady?'

'No. For Claudia.' I realised that this was not helpful but was not sure how to elaborate.

'And Claudia is'—she made circles with her hand—'what age?'

'Forty-one years, three hundred and fifty-six days.'

'Ah,' said Ring Woman, 'so we have a birthday coming up.'

'Just Claudia.' My birthday was thirty-two days away, so it surely did not qualify as 'coming up'. 'Claudia wears scarves, even in hot weather, to cover lines on her neck which she considers unattractive. So the scarf does not need to be functional, only decorative.'

Ring Woman produced a scarf. 'What do you think of this?'

It was remarkably light—and would offer almost zero protection against wind and cold. But it was certainly decorative, as specified.

'Excellent. How much?' We were running to schedule.

'This one is twelve hundred dollars.'

I opened my wallet and extracted my credit card.

'Whoa whoa *whoa*,' said Rosie. 'I think we'd like to see what else you have before we rush into anything.'

I turned to Rosie. 'Our four minutes is almost up.'

Ring Woman put three more scarves on the counter. Rosie looked at one. I copied her, looking at another. It seemed nice. They all seemed nice. I had no framework for discrimination.

It continued. Ring Woman kept throwing more scarves on the counter and Rosie and I looked at them. Ant Woman came to help. I finally identified one that I could comment intelligently on.

'This scarf has a fault! It's not symmetrical. Symmetry is a key component of human beauty.'

Rosie had a brilliant response. 'Maybe the scarf's lack of symmetry will highlight Claudia's symmetry.'

Ant Woman produced a pink scarf with fluffy bits. Even I could see that Claudia would not approve and dropped it immediately on the reject pile.

'What's wrong with it?' said Rosie.

'I don't know. It's unsuitable.'

'Come on,' she said, 'you can do better than that. Imagine who might wear it.'

'Barbara Cartland,' said Ring Woman.

I was not familiar with this name, but the answer suddenly came to me. 'The Dean! At the ball.'

Rosie burst out laughing. 'Corrrrr-ect.' She pulled another scarf from the pile. 'What about this one?' It was virtually transparent.

'Julie,' I said automatically, then explained to Rosie and the two women about the Asperger's counsellor and her revealing costume. Presumably she would not want a scarf to reduce its impact.

'This one?'

It was a scarf that I had quite liked because of its bright colours, but Rosie had rejected as too 'loud'.

'Bianca.'

'Exactly.' Rosie had not stopped laughing. 'You know more about clothes than you think you do.'

Ant Woman produced a scarf covered in pictures of birds. I picked it up—the pictures were remarkably accurate. It was quite beautiful.

'Birds of the world,' Ant Woman said.

'Oh my God, no!' said Rosie. 'Not for Claudia.'

'Why not? It's extremely interesting.'

'Birds of the world! Think about it. Gene.'

Scarves were being sourced from multiple locations, piling rapidly, being evaluated, tossed aside. It was happening so quickly that I was reminded of the Great Cocktail Night, except that we were the customers. I wondered if the women were enjoying their work as much as I had.

In the end I left the choice to Rosie. She chose the first scarf that they had shown us.

As we walked out of the store, Rosie said, 'I think I just wasted an hour of your life.'

'No, no, the outcome was irrelevant,' I said. 'It was so entertaining.'

'Well,' said Rosie, 'any time you need entertaining, I could use a pair of Manolo Blahniks.' From the word 'pair', I guessed that she was referring to shoes.

'Do we have time?' We had already used the time that Rosie had intended for the hotel visit.

'I'm kidding, I'm kidding.'

It was fortunate, as we had to move quickly to arrive

at the Eslers' on schedule. But Rosie needed to change. There was a bathroom at Union Square station. Rosie dashed in and reappeared looking amazingly different.

'That was incredible,' I said. 'So quick.'

Rosie looked at me. 'You're going like that?' Her tone suggested dissatisfaction.

'These are my clothes,' I said. 'I have a spare shirt.'

'Show it to me.'

I reached into the bag to get the alternative shirt, which I doubted Rosie would prefer, and remembered Claudia's gift. I showed the shirt to Rosie.

'It was a gift from Claudia,' I said. 'I've got jeans as well, if that helps.'

'All hail Claudia,' said Rosie. 'She earned the scarf.'

'We'll be late.'

'Politely late is fine.'

Isaac and Judy Esler had an apartment in Williamsburg. My US cell phone card was working to specification, and we were able to navigate by GPS to the location. I hoped that forty-six minutes met Rosie's definition of 'politely late'.

'Austin, remember,' said Rosie as she rang the bell.

Judy answered the door. I estimated her age as fifty and her BMI as twenty-six. She spoke with a New York accent, and was concerned that we might have become lost. Her husband Isaac was a caricature of a psychiatrist: mid-fifties, short, receding hair, black goatee beard, BMI nineteen. He was not as friendly as his wife.

They offered us martinis. I remembered the effect this drink had on me during the preparation for the Great Cocktail Night and resolved that I would have no more than three. Judy had made some fish-based canapés, and asked for details of our trip. She wanted to know whether we had been to New York before, what season it was in Australia (not a challenging question) and whether we planned to do any shopping and see any museums. Rosie handled all of these questions.

'Isaac's off to Chicago in the morning,' said Judy. 'Tell them what you'll be doing there.'

'Just a conference,' said Isaac. He and I did not need to do a great deal of talking to ensure the conversation continued.

He did ask me one thing before we moved to the dining room. 'What do you do, Austin?'

'Austin runs a hardware store,' said Rosie. 'A very successful one.'

Judy served a delicious meal based on farmed salmon, which she assured Rosie was sustainable. I had eaten very little of the poor-quality aeroplane food, and enjoyed Judy's meal immensely. Isaac opened some pinot gris from Oregon and was generous in refilling my glass. We talked about New York and the differences between Australian and American politics.

'Well,' said Judy, 'I'm so glad you could come. It makes up a little for missing the reunion. Isaac was so sorry not to be there.'

'Not really,' said Isaac. 'Revisiting the past is not something to do lightly.' He ate the last piece of fish from his plate and looked at Rosie. 'You look a lot like your mother. She would have been a bit younger than you when I last saw her.'

Judy said, 'We got married the day after the graduation and moved here. Isaac had the biggest hangover at the wedding. He'd been a bad boy.' She smiled.

'I think that's enough telling tales, Judy,' said Isaac. 'It was all a long time ago.'

He stared at Rosie. Rosie stared at him.

Judy picked up Rosie's plate and mine, one in each hand. I decided that this was the moment to act, with everyone distracted. I stood and picked up Isaac's plate in one hand and then Judy's. Isaac was too busy playing the staring game with Rosie to object. I took the plates to the kitchen, swabbing Isaac's fork on the way.

'I imagine Austin and Rosie are exhausted,' said Judy when we returned to the table.

'You said you're a hardware man, Austin?' Isaac stood up. 'Can you spare five minutes to look at a tap for me? It's probably a job for a plumber, but maybe it's just a washer.'

'He means faucet,' said Judy, presumably forgetting we came from the same country as Isaac.

Isaac and I went down the stairs to the basement. I was confident I could help with the tap problem. My school holidays had been spent providing advice of exactly this kind. But as we reached the bottom of the stairs, the lights went out. I wasn't sure what had happened. A power failure?

'You okay, Don?' said Isaac, sounding concerned.

'I'm okay,' I said. 'What happened?'

'What happened is that you answered to Don, Austin.'

We stood there in the dark. I doubted that there were social conventions for dealing with interrogation by a psychiatrist in a dark cellar.

'How did you know?' I asked.

'Two unsolicited communications from the same

university in a month. An internet search. You make good dancing partners.'

More silence and darkness.

'I know the answer to your question. But I made a promise that I would not reveal it. If I thought it was a matter of life or death, or a serious mental health issue, I would reconsider. But I see no reason to break the promise, which was made because the people involved had thought hard about what would be right. You came a long way for my DNA, and I'm guessing you got it when you cleared the plates. You might want to think beyond your girlfriend's wishes before you proceed.'

He turned on the light.

Something bothered me as we walked up the stairs. At the top, I stopped. 'If you knew what I wanted, why did you let us come to your house?'

'Good question,' he said. 'Since you asked the question, I'm sure you can work out the answer. I wanted to see Rosie.'

24

Thanks to carefully timed use of sleeping pills, I woke without any feeling of disorientation, at 7.06 a.m.

Rosie had fallen asleep in the train on the way to the hotel. I had decided not to tell her immediately about the basement encounter, nor mention what I had observed on the sideboard. It was a large photo of Judy and Isaac's wedding. Standing beside Isaac, dressed in the formal clothes required of a best man, was Geoffrey Case, who had only three hundred and seventy days to live. He was smiling.

I was still processing the implications myself, and Rosie would probably have an emotional response that could spoil the New York experience. She was impressed that I had collected the DNA, and even more impressed that I had acted so unobtrusively when I picked up the dishes to assist.

'You're in danger of learning some social skills.'

The hotel was perfectly comfortable. After we checked in, Rosie said that she had been worried that I would expect her to share a room in exchange for paying for her trip to New York. Like a prostitute! I was highly insulted. She seemed pleased with my reaction.

I had an excellent workout at the hotel gym, and returned to find the message light blinking. Rosie.

'Where were you?' she said.

'In the gym. Exercise is critical in reducing the effects of jet lag. Also sunlight. I've planned to walk twenty-nine blocks in sunlight.'

'Aren't you forgetting something? Today is my day. And tomorrow. I own you until midnight Monday. Now get your butt down here. I'm hanging out for breakfast.'

'In my gym clothes?'

'No, Don, not in your gym clothes. Shower, dress. You have ten minutes.'

'I always have my breakfast before I shower.'

'How old are you?' said Rosie, aggressively. She didn't wait for the answer. 'You're like an old man—I always have my breakfast before I shower, don't sit in my chair, that's where I sit...*Do not fuck with me, Don Tillman.*' She said the last words quite slowly. I decided it was best not to fuck with her. By midnight tomorrow it would be over. In the interim, I would adopt the dentist mindset.

It seemed I was in for a root-canal filling. I arrived downstairs and Rosie was immediately critical.

'How long have you had that shirt?'

'Fourteen years,' I said. 'It dries very quickly. Perfect for travelling.' In fact it was a specialised walking shirt, though fabric technology had progressed significantly since it was made.

'Good,' said Rosie. 'It doesn't owe you anything. Upstairs. Other shirt.'

'It's wet.'

'I mean Claudia's shirt. And the jeans while you're at it. I'm not walking around New York with a bum.'

When I came down for the second attempt at

breakfast, Rosie smiled. 'You know, you're not such a bad-looking guy underneath.' She stopped and looked at me. 'Don, you're not enjoying this, are you? You'd rather be by yourself in the museum, right?' She was extremely perceptive. 'I get that. But you've done all these things for me, you've brought me to New York, and, by the way, I haven't finished spending your money yet. So I want to do something for you.'

I could have argued that her *wanting* to do something for me meant she was ultimately acting in her own interests, but it might provoke more of the 'don't fuck with me' behaviour.

'You're in a different place, you're in different clothes. When the medieval pilgrims used to arrive at Santiago after walking hundreds of kilometres they burned their clothes to symbolise that they'd changed. I'm not asking you to burn your clothes—yet. Put them on again on Tuesday. Just be open to something different. Let me show you my world for a couple of days. Starting with breakfast. We're in the city with the best breakfasts in the world.'

She must have seen that I was resisting.

'Hey, you schedule your time so you don't waste it, right?'

'Correct.'

'So, you've committed to two days with me. If you shut yourself down, you're wasting two days of your life that someone is trying to make exciting and productive and fun for you. I'm going to—' She stopped. 'I left the guidebook in my room. When I come down, we're going to breakfast.' She turned and walked to the elevators.

I was disturbed by Rosie's logic. I had always justified my schedule in terms of efficiency. But was my
allegiance to efficiency or was it to the schedule itself?
Was I really like my father, who had insisted on sitting
in the same chair every night? I had never mentioned
this to Rosie. I had my own special chair too.

There was another argument that she had not presented, because she could not have known it. In the last
eight weeks I had experienced two of the three best
times of my adult life, assuming all visits to the Museum
of Natural History were treated as one event. They had
both been with Rosie. Was there a correlation? It was
critical to find out.

By the time Rosie came back I had performed a
brain reboot, an exercise requiring a considerable effort
of will. But I was now configured for adaptability.

'So?' she said.

'So, how do we find the world's best breakfast?'

We found the World's Best Breakfast around the corner.
It may have been the unhealthiest breakfast I had ever
eaten, but I would not put on significant weight, nor lose
fitness, brain acuity or martial arts skills if I neglected
them for two days. This was the mode my brain was
now operating in.

'I can't believe you ate all that,' said Rosie.

'It tasted so good.'

'No lunch. Late dinner,' she said.

'We can eat any time.'

Our server approached the table. Rosie indicated the
empty coffee cups. 'They were great. I think we could
both manage another.'

'Huh?' said the server. It was obvious that she hadn't understood Rosie. It was also obvious that Rosie had very poor taste in coffee—or she had done as I had and ignored the label 'coffee' and was enjoying it as an entirely new beverage. The technique was working brilliantly.

'One regular coffee with cream and one regular coffee without cream…please,' I said.

'Sure.'

This was a town where people talked straight. My kind of town. I was enjoying speaking American: cream instead of milk, elevator instead of lift, check instead of bill. I had memorised a list of differences between American and Australian usage prior to my first trip to the US, and had been surprised at how quickly my brain was able to switch into using them automatically.

We walked uptown. Rosie was looking at a guidebook called *Not for Tourists*, which seemed a very poor choice.

'Where are we going?' I asked.

'We're not going anywhere. We're there.'

We were outside a clothing store. Rosie asked if it was okay to go inside.

'You don't have to ask,' I said. 'You're in control.'

'I do about shops. It's a girl thing. I was going to say, "I suppose you've been on Fifth Avenue before", but I don't suppose anything with you.'

The situation was symmetrical. I knew not to suppose anything about Rosie, or I would have been surprised by her describing herself as a 'girl', a term that I understood to be unacceptable to feminists when referring to adult women.

Rosie was becoming remarkably perceptive about me. I had never been beyond the conference centres and the museum, but with my new mind configuration, I was finding everything fascinating. A whole shop for cigars. The prices of jewellery. The Flatiron Building. The sex museum. Rosie looked at the last of these, and chose not to go in. This was probably a good decision—it might be fascinating, but the risk of a faux pas would be very high.

'Do you want to buy anything?' said Rosie.

'No.'

A few minutes later, a thought occurred to me. 'Is there somewhere that sells men's shirts?'

Rosie laughed. 'On Fifth Avenue, New York City. Maybe we'll get lucky.' I detected sarcasm, but in a friendly way. We found a new shirt of the same genre as the Claudia shirt at a huge store called Bloomingdale's, which was not, in fact, on Fifth Avenue. We could not choose between two candidate shirts and bought both. My wardrobe would be overflowing!

We arrived at Central Park.

'We're skipping lunch, but I could handle an ice-cream,' said Rosie. There was a vendor in the park, and he was serving both cones and prefabricated confections.

I was filled with an irrational sense of dread. I identified it immediately. But I had to know. 'Is the flavour important?'

'Something with peanuts. We're in the States.'

'All ice-creams taste the same.'

'Bullshit.'

I explained about tastebuds.

'Wanna bet?' said Rosie. 'If I can tell the difference

between peanut and vanilla, two tickets to *Spiderman*. On Broadway. Tonight.'

'The textures will be different. Because of the peanuts.'

'Any two. Your choice.'

I ordered an apricot and a mango. 'Close your eyes,' I said. It wasn't really necessary: the colours were almost identical, but I didn't want her to see me tossing a coin to decide which one to show her. I was concerned that with her psychological skills she might guess my sequence.

I tossed the coin and gave her an ice-cream.

'Mango,' guessed Rosie, correctly. Toss, heads again. 'Mango again.' She picked the mango correctly three times, then the apricot, then the apricot again. The chances of her achieving this result randomly were one in thirty-two. I could be ninety-seven per cent confident she was able to differentiate. Incredible.

'So, *Spiderman* tonight?'

'No. You got one wrong.'

Rosie looked at me, very carefully, then burst out laughing. 'You're bullshitting me, aren't you? I can't believe it, you're making jokes.'

She gave me an ice-cream. 'Since you don't care, you can have the apricot.'

I looked at it. What to say? She had been licking it.

Once again she read my mind. 'How are you going to kiss a girl if you won't share her ice-cream?'

For several minutes, I was suffused with an irrational feeling of enormous pleasure, basking in the success of my joke, and parsing the sentence about the kiss: Kiss *a* girl, share *her* ice-cream—it was third-person, but surely not unrelated to the girl who was sharing her ice-cream right now with Don Tillman in his new shirt and jeans as we walked among the trees in Central Park, New York City, on a sunny Sunday afternoon.

I needed the hundred and fourteen minutes of time-out back at the hotel, although I had enjoyed the day immensely. Shower, email, relaxation exercises combined with stretches. I emailed Gene, copying in Claudia, with a summary of our activities.

Rosie was three minutes late for our 7.00 p.m. foyer meeting. I was about to call her room when she arrived wearing clothes purchased that day—white jeans and a blue t-shirt thing—and the jacket she had worn the previous evening. I remembered a Gene-ism, something I had heard him say to Claudia. 'You're looking very elegant,' I said. It was a risky statement, but her reaction appeared to be positive. She did look very elegant.

We had cocktails at a bar with the World's Longest Cocktail List, including many I did not know, and we saw *Spiderman*. Afterwards, Rosie felt the story was a bit predictable but I was overwhelmed by everything, in a hugely positive way. I had not been to the theatre since I was a child. I could have ignored the story and focused entirely on the mechanics of the flying. It was just incredible.

We caught the subway back to the Lower East Side. I was hungry, but did not want to break the rules by suggesting that we eat. But Rosie had this planned too. A 10.00 p.m. booking at a restaurant called Momofuku Ko. We were on Rosie time again.

'This is my present to you for bringing me here,' she said.

We sat at a counter for twelve where we could watch

216

the chefs at work. There were few of the annoying formalities that make restaurants so stressful.

'Any preferences, allergies, dislikes?' asked the chef.

'I'm vegetarian, but I eat sustainable seafood,' said Rosie. 'He eats everything—and I mean everything.'

I lost count of the courses. I had sweetbreads and foie gras (first time!) and sea urchin roe. We drank a bottle of rosé champagne. I talked to the chefs and they told me what they were doing. I ate the best food I had ever eaten. And I did not need to wear a jacket in order to eat. In fact, the man sitting beside me was wearing a costume that would have been extreme at the Marquess of Queensbury, including multiple facial piercings. He heard me speaking to the chef and asked me where I was from. I told him.

'How are you finding New York?'

I told him I was finding it highly interesting, and explained how we had spent our day. But I was conscious that, under the stress of talking to a stranger, my manner had changed—or, to be more precise, *reverted*—to my usual style. During the day, with Rosie, I had felt relaxed, and had spoken and acted differently, and this continued in my conversation with the chef, which was essentially a professional exchange of information. But informal social interaction with another person had triggered my regular behaviour. And my regular behaviour and speaking style is, I am well aware, considered odd by others. The man with the piercings must have noticed.

'You know what I like about New York?' he said. 'There are so many weird people that nobody takes any notice. We all just fit right in.'

'How was it?' said Rosie as we walked back to the hotel.

'The best day of my adult life,' I said. Rosie seemed so happy with my response that I decided not to finish the sentence: 'excluding the Museum of Natural History.'

'Sleep in,' she said. '9.30 here and we'll do the brunch thing again. Okay?'

It would have been totally irrational to argue.

25

'Did I cause any embarrassment?'

Rosie had been concerned that I might make inappropriate comments during our tour of the World Trade Center site. Our guide, a former firefighter named Frank, who had lost many of his colleagues in the attack, was incredibly interesting and I asked a number of technical questions that he answered intelligently and, it seemed to me, enthusiastically.

'You may have changed the tone a bit,' she said. 'You sort of moved the attention away from the emotional impact.' So, I had reduced the sadness. Good.

Monday was allocated to visiting popular tourist sights. We had breakfast at Katz's Deli, where a scene for a film called *When Harry Met Sally* was shot. We went to the top of the Empire State Building, famous as a location for *An Affair to Remember*. We visited MOMA and the Met, which were excellent.

We were back at the hotel early—4.32 p.m.

'Back here at 6.30,' said Rosie.

'What are we having for dinner?'

'Hot dogs. We're going to the baseball.'

I *never* watch sport. Ever. The reasons are obvious—or should be to anyone who values their time. But my reconfigured mind, sustained by huge doses of positive reinforcement, accepted the proposition. I spent the next hundred and eighteen minutes on the internet, learning about the rules and the players.

On the subway, Rosie had some news for me. Before she left Melbourne, she had sent an email to Mary Keneally, a researcher working in her field at Columbia University. She had just received a reply and Mary could see her tomorrow. But she wouldn't be able to make it to the Museum of Natural History. She could come Wednesday, but would I be okay by myself tomorrow? Of course I would.

At Yankee Stadium we got beer and hot dogs. A man in a cap, estimated age thirty-five, estimated BMI forty (i.e. dangerously fat), sat beside me. He had three hot dogs! The source of the obesity was obvious.

The game started, and I had to explain to Rosie what was happening. It was fascinating to see how the rules worked in a real game. Every time there was an event on the field, Fat Baseball Fan would make an annotation in his book. There were runners on second and third when Curtis Granderson came to the plate and Fat Baseball Fan spoke to me. 'If he bats in both of these guys he'll be heading the league on RBI. What are the odds?'

I didn't know what the odds were. All I could tell him was that they were somewhere between 9.9 and 27.2 per cent based on the batting average and percentage of home runs listed in the profile I had read. I had not had time to memorise the statistics for doubles and triples. Fat Baseball Fan nevertheless seemed impressed and we began a very interesting conversation. He showed me how to mark the program with symbols to represent the various events, and how the more sophisticated statistics worked. I had no idea sport could be so intellectually stimulating.

Rosie got more beer and hot dogs and Fat Baseball Fan started to tell me about Joe DiMaggio's 'streak' in 1941 which he claimed was a uniquely odds-defying achievement. I was doubtful, and the conversation was just getting interesting when the game ended, so he suggested we take the subway to a bar in Midtown. As Rosie was in charge of the schedule, I asked for her opinion, and she agreed.

The bar was noisy and there was more baseball playing on a large television screen. Some other men, who did not appear to have previously met Fat Baseball Fan, joined our discussion. We drank a lot of beer, and talked about baseball statistics. Rosie sat on a stool with her drink and observed. It was late when Fat Baseball Fan, whose actual name was Dave, said he had to go home. We exchanged email addresses and I considered that I had made a new friend.

Walking back to the hotel, I realised that I had behaved in stereotypical male fashion, drinking beer in a bar, watching television and talking about sport. It is generally known that women have a negative attitude to such behaviour. I asked Rosie if I had offended her.

'Not at all. I had fun watching you being a guy—fitting in.'

I told her that this was a highly unusual response from a feminist, but that it would make her a very attractive partner to conventional men.

'If I was interested in conventional men.'

It seemed a good opportunity to ask a question about Rosie's personal life.

'Do you have a boyfriend?' I hoped I had used an appropriate term.

'Sure, I just haven't unpacked him from my suitcase,' she said, obviously making a joke. I laughed, then pointed out that she hadn't actually answered my question.

'Don,' she said, 'don't you think that if I had a boyfriend you might have heard about him by now?'

It seemed to me entirely possible that I would not have heard about him. I had asked Rosie very few personal questions outside the Father Project. I did not know any of her friends, except perhaps Stefan who I had concluded was not her boyfriend. Of course, it would have been traditional to bring any partner to the faculty ball, and not to offer me sex afterwards, but not everyone was bound by such conventions. Gene was the perfect example. It seemed entirely possible that Rosie had a boyfriend who did not like dancing or socialising with academics, was out of town at the time, or was in an open relationship with her. She had no reason to tell me. In my own life, I had rarely mentioned Daphne or my sister to Gene and Claudia or vice versa. They belonged to different parts of my life. I explained this to Rosie.

'Short answer, no,' she said. We walked a bit further. 'Long answer: you asked what I meant about being fucked-up by my father. Psychology 101—our first relationship with a male is with our fathers. It affects how we relate to men forever. So, lucky me, I get a choice of two. Phil, who's fucked in the head, or my real father who walked away from me and my mother. And I get this choice when I'm twelve years old and Phil sits me down and has this "I wish your mother could be here to tell you" talk with me. You know, just the standard stuff your dad tells you at twelve—I'm not your dad, your mum who died before you could know her properly isn't the perfect person you thought she was, and you're only here because of your mother being easy and I wish you weren't so I could go off and have a life.'

'He said that to you?'

'Not in those words. But that's what he meant.'

I thought it highly unlikely that a twelve-year-old—even a female future psychology student—could correctly deduce an adult male's unspoken thoughts. Sometimes it is better to be aware of one's incompetence in these matters, as I am, than to have a false sense of expertise.

'So, I don't trust men. I don't believe they're what they say they are. I'm afraid they're going to let me down. That's my summary from seven years of studying psychology.'

This seemed a very poor result for seven years of effort, but I assumed she was omitting the more general knowledge provided by the course.

'You want to meet tomorrow evening?' said Rosie. 'We can do whatever you want to do.'

I had been thinking about my plans for the next day.

'I know someone at Columbia,' I said. 'Maybe we could go there together.'

'What about the museum?'

'I've already compressed four visits into two. I can compress two into one.' There was no logic in this, but I had drunk a lot of beer, and I just felt like going to Columbia. *Go with the flow.*

'See you at eight—and don't be late,' said Rosie. Then she kissed me. It was not a passionate kiss; it was on the cheek, but it was disturbing. Neither positive nor negative, just disturbing.

I emailed David Borenstein at Columbia then Skyped Claudia and told her about the day, omitting the kiss.

'Sounds like she's made a big effort,' said Claudia.

This was obviously true. Rosie had managed to select activities that I would normally have avoided, but enjoyed immensely. 'And you're giving her the guided tour of the Museum of Natural History on Wednesday?'

'No, I'm going to look at the crustaceans and the Antarctic flora and fauna.'

'Try again,' said Claudia.

26

We took the subway to Columbia. David Borenstein had not replied to my email. I did not mention this to Rosie who invited me to her meeting, if it did not clash with mine.

'I'll say you're a fellow researcher,' she said. 'I'd like you to see what I do when I'm not mixing drinks.'

Mary Keneally was an associate professor of psychiatry in the Medical Faculty. I had never asked Rosie the topic of her PhD. It turned out to be *Environmental Risks for Early Onset Bipolar Disorder*, a serious scientific topic. Rosie's approach appeared sound and well considered. She and Mary talked for fifty-three minutes, and then we all went for coffee.

'At heart,' Mary said to Rosie, 'you're a psychiatrist rather than a psychologist. You've never thought of transferring to Medicine?'

'I came from a medical family,' said Rosie. 'I sort of rebelled.'

'Well, when you've finished rebelling, we've got a great MD program here.'

'Right,' said Rosie. 'Me at Columbia.'

'Why not? In fact, since you've come all this way...' She made a quick phone call, then smiled. 'Come and meet the Dean.'

As we walked back to the Medical building, Rosie said to me, 'I hope you're suitably impressed.' We arrived at the Dean's office and he stepped out to meet us.

'Don,' he said. 'I just got your email. I haven't had a chance to reply.' He turned to Rosie. 'I'm David Borenstein. And you're with Don?'

We all had lunch at the faculty club. David told Rosie that he had supported my O-1 visa application. 'I didn't lie,' he said. 'Any time Don feels like joining the main game, there's a job for him here.'

Coal-oven pizza is supposedly environmentally unsound, but I treat statements of this kind with great suspicion. They are frequently emotionally based rather than scientific and ignore full life-cycle costs. Electricity good, coal bad. But where does the electricity come from? Our pizza at Arturo's was excellent. World's Best Pizza.

I was interested in one of the statements Rosie had made at Columbia.

'I thought you admired your mother. Why wouldn't you want to be a doctor?'

'It wasn't my mother. My father's a doctor too. Remember? That's what we're here for.' She poured the rest of the red wine into her glass. 'I thought about it. I did the GAMSAT, like I told Peter Enticott. And I did get seventy-four. Suck on that.' Despite the aggressive words, her expression remained friendly. 'I thought that doing Medicine would be a sign of some sort of obsession with my real father. Like I was following him rather than Phil. Even I could see that was a bit fucked-up.'

Gene frequently states that psychologists are

incompetent at understanding themselves. Rosie seemed to have provided good evidence for that proposition. Why avoid something that she would enjoy and be good at? And surely three years of undergraduate education in psychology plus several years of postgraduate research should have provided a more precise classification of her behavioural, personality and emotional problems than 'fucked-up'. Naturally I did not share these thoughts.

We were first in line when the museum opened at 10.30 a.m. I had planned the visit according to the history of the universe, the planet and life. Thirteen billion years of history in six hours. At noon, Rosie suggested we delete lunch from the schedule to allow more time with the exhibits. Later, she stopped at the reconstruction of the famous Laetoli footprints made by hominids approximately 3.6 million years ago.

'I read an article about this. It was a mother and child, holding hands, right?'

It was a romantic interpretation, but not impossible.

'Have you ever thought of having children, Don?'

'Yes,' I said, forgetting to deflect this personal question. 'But it seems both unlikely and inadvisable.'

'Why?'

'Unlikely, because I have lost confidence in the Wife Project. And inadvisable because I would be an unsuitable father.'

'Why?'

'Because I'd be an embarrassment to my children.'

Rosie laughed. I thought this was very insensitive, but she explained, 'All parents are an embarrassment to their kids.'

'Including Phil?'

She laughed again. 'Especially Phil.'

At 4.28 p.m. we had finished the primates. 'Oh no, we're done?' said Rosie. 'Is there something else we can see?'

'We have two more things to see,' I said. 'You may find them dull.'

I took her to the room of balls—spheres of different sizes showing the scale of the universe. The display is not dramatic, but the information is. Non-scientists, non-*physical*-scientists, frequently have no idea of scale—how small we are compared to the size of the universe, how big compared to the size of a neutrino. I did my best to make it interesting.

Then we went up in the elevator and joined the Heilbrunn Cosmic Pathway, a one hundred and ten metre spiral ramp representing a timeline from the big bang to the present. It is just pictures and photos and occasional rocks and fossils on the wall, and I didn't even need to look at them, because I know the story, which I related as accurately and dramatically as I could, putting all that we had seen during the day into context, as we walked down and around until we reached the ground level and the tiny vertical hairline representing all of recorded human history. It was almost closing time now, and we were the only people standing there. On other occasions, I have listened to people's reactions as they reach the end. 'Makes you feel a bit unimportant, doesn't it?' they say. I suppose that is one way of looking at it—how the age of the universe somehow diminishes our lives or the events of history or Joe DiMaggio's streak.

But Rosie's response was a verbal version of mine. 'Wow,' she said, very quietly, looking back at the vastness of it all. Then, in this vanishingly small moment in the history of the universe, she took my hand, and held it all the way to the subway.

27

We had one critical task to perform before leaving New York the following morning. Max Freyberg, the cosmetic surgeon and potential biological father of Rosie, who was 'booked solid', had agreed to see us for fifteen minutes at 6.45 p.m. Rosie had told his secretary she was writing a series of articles for a publication about successful alumni of the university. I was carrying Rosie's camera and would be identified as a photographer.

Getting the appointment had been difficult enough, but it had become apparent that collecting the DNA would be far more difficult in a working environment than in a social or domestic location. I had set my brain the task of solving the problem before we departed for New York, and had expected it to have found a solution through background processing, but it had apparently been too occupied with other matters. The best I could think of was a spiked ring that would draw blood when we shook hands, but Rosie considered this socially infeasible.

She suggested clipping a hair, either surreptitiously or after identifying it as a stray that would mar the photo. Surely a cosmetic surgeon would care about his appearance. Unfortunately a clipped hair was unlikely to yield an adequate sample—it needed to be plucked to obtain a follicle. Rosie packed a pair of tweezers. For once I hoped I might have to spend fifteen minutes in a smoke-filled room. A cigarette butt would solve our problem. We would have to be alert to opportunities.

Dr Freyberg's rooms were in an older-style building on the Upper West Side. Rosie pushed the buzzer and a security guard appeared and took us up to a waiting area where the walls were totally covered with framed certificates and letters from patients praising Dr Freyberg's work.

Dr Freyberg's secretary, a very thin woman (BMI estimate sixteen) of about fifty-five with disproportionately thick lips, led us into his office. More certificates! Freyberg himself had a major fault: he was completely bald. The hair-plucking approach would not be viable. Nor was there any evidence that he was a smoker.

Rosie conducted the interview very impressively. Freyberg described some procedures that seemed to have minimal clinical justification, and talked about their importance to self-esteem. It was fortunate that I had been allocated the silent role, as I would have been strongly tempted to argue. I was also struggling to focus. My mind was still processing the hand-holding incident.

'I'm sorry,' said Rosie, 'but could I bother you for something to drink?'

Of course! The coffee swab solution.

'Sure,' said Freyberg. 'Tea, coffee?'

'Coffee would be great,' said Rosie. 'Just black. Will you have one yourself?'

'I'm good. Let's keep going.' He pushed a button on his intercom. 'Rachel. One black coffee.'

'You should have a coffee,' I said to him.

'Never touch it,' said Freyberg.

'Unless you have a genetic intolerance of caffeine, there are no proven harmful effects. On the contrary—'

'What magazine is this for again?'

The question was straightforward and totally predictable. We had agreed the name of the fictitious university publication in advance, and Rosie had already used it in her introduction.

But my brain malfunctioned. Rosie and I spoke simultaneously. Rosie said, *'Faces of Change.'* I said, *'Hands of Change.'*

It was a minor inconsistency that any rational person would have interpreted as a simple, innocent error, which in fact it was. But Freyberg's expression indicated disbelief and he immediately scribbled on a notepad. When Rachel brought the coffee, he gave her the note. I diagnosed paranoia and started to think about escape plans.

'I need to use the bathroom,' I said. I planned to phone Freyberg from the bathroom, so Rosie could escape while he took the call.

I walked towards the exit, but Freyberg blocked my path.

'Use my private one,' he said. 'I insist.'

He led me through the back of his office, past Rachel to a door marked 'Private' and left me there. There was no way to exit without returning the way we had come. I took out my phone, called 411—directory assistance— and they connected me to Rachel. I could hear the phone ring and Rachel answer. I kept my voice low.

'I need to speak to Dr Freyberg,' I said. 'It's an emergency.' I explained that my wife was a patient of

Dr Freyberg and that her lips had exploded. I hung up and texted Rosie: *Exit now*.

The bathroom was in need of Eva's services. I managed to open the window, which had obviously not been used for a long time. We were four floors up, but there seemed to be plenty of handholds on the wall. I eased myself through the window and started climbing down, slowly, focusing on the task, hoping Rosie had escaped successfully. It had been a long time since I had practised rockclimbing and the descent was not as simple as it first seemed. The wall was slippery from rain earlier in the day and my running shoes were not ideal for the task. At one point I slipped and only just managed to grasp a rough brick. I heard shouts from below.

When I finally reached the ground, I discovered that a small crowd had formed. Rosie was among them. She flung her arms around me. 'Oh my God, Don, you could have killed yourself. It didn't matter that much.'

'The risk was minor. It was just important to ignore the height issue.'

We headed for the subway. Rosie was quite agitated. Freyberg had thought that she was some sort of private investigator, working on behalf of a dissatisfied patient. He was trying to have the security personnel detain her. Whether his position was legally defensible or not, we would have been in a difficult position.

'I'm going to get changed,' said Rosie. 'Our last night in New York City. What do you want to do?'

My original schedule specified a steakhouse, but now that we were in the pattern of eating together, I would need to select a restaurant suitable for a sustainable-seafood-eating 'vegetarian'.

'We'll work it out,' she said. 'Lots of options.'

It took me three minutes to change my shirt. I waited downstairs for Rosie for another six. Finally I went up to her room and knocked. There was a long wait. Then I heard her voice.

'How long do you think it takes to have a shower?'

'Three minutes, twenty seconds,' I said, 'unless I wash my hair, in which case it takes an extra minute and twelve seconds.' The additional time was due primarily to the requirement that the conditioner remain in place for sixty seconds.

'Hold on.'

Rosie opened the door wearing only a towel. Her hair was wet, and she looked extremely attractive. I forgot to keep my eyes directed towards her face.

'Hey,' she said. 'No pendant.' She was right. I couldn't use the pendant excuse. But she didn't give me a lecture on inappropriate behaviour. Instead, she smiled and stepped towards me. I wasn't sure if she was going to take another step, or if I should. In the end, neither of us did. It was an awkward moment but I suspected we had both contributed to the problem.

'You should have brought the ring,' said Rosie.

For a moment, my brain interpreted 'ring' as 'wedding ring', and began constructing a completely incorrect scenario. Then I realised that she was referring to the spiked ring I had proposed as a means of obtaining Freyberg's blood.

'To come all this way and not get a sample.'

'Fortunately, we have one.'

'You got a sample? How?'

'His bathroom. What a slob. He should get his prostate checked. The floor—'

'Stop,' said Rosie. 'Too much information. But nice work.'

'Very poor hygiene,' I told her. 'For a surgeon. A pseudo-surgeon. Incredible waste of surgical skill—inserting synthetic materials purely to alter appearance.'

'Wait till you're fifty-five and your partner's forty-five and see if you say the same thing.'

'You're supposed to be a feminist,' I said, though I was beginning to doubt it.

'It doesn't mean I want to be unattractive.'

'Your appearance should be irrelevant to your partner's assessment of you.'

'Life is full of should-be's,' said Rosie. 'You're the geneticist. Everyone notices how people look. Even you.'

'True. But I don't allow it to affect my evaluation of them.'

I was on dangerous territory: the issue of Rosie's attractiveness had got me into serious trouble on the night of the faculty ball. The statement was consistent with my beliefs about judging people and with how I would wish to be judged myself. But I had never had to apply these beliefs to someone standing opposite me in a hotel bedroom wearing only a towel. It dawned on me that I had not told the full truth.

'Ignoring the testosterone factor,' I added.

'Is there a compliment buried in there somewhere?'

The conversation was getting complicated. I tried to clarify my position. 'It would be unreasonable to give you credit for being incredibly beautiful.'

What I did next was undoubtedly a result of my thoughts being scrambled by a sequence of extraordinary and traumatic incidents in the preceding few hours: the hand-holding, the escape from the cosmetic

235

surgery and the extreme impact of the world's most beautiful woman standing naked under a towel in front of me.

Gene should also take some blame for suggesting that earlobe size was a predictor of sexual attraction. Since I had never been so sexually attracted to a woman before, I was suddenly compelled to examine her ears. In a moment that was, in retrospect, similar to the critical incident in George sDuhamel's *Confession de Minuit*, I reached out and brushed her hair aside. But in this case, amazingly, the response was different from that documented in the novel we had studied in French class. Rosie put her arms around me and kissed me.

I think it is likely that my brain is wired in a nonstandard configuration, but my ancestors would not have succeeded in breeding without understanding and responding to basic sexual signals. That aptitude was hardwired in. I kissed Rosie back. She responded.

We pulled apart for a moment. It was obvious that dinner would be delayed. Rosie studied me and said, 'You know, if you changed your glasses and your haircut, you could be Gregory Peck in *To Kill a Mockingbird*.'

'Is that good?' I assumed, given the circumstances, that it was, but wanted to hear her confirm it.

'He was only the sexiest man that ever lived.'

We looked at each other some more, and I moved to kiss her again. She stopped me.

'Don, this is New York. It's like a holiday. I don't want you to assume it means anything more.'

'What happens in New York stays in New York, right?' It was a line Gene had taught me for conference use. I had never needed to employ it before. It felt a little odd, but appropriate for the circumstances. It was obviously important that we both agreed there was no emotional continuation. Although I did not have a wife at home like Gene, I had a concept of a wife that was very different from Rosie, who would presumably step out on the balcony for a cigarette after sex. Oddly, the prospect didn't repel me as much as it should have.

'I have to get something from my room,' I said.

'Good thinking. Don't take too long.'

My room was only eleven floors above Rosie's, so I walked up the stairs. Back in my room, I showered, then thumbed through the book Gene had given me. He had been right after all. Incredible.

I descended the stairs to Rosie's room. Forty-three minutes had passed. I knocked on the door, and Rosie answered, now wearing a sleeping costume that was, in fact, more revealing than the towel. She was holding two glasses of champagne.

'Sorry, it's gone a bit flat.'

I looked around the room. The bed cover was turned down, the curtains were closed and there was just one bedside lamp on. I gave her Gene's book.

'Since this is our first—and probably only—time, and you are doubtless more experienced, I recommend that you select the position.'

Rosie thumbed through the book, then started again. She stopped at the first page where Gene had written his symbol.

'Gene gave you this?'

'It was a present for the trip.'

I tried to read Rosie's expression, and guessed anger,

but that disappeared and she said, in a non-angry tone, 'Don, I'm sorry, I can't do this. I'm really sorry.'

'Did I say something wrong?'

'No, it's me. I'm really sorry.'

'You changed your mind while I was gone?'

'Yeah,' said Rosie. 'That's what happened. I'm sorry.'

'Are you sure I didn't do something wrong?' Rosie was my friend and the risk to our friendship was now at the forefront of my mind. The sex issue had evaporated.

'No, no, it's me,' she said. 'You were incredibly considerate.'

It was a compliment I was unaccustomed to receiving. A very satisfying compliment. The night had not been a total disaster.

I could not sleep. I had not eaten and it was only 8.55 p.m. Claudia and Gene would be at work now, back in Melbourne, and I did not feel like talking to either of them. I considered it inadvisable to contact Rosie again, so I rang my remaining friend. Dave had eaten already, but we walked to a pizza restaurant and he ate a second dinner. Then we went to a bar and watched baseball and talked about women. I do not recall much of what either of us said, but I suspect that little of it would have been useful in making rational plans for the future.

28

My mind had gone blank. That is a standard phrase, and an exaggeration of the situation. My brain stem continued to function, my heart still beat, I did not forget to breathe. I was able to pack my bag, consume breakfast in my room, navigate to JFK, negotiate check-in and board the plane to Los Angeles. I managed to communicate with Rosie to the extent that it was necessary to coordinate these activities.

But reflective functioning was suspended. The reason was obvious—*emotional overload!* My normally well-managed emotions had been allowed out in New York—on the advice of Claudia, *a qualified clinical psychologist*—and had been dangerously overstimulated. Now they were running amok in my brain, crippling my ability to think. And I needed all my thinking ability to analyse the problem.

Rosie had the window seat and I was by the aisle. I followed the pre-take-off safety procedures, for once not dwelling on their unjustified assumptions and irrational priorities. In the event of impending disaster, we would all have something to do. I was in the opposite position. Incapacitated.

Rosie put her hand on my arm. 'How are you feeling, Don?'

I tried to focus on analysing one aspect of the experience and the corresponding emotional reaction. I knew where to start. Logically, I did not need to go back to my room to get Gene's book. Showing a book to Rosie was not part of the original scenario I had planned back in Melbourne when I prepared for a sexual encounter. I may be socially inept, but with the kiss underway, and Rosie wearing only a towel, there should have been no difficulties in proceeding. My knowledge of positions was a bonus, but probably irrelevant the first time.

So why did my instincts drive me to a course of action that ultimately sabotaged the opportunity? The first-level answer was obvious. They were telling me not to proceed. But why? I identified three possibilities.

1. I was afraid that I would fail to perform sexually.

It did not take long to dismiss this possibility. I might well have been less competent than a more experienced person and could even have been rendered impotent by fear, though I considered this unlikely. But I was accustomed to being embarrassed, even in front of Rosie. The sexual drive was much stronger than any requirement to protect my image.

2. No condom.

I realised, on reflection, that Rosie had probably assumed that I had left her room to collect or purchase a condom. Obviously I should have obtained one, in line with all recommendations on safe sex, and presumably the concierge would have some for emergencies, along with spare toothbrushes and razors. The fact that I did not do so was further evidence that subconsciously I did not expect to proceed. Gene had once told me a story about racing around Cairo in a taxi trying to find a condom vendor. My motivation had clearly not been as strong.

3. I could not deal with the emotional consequences.

The third possibility only entered my mind after I eliminated the first and second. I immediately knew—instinctively!—that it was the correct one. My brain was already emotionally overloaded. It was not the death-defying climb from the surgeon's window or the memory of being interrogated in a dark cellar by a bearded psychiatrist who would stop at nothing to protect his secret. It was not even the experience of holding Rosie's hand from the museum to the subway, although that was a contributor. It was the total experience of hanging out with Rosie in New York.

My instincts were telling me that if I added any more to this experience—if I added the literally mind-blowing experience of having sex with her—my emotions would take over my brain. And they would drive me towards a relationship with Rosie. That would be a disaster for two reasons. The first was that she was totally unsuitable in the longer term. The second was that she had made it clear that such a relationship would not extend beyond our time in New York. These reasons were completely contradictory, mutually exclusive, and based on entirely different premises. I had no idea which one was correct.

We were in the final stages of our descent into LAX. I turned to Rosie. It had been several hours since she asked her question, and I had now given it considerable thought. How was I feeling?

'Confused,' I said to her.

I expected her to have forgotten the question, but perhaps the answer made sense in any case.

'Welcome to the real world.'

I managed to stay awake for the first six hours of the fifteen-hour flight home from LA in order to reset my internal clock, but it was difficult.

Rosie had slept for a few hours then watched a movie. I looked over, and saw that she was crying. She removed her headphones and wiped her eyes.

'You're crying,' I said. 'Is there a problem?'

'Sprung,' said Rosie. 'It's just a sad story. *Bridges of Madison County*. I presume you don't cry at movies.'

'Correct.' I realised that this might be viewed as a negative, so added, in defence, 'It seems to be a predominantly female behaviour.'

'Thanks for that.' Rosie went quiet again but seemed to have recovered from the sadness that the movie had stimulated.

'Tell me,' she said, 'do you feel anything when you watch a movie? You've seen *Casablanca*?'

I was familiar with this question. Gene and Claudia had asked it after we watched a DVD together. So my answer was the result of reflection.

'I've seen several romantic movies. The answer is no.

Unlike Gene and Claudia, and apparently the majority of the human race, I am not emotionally affected by love stories. I don't appear to be wired for that response.'

I visited Claudia and Gene for dinner on the Sunday night. I was feeling unusually jet-lagged, and as a result had some difficulty in providing a coherent account of the trip. I tried to talk about my meeting with David Borenstein at Columbia, what I saw at the museums, and the meal at Momofuku Ko, but they were *obsessed* with grilling me about my interactions with Rosie. I could not reasonably be expected to remember every detail. And obviously I could not talk about the Father Project activities.

Claudia was very pleased with the scarf, but it provided another opportunity for interrogation. 'Did Rosie help you choose this?'

Rosie, Rosie, Rosie.

'The sales assistant recommended it. It was very straightforward.'

As I left, Claudia said, 'So, Don, are you planning to see Rosie again?'

'Next Saturday,' I said, truthfully, not bothering to tell her that it was not a social occasion—we had scheduled the afternoon to analyse the DNA.

She seemed satisfied.

I was eating lunch alone in the University Club, reviewing the Father Project file, when Gene arrived with his meal and a glass of wine and sat opposite me. I tried to put the file away, but succeeded only in giving him the correct impression that I was trying to hide something.

Gene suddenly looked over at the service counter, behind me.

'Oh God!' he said.

I turned to look and Gene snatched the folder, laughing.

'That's private,' I said, but Gene had opened it. The photo of the graduating class was on top.

Gene seemed genuinely surprised. 'My God. Where did you get this?' He was studying the photo intently. 'It must be thirty years old. What's all the scribble?'

'Organising a reunion,' I said. 'Helping a friend. Weeks ago.' It was a good answer, considering the short time I had to formulate it, but it did have a major defect. Gene detected it.

'A friend? Right. One of your many friends. You should have invited me.'

'Why?'

'Who do you think took the photo?'

Of course. Someone had been required to take the photo. I was too stunned to speak.

'I was the only outsider,' said Gene. 'The genetics tutor. Big night—everyone pumped, no partners. Hottest ticket in town.'

Gene pointed to a face in the photo. I had always focused on the males, and never looked for Rosie's mother. But now that Gene was pointing to her, she was easy to identify. The resemblance was obvious, including the red hair, although the colour was less dramatic than Rosie's. She was standing between Isaac Esler and Geoffrey Case. As in Isaac Esler's wedding photo, Case was smiling broadly.

'Bernadette O'Connor.' Gene sipped his wine. 'Irish.'

I was familiar with the tone of Gene's statement. There was a reason for him remembering this particular woman, and it was not because she was Rosie's mother. In fact, it seemed that he didn't know the connection, and I made a quick decision not to inform him.

His finger moved one space to the left.

'Geoffrey Case. Not a great return on his tuition fees.'

'He died, correct?'

'Killed himself.'

This was new information. 'Are you sure?'

'Of course I'm sure,' said Gene. 'Come on, what's this about?'

I ignored the question. 'Why did he do it?'

'Probably forgot to take his lithium,' said Gene. 'He had bipolar disorder. Life of the party on a good day.' He looked at me. I assumed he was about to interrogate me as to the reason for my interest in Geoffrey Case and the reunion, and I was thinking frantically to invent a plausible explanation. I was saved by an empty pepper grinder. Gene gave it a twist, then walked away to exchange it. I used a table napkin to swab his wine glass and left before he returned.

29

I cycled to the university on Saturday morning with an unidentifiable, and therefore disconcerting, emotion. Things were settling back into their normal pattern. The day's testing would mark the end of the Father Project. At worst, Rosie might find a person that we had overlooked—another tutor or caterer or perhaps someone who had left the party early—but a single additional test would not take long. And I would have no reason to see Rosie again.

We met at the lab. There were three samples to test: the swab from Isaac Esler's fork, a urine sample on toilet paper from Freyberg's floor, and Gene's table napkin. I had still not told Rosie about the handkerchief from Margaret Case, but was anxious to get a result on Gene's sample. There was a strong possibility that Gene was Rosie's father. I tried not to think about it, but it was consistent with Gene's reaction to the photo, his identification of Rosie's mother, and his history of casual sex.

'What's the napkin?' asked Rosie.

I was expecting this question.

'Retest. One of the earlier samples was contaminated.'

My improving ability at deception was not enough

to fool Rosie. 'Bullshit. Who is it? It's Case, isn't it? You got a sample for Geoffrey Case.'

It would have been easy to say yes but identifying the sample as Case's would create great confusion if it tested positive. A web of lies.

'I'll tell you if it's the one,' I said.

'Tell me now,' said Rosie. 'It *is* the one.'

'How can you know?'

'I just know.'

'You have zero evidence. Isaac Esler's story makes him an excellent candidate. He was committed to getting married to someone else right after the party. He admits to being drunk. He was evasive at dinner. He's standing next to your mother in the photo.'

This was something we had not discussed before. It was such an obvious thing to have checked. Gene had once given me an exercise to do at conferences: 'If you want to know who's sleeping with who, just look at who they sit with at breakfast.' Whoever Rosie's mother had been with that night would likely be standing next to her. Unless of course he was required to take the photo.

'My intuition versus your logic. Wanna bet?'

It would have been unfair to take the bet. I had the advantage of the knowledge from the basement encounter. Realistically, I considered Isaac Esler, Gene and Geoffrey Case to be equally likely. I had mulled over Esler's reference to 'people involved' and concluded that it was ambiguous. He might have been protecting his friend but he could equally have been hiding behind him. Though, if Esler was not himself the father, he could simply have told me to test his sample. Perhaps his plan was to confuse me, in which case it had succeeded,

247

but only temporarily. Esler's deceptive behaviour had caused me to review an earlier decision. If we reached a point where we had eliminated all other candidates, including Esler, I would test the sample I had collected from Margaret Case.

'Anyway it's definitely not Freyberg,' said Rosie, interrupting my thinking.

'Why not?' Freyberg was the least likely, but certainly not impossible.

'Green eyes. I should have thought of it at the time.'

She interpreted my expression correctly: disbelief.

'Come on, you're the geneticist. He's got green eyes so he can't be my father. I checked it on the internet.'

Amazing. She retains a professor of genetics, an alien of extraordinary abilities, to help find her father, she travels for a week spending almost every minute of the waking day with him, yet when she wants the answer to a question on genetics she goes to the internet.

'Those models are simplifications.'

'Don, my mother had blue eyes. I have brown eyes. My real father had to have brown eyes, right?'

'Wrong,' I said. 'Highly likely but not certain. The genetics of eye colour are extremely complex. Green is possible. Also blue.'

'A medical student—a doctor—would know that, wouldn't she?'

Rosie was obviously referring to her mother. I thought it was probably not the right time to give Rosie a detailed account of the deficiencies in medical education.

I just said, 'Highly *un*likely. Gene used to teach genetics to medical students. That's a typical Gene simplification.'

'Fuck Gene,' said Rosie. 'I am so over Gene. Just test the napkin. It's the one.' But she sounded less sure.

'What are you going to do when you find out?'

This question should have been asked earlier. Failure to raise it was another result of lack of planning but, now that I could picture Gene as the father, Rosie's future actions became more relevant to me.

'Funny you should ask,' said Rosie. 'I said it was about closure. But I think, subconsciously, I had this fantasy that my real father would come riding in and... deal with Phil.'

'For failing to keep the Disneyland promise? It would surely be difficult to devise a suitable punishment after so much time.'

'I said it was a fantasy,' she said. 'I saw him as some sort of hero. But now I know it's one of three people, and I've met two of them. Isaac Esler: "We must not revisit the past lightly." Max Freyberg: "I consider myself a restorer of self-esteem." Wankers, both of them. Just weak guys who ran away.'

The lack of logic here was astounding. At most, one of them had deserted her.

'Geoffrey Case...' I began, thinking Rosie's characterisation would not apply to him, but if Rosie knew about the manner of his death she might interpret it as a means of escaping his responsibilities.

'I know, I know. But if it turns out to be someone else, some middle-aged guy who's pretending to be something he isn't, then time's up, arsehole.'

'You're planning to expose him?' I asked, horrified. Suddenly it struck me that I could be involved in causing great pain to someone, very possibly my best friend.

To his whole family! Rosie's mother had not wanted Rosie to know. Perhaps this was why. By default, Rosie's mother knew more about human behaviour than I did.

'Correct.'

'But you'll be inflicting pain. For no compensatory gain.'

'*I'll* feel better.'

'Incorrect,' I said. 'Research shows that revenge adds to the distress of the victim—'

'That's my choice.'

There was the possibility that Rosie's father was Geoffrey Case, in which case all three samples would test negative, and it would be too late for Rosie to wreak her revenge. I did not want to rely on that possibility.

I turned off the machine.

'Stop,' said Rosie. 'I have a right to know.'

'Not if it causes suffering.'

'What about me?' she said. 'Don't you care about me?' She was becoming emotional. I felt very calm. Reason was in control again. My thoughts were straight.

'I care about you enormously. So I can't contribute to you doing something immoral.'

'Don, if you don't do the test, I'm never going to speak to you again. Ever.'

This information was painful to process, but rationally entirely predictable.

'I'd assumed that was inevitable,' I said. 'The project will be complete, and you've indicated no further interest in the sexual aspect.'

'So it's my fault?' said Rosie. 'Of course it's my fault. I'm not a fucking non-smoking teetotal chef with a PhD. I'm not *organised*.'

'I've deleted the non-drinking requirement.' I realised that she was referring to the Wife Project. But what was she saying? That she was evaluating herself according to the criteria of the Wife Project? Which meant—

'You considered me as a partner?'

'Sure,' she said. 'Except for the fact that you have no idea of social behaviour, your life's ruled by a whiteboard and you're incapable of feeling love—you're perfect.'

She walked out, slamming the door behind her.

I turned the machine on. Without Rosie in the room, I could safely test the samples and then decide what to do with them. Then I heard the door open again. I turned around, expecting to see Rosie. Instead it was the Dean.

'Working on your secret project, Professor Tillman?'

I was in serious trouble. In all previous encounters with the Dean, I had been following the rules, or the infraction had been too minor to punish. Using the DNA machine for private purposes was a substantial breach of the Genetics Department regulations. How much did she know? She did not normally work on weekends. Her presence was not an accident.

'Fascinating stuff, according to Simon Lefebvre,' said the Dean. 'He comes into my office and asks me about a project in my own faculty. One that apparently requires that we collect his DNA. As you do. I gather there was some sort of joke involved. Pardon my lack of humour, but I was at a slight disadvantage—having never heard of the project. Surely, I thought, I would have seen the proposal when it went to the ethics committee.'

Up to this point, the Dean had seemed cool and rational. Now she raised her voice.

'I've been trying for two years to get the Medical Faculty to fund a joint research project—and you decide not only to behave grossly unethically but to do it to the man who holds the purse strings. I want a written report. If it doesn't include an ethics approval that I somehow haven't seen yet, we'll be advertising an associate professor position.'

The Dean stopped at the door.

'I'm still holding your complaint about Kevin Yu. You might want to think about that. And I'll have your lab key, thank you.'

The Father Project was over. Officially.

Gene came into my office the following day as I was completing an EPDS questionnaire.

'Are you okay?' he said. This was a timely question.

'I suspect not. I'll tell you in approximately fifteen seconds.' I completed the questionnaire, calculated the result, and passed it to Gene. 'Sixteen,' I told him. 'Second-highest score ever.'

Gene looked at it. '*Edinburgh Postnatal Depression Scale*. Do I have to point out that you haven't had a baby recently?'

'I don't answer the baby-related questions. It was the only depression instrument Claudia had at home when my sister died. I've continued using it for consistency.'

'This is what we call "getting in touch with our feelings", is it?' said Gene.

I sensed that the question was rhetorical and did not reply.

'Listen,' he said, 'I think I can fix this thing for you.'

'You have news from Rosie?'

'For Chrissakes, Don,' said Gene. 'I have news from the *Dean*. I don't know what you've been doing, but DNA testing without ethics approval!—that's "career over".'

I knew this. I had decided to phone Amghad, the golf club boss, and ask him about the cocktail bar partnership. It seemed like time to do something different. It had been a weekend of rude awakenings. I had arrived home after the interaction with the Dean to find that Eva, my housekeeper, had filled in a copy of the Wife Project questionnaire. On the front, she had written: 'Don. Nobody is perfect. Eva.' In my state of heightened vulnerability, I had been extremely affected by this. Eva was a good person whose short skirts were perhaps intended to attract a partner and who would have been embarrassed by her relatively low socio-economic status as she answered questions about postgraduate qualifications and appreciation of expensive food. I reflected on all the women who had completed my questionnaire, hoping that they might find a partner. Hoping that partner might be me, even though they did not know much about me and would probably be disappointed if they did.

I had poured myself a glass of pinot noir and gone out to the balcony. The city lights reminded me of the lobster dinner with Rosie that, contrary to the predictions of the questionnaire, had been one of the most enjoyable meals of my life. Claudia had told me I was being too picky but Rosie had demonstrated in New York that my assessment of what would make me happy was totally incorrect. I sipped the wine slowly and watched the view change. A window went dark, a traffic light changed from red to green, an ambulance's flashing lights bounced off the buildings. And it dawned on me that I had not designed the questionnaire to find a woman I could accept, but to find someone who might accept me.

Regardless of what decisions I might make as a result of my experiences with Rosie, I would not use the questionnaire again. The Wife Project was over.

Gene had more to say. 'No job, no structure, no schedule. You'll fall apart.' He looked at the depression questionnaire again. 'You're falling apart already. Listen. I'm going to say that it was a Psych Department project. We'll make up an ethics application, and you can say you thought it had been approved.'

Gene was obviously doing his best to be helpful. I smiled for his benefit.

'Does that take a few points off the score?' he said, waving the EPDS questionnaire.

'I suspect not.'

There was a silence. Neither of us apparently had anything to say. I expected Gene to leave. But he tried again.

'Help me here, Don. It's Rosie, isn't it?'

'It makes no sense.'

'Let me put this simply,' said Gene. 'You're unhappy —so unhappy that you've lost perspective on your career, your reputation, your holy schedule.'

This was true.

'Shit, Don, you broke the rules. Since when do you break rules?'

It was a good question. I respect rules. But in the last ninety-nine days, I had broken many rules, legal, ethical and personal. I knew exactly when it had started. The day Rosie walked into my office and I hacked into Le Gavroche's reservation system so I could go on a date with her.

'All this because of a woman?' said Gene.

'Apparently. It's totally irrational.' I felt embarrassed. It was one thing to make a social error, another to admit that rationality had deserted me.

'It's only irrational if you believe in your questionnaire.'

'The EPDS is highly—'

'I'm talking about your "Do you eat kidneys?" questionnaire. I'd say genetics one, questionnaire nil.'

'You consider the situation with Rosie to be the result of genetic compatibility?'

'You have such a way with words,' Gene said. 'If you want to be a bit more romantic about it, I'd say you were in love.'

This was an extraordinary statement. It also made absolute sense. I had assumed that romantic love would always be outside my realm of experience. But it perfectly accounted for my current situation. I wanted to be sure.

'This is your professional opinion? As an expert on human attraction?'

Gene nodded.

'Excellent.' Gene's insight had transformed my mental state.

'Not sure how that helps,' said Gene.

'Rosie identified three faults. Fault number one was

the inability to feel love. There are only two left to rectify.'

'And they would be?'

'Social protocols and adherence to schedules. Trivial.'

30

I booked a meeting with Claudia at the usual café to discuss social behaviour. I realised that improving my ability to interact with other humans would require some effort and that my best attempts might not convince Rosie. But the skills would be useful in their own right.

I had, to some extent, become comfortable with being socially odd. At school, I had been the unintentional class clown, and eventually the intentional one. It was time to grow up.

The server approached our table. 'You order,' said Claudia.

'What would you like?'

'A skinny decaf latte.'

This is a ridiculous form of coffee, but I did not point it out. Claudia would surely have received the message from previous occasions and would not want it repeated. It would be annoying to her.

'I'd like a double espresso,' I said to the server, 'and my friend will have a skinny decaf latte, no sugar, please.'

'Well,' said Claudia. 'Something's changed.'

I pointed out that I had been successfully and politely ordering coffee all my life, but Claudia insisted that my mode of interaction had changed in subtle ways.

'I wouldn't have picked New York City as the place to learn to be genteel,' she said, 'but there you go.'

I told her that, on the contrary, people had been extremely friendly, citing my experience with Dave the Baseball Fan, Mary the bipolar-disorder researcher, David Borenstein the Dean of Medicine at Columbia, and the chef and weird guy at Momofuku Ko. I mentioned that we had dined with the Eslers, describing them as friends of Rosie's family. Claudia's conclusion was simple. All this unaccustomed social interaction, plus that with Rosie, had dramatically improved my skills.

'You don't need to try with Gene and me, because you're not out to impress us or make friends with us.'

While Claudia was right about the value of practice, I learn better from reading and observation. My next task was to download some educational material.

I decided to begin with romantic films specifically mentioned by Rosie. There were four: *Casablanca*, *The Bridges of Madison County*, *When Harry Met Sally* and *An Affair to Remember*. I added *To Kill a Mockingbird* and *The Big Country* for Gregory Peck, whom Rosie had cited as the sexiest man ever.

It took a full week to watch all six, including time for pausing the DVD player and taking notes. The films were incredibly useful, but also highly challenging. The emotional dynamics were so complex! I persevered, drawing on movies recommended by Claudia about male-female relationships with both happy and unhappy outcomes. I watched *Hitch, Gone with the Wind, Bridget*

Jones's Diary, Annie Hall, Notting Hill, Love Actually and *Fatal Attraction*.

Claudia also suggested I watch *As Good as It Gets*, 'just for fun'. Although her advice was to use it as an example of what *not* to do, I was impressed that the Jack Nicholson character handled a jacket problem with more finesse than I had. It was also encouraging that, despite serious social incompetence, a significant difference in age between him and the Helen Hunt character, probable multiple psychiatric disorders and a level of intolerance far more severe than mine, he succeeded in winning the love of the woman in the end. An excellent choice by Claudia.

Slowly I began to make sense of it all. There were certain consistent principles of behaviour in male-female romantic relationships, including the prohibition of infidelity. That rule was in my mind when I met with Claudia again for social practice.

We worked through some scenarios.

'This meal has a fault,' I said. The situation was hypothetical. We were only drinking coffee. 'That would be too confrontational, correct?'

Claudia agreed. 'And don't say fault, or error. That's computer talk.'

'But I can say "I'm sorry, it was an error of judgment, entirely my fault", correct? That use of "fault" is acceptable?'

'Correct,' said Claudia and then laughed. 'I mean yes. Don, this takes years to learn.'

I didn't have years. But I am a quick learner and was in human-sponge mode. I demonstrated.

'I'm going to construct an objective statement

followed by a request for clarification, and preface it with a platitude: "Excuse me. I ordered a rare steak. Do you have a different definition of rare?"'

'Good start, but the question's a bit aggressive.'

'Not acceptable?'

'In New York maybe. Don't blame the waiter.'

I modified the question. 'Excuse me. I ordered a rare steak. Could you check that my order was processed correctly?'

Claudia nodded. But she did not look entirely happy. I was paying great attention to expressions of emotion and I had diagnosed hers correctly.

'Don. I'm impressed, but…changing to meet someone else's expectations may not be a good idea. You may end up resenting it.'

I didn't think this was likely. I was learning some new protocols, that was all.

'If you really love someone,' Claudia continued, 'you have to be prepared to accept them as they are. Maybe you hope that one day they get a wake-up call and make the changes for their own reasons.'

This last statement connected with the fidelity rule that I had in my mind at the beginning of the discussion. I did not need to raise the subject now. I had the answer to my question. Claudia was surely talking about Gene.

I organised a run with Gene for the following morning. I needed to speak to him in private, somewhere he could not escape. I started my personal lecture as soon as we were moving. My key point was that infidelity was totally unacceptable. Any benefits were outweighed by the risk of total disaster. Gene had been divorced once already. Eugenie and Carl—

Gene interrupted, breathing heavily. In my effort to get the message across unambiguously and forcefully, I had been running faster than normal. Gene is significantly less fit than I am and my fat-burning low-heart-rate jogs are major cardiovascular workouts for him.

'I hear you,' said Gene. 'What've you been reading?'

I told him about the movies I had been watching, and their idealised representation of acceptable and unacceptable behaviour. If Gene and Claudia had owned a rabbit, it would have been in serious danger from a disgruntled lover. Gene disagreed, not about the rabbit, but about the impact of his behaviour on his marriage.

'We're psychologists,' he said. 'We can handle an open marriage.'

I ignored his incorrect categorisation of himself as a real psychologist, and focused on the critical issue: all authorities and moral codes consider fidelity critical. Even theories of evolutionary psychology concede that if a person discovers that their partner is unfaithful, they will have strong reasons for rejecting them.

'You're talking about men there,' said Gene. 'Because they can't afford the risk of raising a child who doesn't have their genes. Anyway, I thought you were all about overcoming instinct.'

'Correct. The male instinct is to cheat. You need to overcome it.'

'Women accept it as long as you don't embarrass them with it. Look at France.'

I cited a counter-example from a popular book and film.

'*Bridget Jones's Diary*?' said Gene. 'Since when are

we expected to behave like characters in chick flicks?' He stopped and doubled over, gasping for breath. It gave me the opportunity to present him with the evidence without interruption. I finished by pointing out that he loved Claudia and that he should therefore be prepared to make all necessary sacrifices.

'I'll think about it when I see you changing the habits of a lifetime,' he said.

I had thought that eliminating my schedule would be relatively straightforward. I had just spent eight days without it and while I had faced numerous problems they were not related to inefficiency or unstructured time. But I had not factored in the impact of the enormous amount of turmoil in my life. As well as the uncertainty around Rosie, the social skills project and the fear that my best friends were on the path to domestic disintegration, I was about to lose my job. The schedule of activities felt like the only stable thing in my life.

In the end, I made a compromise that would surely be acceptable to Rosie. Everyone keeps a timetable of their regular commitments, in my case lectures, meetings and martial arts classes. I would allow myself these. I would put appointments in my diary, *as other people did*, but reduce standardisation. Things could change week by week. Reviewing my decision, I could see that the abandonment of the Standardised Meal System, the aspect of my schedule that provoked the most comment, was the only item requiring immediate attention.

My next market visit was predictably strange. I arrived at the seafood stall and the proprietor turned to pull a lobster from the tank.

'Change of plan,' I said. 'What's good today?'

'Lobster,' he said, in his heavily accented English. 'Lobster good every Tuesday for you.' He laughed, and waved his hand at his other customers. He was making a joke about me. Rosie had a facial expression that she used when she said, 'Don't fuck with me.' I tried the expression. It seemed to work by itself.

'I'm joking,' he said. 'Swordfish is beautiful. Oysters. You eat oysters?'

I ate oysters, though I had never prepared them at home. I ordered them unshucked as quality restaurants promoted their oysters as being freshly shucked.

I arrived home with a selection of food not associated with any particular recipe. The oysters proved challenging. I could not get a knife in to open them without risking injury to my hand through slippage. I could have looked up the technique on the internet, but it would have taken time. This was why I had a schedule based around familiar items. I could remove the meat from a lobster with my eyes closed while my brain worked on a genetics problem. What was wrong with standardisation? Another oyster failed to provide an opening for my knife. I was getting annoyed and about to throw the full dozen in the bin when I had an idea.

I put one in the microwave and heated it for a few seconds. It opened easily. It was warm but delicious. I tried a second, this time adding a squeeze of lemon juice and a grind of pepper. Sensational! I could feel a whole world opening up to me. I hoped the oysters were sustainable, because I wanted to share my new skills with Rosie.

31

My focus on self-improvement meant that I had little time to consider and respond to the Dean's threat of dismissal. I had decided not to take up Gene's offer to construct an alibi; now that the breach of rules was in my conscious mind, it would be a violation of my personal integrity to compound the error.

I succeeded in suppressing thoughts of my professional future, but could not stop the Dean's parting comment about Kevin Yu and my plagiarism complaint from intruding into my conscious mind. After much thought, I concluded that the Dean was not offering me an unethical deal: 'Withdraw the complaint and you can keep your job.' What she said was bothering me because I had myself broken the rules in pursuing the Father Project. Gene had once told me a religious joke when I questioned the morality of his behaviour.

Jesus addresses the angry mob who are stoning a prostitute: 'Let he who is without sin cast the first stone.' A stone flies through the air and hits the woman. Jesus turns around and says, 'Sometimes you really piss me off, Mother.'

I could no longer be equated with the Virgin Mary. I had been corrupted. I was like everyone else. My stone-casting credibility had been significantly compromised.

I summoned Kevin to a meeting in my office. He was from mainland China, and aged approximately twenty-eight (estimated BMI nineteen). I interpreted his expression and demeanour as 'nervous'.

I had his essay, partly or entirely written by his tutor, in my hand and showed it to him. I asked the obvious question: Why had he not written it himself?

He averted his gaze—which I interpreted as a cultural signal of respect rather than of shiftiness—but instead of answering my question, he started to explain the consequences of his probable expulsion. He had a wife and child in China, and had not yet told them of the problem. He hoped someday to emigrate, or, if not, at least to work in genetics. His unwise behaviour would mean the end of his dreams and those of his wife, who had managed for almost four years without him. He was crying.

In the past, I would have regarded this as sad but irrelevant. A rule had been broken. But now I was also a rule-breaker. I had not broken the rules deliberately, or at least not with any conscious thought. Perhaps Kevin's behaviour had been similarly unconsidered.

I asked Kevin, 'What are the principal arguments advanced against the use of genetically modified crops?' The essay had been on the ethical and legal issues raised by advances in genetics. Kevin gave a comprehensive summary. I followed with further questions, which Kevin also answered well. He seemed to have a good knowledge of the topic.

'Why didn't you write this yourself?' I asked.

'I am a scientist. I am not confident writing in English about moral and cultural questions. I wanted to be sure not to fail. I did not think.'

I did not know how to respond to Kevin. Acting without thinking was anathema to me, and I did not want to encourage it in future scientists. Nor did I want my own weakness to affect a correct decision regarding Kevin. I would pay for my own error in this regard, as I deserved to. But losing my job would not have the same consequences for me as expulsion would for Kevin. I doubted he would be offered a potentially lucrative partnership in a cocktail bar as an alternative.

I thought for quite a long time. Kevin just sat. He must have realised that I was considering some form of reprieve. But I was incredibly uncomfortable in this position of judgment as I weighed the impact of various decisions. Was this what the Dean had to do every day? For the first time, I felt some respect for her.

I was not confident I could solve the problem in a short time. But I realised that it would be cruel to leave Kevin wondering if his life had been destroyed.

'I understand…' I started, and realised that this was not a phrase I was accustomed to using when talking about people. I stopped the sentence and thought for a while longer. 'I will create a supplementary task—probably an essay on personal ethics. As an alternative to expulsion.'

I interpreted Kevin's expression as ecstatic.

I was conscious that there was more to social skills than knowing how to order coffee and being faithful to your partner. Since my school days, I had selected my clothes without regard to fashion. I started out not caring how I looked, then discovered that people found what I wore amusing. I enjoyed being seen as someone not tied to the norms of society. But now I had no idea how to dress.

I asked Claudia to buy me some suitable clothes. She had proved her expertise with the jeans and shirt, but she insisted on me accompanying her.

'I may not be around forever,' she said. After some reflection, I deduced that she was talking not about death, but about something more immediate: marriage failure! I had to find a way to convince Gene of the danger.

The actual shopping took a full morning. We went to several shops, acquiring shoes, trousers, a jacket, a second pair of jeans, more shirts, a belt and even a tie.

I had more shopping to do, but I did not require Claudia's help. A photo was sufficient to specify my requirements. I visited the optometrist, the hairdresser (not my regular barber) and the menswear shop. Everyone was extremely helpful.

My schedule and social skills had now been brought into line with conventional practice, to the best of my ability within the time I had allocated. The Don Project was complete. It was time to commence the Rosie Project.

There was a mirror on the inside of the closet in my office which I had never needed before. Now I used it to review my appearance. I expected I would have only one chance to cut through Rosie's negative view of me and produce an emotional reaction. I wanted her to fall in love with me.

Protocol dictated that I should not wear a hat indoors, but I decided that the PhD students' area could be considered public. On that basis, it would be acceptable. I checked the mirror again. Rosie had been right.

In my grey three-piece suit, I could be mistaken for Gregory Peck in *To Kill a Mockingbird*. Atticus Tillman. World's sexiest man.

Rosie was at her desk. So was Stefan, looking unshaven as always. I had my speech prepared.

'Good afternoon, Stefan. Hi, Rosie. Rosie, I'm afraid it's short notice but I was wondering if you'd join me for dinner this evening. There's something I'd like to share with you.'

Neither spoke. Rosie looked a little stunned. I looked at her directly. 'That's a charming pendant,' I said. 'I'll pick you up at 7.45.' I was shaking as I walked away, but I had given it my best effort. Hitch from *Hitch* would have been pleased with me.

I had two more visits to make before my evening date with Rosie.

I walked straight past Helena. Gene was in his office looking at his computer. On the screen was a photo of an Asian woman who was not conventionally attractive. I recognised the format—she was a Wife-Project Applicant. Place of Birth—North Korea.

Gene looked at me strangely. My Gregory Peck costume was doubtless unexpected but appropriate for my mission.

'Hi, Gene.'

'What's with the "Hi"? What happened to "Greetings"?'

I explained that I had eliminated a number of unconventional mannerisms from my vocabulary.

'So Claudia tells me. You didn't think your regular mentor was up to the job?'

I wasn't sure what he meant.

He explained. 'Me. You didn't ask me.'

This was correct. Feedback from Rosie had prompted me to reassess Gene's social competence, and my recent work with Claudia and the movie exemplars had confirmed my suspicion that his skills applied to a limited domain, and that he was not employing them in the best interests of himself and his family.

'No,' I told him. 'I wanted advice on socially appropriate behaviour.'

'What's that supposed to mean?'

'Obviously, you're similar to me. That's why you're my best friend. Hence this invitation.' There had been a great deal of preparation for this day. I gave Gene an envelope. He did not open it but continued the conversation.

'I'm like you? No offence, Don, but your behaviour—your old behaviour—was in a class of its own. If you want my opinion, you hid behind a persona that you thought people found amusing. It's hardly surprising people saw you as a…buffoon.'

This was exactly my point. But Gene was not making the connection. As his buddy, it was my duty to behave as an adult male and give it to him straight.

I walked over to his map of the world, with a pin for every conquest. I checked it for what I hoped would be the last time. Then I stabbed it with my finger, to create an atmosphere of threat.

'Exactly,' I said. 'You think people see you as a Casanova. You know what? I don't care what other people think of you, but if you want to know, they think you're a jerk. And they're right, Gene. You're fifty-six years old with a wife and two kids, though for how much longer I don't know. Time you grew up. I'm telling you that as a friend.'

I watched Gene's face. I was getting better at reading emotions, but this was a complex one. Shattered, I think.

I was relieved. The basic male-male tough advice protocol had been effective. It had not been necessary to slug him.

32

I went back to my office and changed from my Gregory Peck costume into my new trousers and jacket. Then I made a phone call. The receptionist was not prepared to make an appointment for a personal matter, so I booked a fitness evaluation with Phil Jarman, Rosie's father in air quotes, for 4.00 p.m.

As I got up to leave, the Dean knocked and walked in. She signalled for me to follow her. This was not part of my plan, but today was an appropriate day to close this phase of my professional life.

We went down in the lift and then across the campus to her office, not speaking. It seemed that our conversation needed to take place in a formal setting. I felt uncomfortable, which was a rational response to the almost-certain prospect of being dismissed from a tenured position at a prestigious university for professional misconduct. But I had expected this and my feelings came from a different source. The scenario triggered a memory from my first week at high school, of being sent to the headmaster's office as a result of allegedly inappropriate behaviour. The purported misconduct involved a rigorous questioning of our religious education teacher. In retrospect, I understood that she was a well-meaning person, but she used her position of power over an eleven-year-old to cause me considerable distress.

The headmaster was, in fact, reasonably sympathetic, but warned me that I needed to show 'respect'. But he was too late: as I walked to his office I had made the decision that it was pointless to try to fit in. I would be the class clown for the next six years.

I have thought about this event often. At the time my decision felt like a rational response based on my assessment of the new environment, but in retrospect I understood that I was driven by anger at the power structure that suppressed my arguments.

Now as I walked to the Dean's office another thought occurred to me. What if my teacher had been a brilliant theologian, equipped with two thousand years of well-articulated Christian thinking? She would have had more compelling arguments than an eleven-year-old. Would I have then been satisfied? I suspect not. As a scientist, with an allegiance to scientific thinking, I would have had a deep-seated feeling that I was being, as Rosie would say, bullshitted. Was that how Faith Healer had felt?

Had the flounder demonstration been an instance of bullying as heinous as the one committed by my religious education teacher, *even though I was right*?

As we entered the Dean's office for what I expected to be the last time, I took notice of her full name on the door, and a minor confusion was resolved. Professor Charlotte Lawrence. I had never thought of her as 'Charlie', but presumably Simon Lefebvre did.

We entered her office and sat down. 'I see we're in our job interview clothes,' she said. 'I'm sorry you didn't see fit to grace us with them during your time here.'

I did not respond.

'So. No report. No explanation?'

Again, I could not think of anything appropriate to say.

Simon Lefebvre appeared at the door. Obviously this had been planned. The Dean—Charlie—waved him in.

'You can save time by explaining to Simon and me together.'

Lefebvre was carrying the documents that I had given him.

At that point, the Dean's personal assistant, Regina, who is not objectified by having the words 'The Beautiful' included in her name, entered the room.

'Sorry to bother you, Professor,' she said, ambiguously, as we were all professors, for the next few minutes at least, but the context made it clear she was addressing the Dean. 'I've got a problem with your booking at Le Gavroche. They seem to have taken you off the VIP list.'

The Dean's face registered annoyance but she waved Regina away.

Simon Lefebvre smiled at me. 'You could've just sent me this,' he said, referring to the documents. 'No need for the idiot-savant impression. Which I have to concede was beautifully done. As is the proposal. We'll need to run it by the ethics guys, but it's exactly what we're looking for. Genetics and medicine, topic's current, we'll both get publicity.'

I attempted to analyse the Dean's expression. It was beyond my current skill set.

'So congratulations, Charlie,' said Simon. 'You've

got your joint research project. The Medical Research Institute is prepared to put in four mill, which is more than the budget actually specifies, so you're set to go.'

I presumed he meant four million dollars.

He pointed to me. 'Hang on to this one, Charlie. He's a dark horse. And I need him to be part of the project.'

I got my first real return on my investment in improved social skills. I had worked out what was going on. I did not ask a silly question. I did not put the Dean in a position of untenable embarrassment where she might work against her own interests. I just nodded and walked back to my office.

Phil Jarman had blue eyes. I knew this but it was the first thing I noticed. He was in his mid-fifties, about ten centimetres taller than me, powerfully built and extremely fit-looking. We were standing in front of the reception desk at Jarman's Gym. On the wall were newspaper cuttings and photos of a younger Phil playing football. If I had been a medical student without advanced martial arts skills, I would have thought carefully before having sex with this man's girlfriend. Perhaps this was the simple reason that Phil had never been informed of the identity of Rosie's father.

'Get the Prof some gear and get his signature on a waiver form.'

The woman behind the counter seemed puzzled.

'It's just an assessment.'

'New procedure starts today,' said Phil.

'I don't require an assessment,' I began, but Phil seemed to have fixed ideas.

'You booked one,' he said. 'Sixty-five bucks. Let's get you some boxing gloves.'

I wondered if he realised that he had called me 'Prof'. Presumably Rosie had been right, and he had seen the dancing picture. I had not bothered to disguise my name. But at least I knew that he knew who I was. Did he know that I knew that he knew who I was? I was getting quite good at social subtleties.

I changed into a singlet and shorts, which smelled freshly laundered, and we put on boxing gloves. I had only done the occasional boxing workout, but I was not afraid of getting hurt. I had good defensive techniques if necessary. I was more interested in talking.

'Let's see you hit me,' said Phil.

I threw some gentle punches which Phil blocked.

'Come on,' he said. 'Try to hurt me.'

He asked for it.

'Your stepdaughter is trying to locate her real father because she's dissatisfied with you.'

Phil dropped his guard. Very poor form. I could have landed a punch unimpeded if we were in a real bout.

'Stepdaughter?' he said. 'That's what she's calling herself? That's why you're here?'

He threw a hard punch and I had to use a proper block to avoid being hit. He recognised it and tried a hook. I blocked that too and counterpunched. He avoided it nicely.

'Since it's unlikely she'll succeed, we need to fix the problem with you.'

Phil threw a straight hard one at my head. I blocked and stepped away.

'With me?' he said. 'With Phil Jarman? Who built his own business from nothing, who bench-presses a hundred and forty-five kilos, who plenty of women still think is a better deal than some doctor or lawyer. Or egghead.'

He threw a combination and I attacked back. I thought there was a high probability that I could take him down, but I needed to continue the conversation.

'It's none of your business but I was on the school council, coached the senior football team—'

'Obviously these achievements were insufficient,' I said. 'Perhaps Rosie requires something in addition to personal excellence.' In a moment of clarity, I realised what that something might be in my own case. Was all my work in self-improvement in vain? Was I going to end up like Phil, trying to win Rosie's love but regarded with contempt?

Fighting and contemplation are not compatible. Phil's punch took me in the solar plexus. I managed to step back and reduce the force, but went down. Phil stood over me, angry.

'Maybe one day she'll know everything. Maybe that'll help, maybe it won't.' He shook his head hard, as though he was the one who had taken a punch. 'Did I ever call myself her stepfather? Ask her that. I've got no other children, no *wife*. I did all the things—I read to her, got up in the night, took her horseriding. After her mother was gone, I couldn't do a thing right.'

I sat up and shouted. I was angry too. 'You failed to take her to Disneyland. You lied to her.'

I scissored his legs, bringing him down. He didn't fall competently, and hit the floor hard. We struggled and I pinned him. His nose was bleeding badly and there was blood all over my singlet.

'Disneyland!' said Phil. 'She was ten!'

'She told everyone at school. It's still a major problem.'

He tried to break free, but I managed to hold him, despite the impediment of the boxing gloves.

'You want to know when I told her I'd take her to Disneyland? One time. Once. You know when? At her mother's funeral. I was in a wheelchair. I was in rehab for eight months.'

It was a very reasonable explanation. I wished Rosie had provided this background information prior to me holding her stepfather's head on the floor with blood pouring from his nose. I explained to Phil that at my sister's funeral I made an irrational promise to donate to a hospice when the money would have been better applied to research. He seemed to understand.

'I bought her a jewellery box. She'd been on her mother's case forever to buy it. I thought she'd forgotten about Disneyland when I came out of rehab.'

'Predicting the impact of actions on other people is difficult.'

'Amen to that,' said Phil. 'Can we get up?'

His nose was still bleeding and was probably broken, so it was a reasonable request. But I was not prepared to let him go yet.

'Not until we solve the problem.'

It had been a very full day but the most critical task was still ahead. I examined myself in the mirror. The new glasses, vastly lighter, and the revised hair shape made a bigger difference than the clothes.

I put the important envelope in my jacket pocket and the small box in my trouser pocket. As I phoned for a taxi, I looked at my whiteboard. The schedule, now written in erasable marker, was a sea of red writing—my code for the Rosie Project. I told myself that the changes it had produced were worthwhile, even if tonight I failed to achieve the final objective.

33

The taxi arrived and we made an intermediate stop at the flower shop. I had not been inside this shop—or indeed purchased flowers at all—since I stopped visiting Daphne. Daphne for Daphne; obviously the appropriate choice for this evening was roses. The vendor recognised me and I informed her of Daphne's death. After I purchased a dozen long-stemmed red roses, consistent with standard romantic behaviour, she snipped a small quantity of daphne and inserted it in the buttonhole of my jacket. The smell brought back memories of Daphne. I wished she was alive to meet Rosie.

I tried to phone Rosie as the taxi approached her apartment building, but there was no answer. She was not outside when we arrived, and most of the bell buttons did not have names beside them. There was a risk that she had chosen not to accept my invitation.

It was cold and I was shaking. I waited a full ten minutes, then called again. There was still no answer and I was about to instruct the driver to leave when she came running out. I reminded myself that it was I who had changed, not Rosie—I should have expected her to be late. She was wearing the black dress that had stunned me on the night of the Jacket Incident. I gave her the roses. I read her expression as surprised.

Then she looked at me.

'You look different…really different…again,' she said. 'What happened?'

'I decided to reform myself.' I liked the sound of the word: 're-form'. We got in the taxi, Rosie still holding the roses, and travelled the short distance to the restaurant in silence. I was looking for information about her attitude towards me, and thought it best to let her speak first. In fact she didn't say anything until she noticed that the taxi was stopping outside Le Gavroche—the scene of the Jacket Incident.

'Don, is this a joke?'

I paid the driver, exited the taxi and opened Rosie's door. She stepped out but was reluctant to proceed, clutching the roses to her chest with both hands. I put one hand behind her and guided her towards the door, where the maitre d' whom we had encountered on our previous visit was standing in his uniform. Jacket Man.

He recognised Rosie instantly, as evidenced by his greeting. 'Rosie.'

Then he looked at me. 'Sir?'

'Good evening.' I took the flowers from Rosie and gave them to the maitre d'. 'We have a reservation in the name of Tillman. Would you be kind enough to look after these?' It was a standard formula but very confidence-boosting. Everyone seemed very comfortable now that we were behaving in a predictable manner. The maitre d' checked the reservation list. I took the opportunity to smooth over any remaining difficulties and made a small prepared joke.

'My apologies for the misunderstanding last time. There shouldn't be any difficulties tonight. Unless they overchill the white burgundy.' I smiled.

A male waiter appeared, the maitre d' introduced me, briefly complimenting me on my jacket, and we were led into the dining room and to our table. It was all very straightforward.

I ordered a bottle of chablis. Rosie still seemed to be adjusting.

The sommelier appeared with the wine. He was looking around the room, as if for support. I diagnosed nervousness.

'It's at thirteen degrees but if sir would like it less chilled…or more chilled…'

'That will be fine, thank you.'

He poured me a taste and I swirled, sniffed and nodded approval according to the standard protocol. Meanwhile, the waiter who had led us to the table reappeared. He was about forty, BMI approximately twenty-two, quite tall.

'Professor Tillman?' he said. 'My name's Nick and I'm the head waiter. If there's anything you need, or anything that's a problem, just ask for me.'

'Much appreciated, Nick.'

Waiters introducing themselves by name was more in the American tradition. Either this restaurant deliberately chose to do so as a point of difference, or we were being given more personal treatment. I guessed the latter: I was probably marked as a dangerous person. Good. I would need all the support I could get tonight.

Nick handed us menus.

'I'm happy to leave it to the chef,' I said. 'But no meat, and seafood only if it's sustainable.'

Nick smiled. 'I'll speak to the chef and see what he can do.'

281

'I realise it's a little tricky, but my friend lives by some quite strict rules,' I said.

Rosie gave me a very strange look. My statement was intended to make a small point, and I think it succeeded. She tried her chablis and buttered a bread roll. I remained silent.

Finally she spoke.

'All right, Gregory Peck. What are we doing first? The *My Fair Lady* story or the big revelation?'

This was good. Rosie was prepared to discuss things directly. In fact, directness had always been one of Rosie's positive attributes, though on this occasion she had not identified the most important topic.

'I'm in your hands,' I said. Standard polite method for avoiding a choice and empowering the other person.

'Don, stop it. You know who my father is, right? It's Table-Napkin Man, isn't it?'

'Possibly,' I said, truthfully. Despite the positive outcome of the meeting with the Dean, I did not have my lab key back. 'That isn't what I want to share.'

'All right then. Here's the plan. You share your thing; tell me who my father is; tell me what you've done to yourself; we both go home.'

I couldn't put a name to her tone of speech and expression, but it was clearly negative. She took another sip of her wine.

'Sorry.' She looked a little apologetic. 'Go. The sharing thing.'

I had grave doubts about the likely efficacy of my next move, but there was no contingency plan. I had sourced my speech from *When Harry Met Sally*. It resonated best with me and with the situation, and had the additional advantage of the link to our happy time in New York. I hoped Rosie's brain would make that connection, ideally subconsciously. I drank the remainder of my wine. Rosie's eyes followed my glass, then she looked up at me.

'Are you okay, Don?'

'I asked you here tonight because when you realise you want to spend the rest of your life with somebody, you want the rest of your life to start as soon as possible.'

I studied Rosie's expression carefully. I diagnosed stunned.

'Oh my God,' said Rosie, confirming the diagnosis. I followed up while she was still receptive.

'It seems right now that all I've ever done in my life is making my way here to you.'

I could see that Rosie could not place the line from *The Bridges of Madison County* that had produced such a powerful emotional reaction on the plane. She looked confused.

'Don, what are you…what have you done to yourself?'

'I've made some changes.'

'Big changes.'

'Whatever behavioural modifications you require from me are a trivial price to pay for having you as my partner.'

Rosie made a downwards movement with her hand, which I could not interpret. Then she looked around the room and I followed her eyes. Everyone was watching. Nick had stopped partway to our table. I realised that in my intensity I had raised my voice. I didn't care.

'You are the world's most perfect woman. All other women are irrelevant. Permanently. No Botox or implants will be required.'

I heard someone clapping. It was a slim woman of about sixty sitting with another woman of approximately the same age.

Rosie took a drink of her wine, then spoke in a very measured way. 'Don, I don't know where to start. I don't even know who's asking me—the old Don or Billy Crystal.'

'There's no old and new,' I said. 'It's just behaviour. Social conventions. Glasses and haircut.'

'I like you, Don,' said Rosie. 'Okay? Forget what I said about outing my father. You're probably right. I really *really* like you. I have fun with you. The best times. But, you know I couldn't eat lobster every Tuesday. Right?'

'I've abandoned the Standardised Meal System. I've deleted thirty-eight per cent of my weekly schedule, excluding sleep. I've thrown out my old t-shirts. I've eliminated all of the things you didn't like. Further changes are possible.'

'You changed yourself for me?'

'Only my behaviour.'

Rosie was silent for a while, obviously processing the new information.

'I need a minute to think,' she said. I automatically started the timer on my watch. Suddenly Rosie started laughing. I looked at her, understandably puzzled at this outburst in the middle of a critical life decision.

'The watch,' she said. 'I say "I need a minute" and you start timing. Don is not dead.'

I waited. I looked at my watch. When there were fifteen seconds left, I assessed that it was likely that she was about to say no. I had nothing to lose. I pulled the small box from my pocket and opened it to reveal the ring

I had purchased. I wished I had not learned to read expressions, because I could read Rosie's now and I knew the answer.

'Don,' said Rosie. 'This isn't what you want me to say. But remember on the plane, when you said you were wired differently?'

I nodded. I knew what the problem was. The fundamental, insurmountable problem of who I was. I had pushed it to the back of my mind since it had surfaced in the fight with Phil. Rosie didn't need to explain. But she did.

'That's inside you. You can't fake—sorry, start again. You can behave perfectly, but if the *feeling's* not there inside...God, I feel so unreasonable.'

'The answer is no?' I said, some small part of my brain hoping that for once my fallibility in reading social cues would work in my favour.

'Don, you don't feel love, do you?' said Rosie. 'You can't really love me.'

'Gene diagnosed love.' I knew now that he had been wrong. I had watched thirteen romantic movies and felt nothing. That was not strictly true. I had felt suspense, curiosity and amusement. But I had not for one moment felt engaged in the love between the protagonists. I had cried no tears for Meg Ryan or Meryl Streep or Deborah Kerr or Vivien Leigh or Julia Roberts.

I could not lie about so important a matter. 'According to your definition, no.'

Rosie looked extremely unhappy. The evening had turned into a disaster.

'I thought my behaviour would make you happy, and instead it's made you sad.'

'I'm upset because you can't love me. Okay?'

This was worse! She wanted me to love her. And I was incapable.

'Don,' she said, 'I don't think we should see each other anymore.'

I got up from the table and walked back to the entrance foyer, out of sight of Rosie and the other diners. Nick was there, talking to the maitre d'. He saw me and came over.

'Can I help you with anything?'

'Unfortunately, there has been a disaster.'

Nick looked worried, and I elaborated. 'A personal disaster. There is no risk to other patrons. Would you prepare the bill, please?'

'We haven't served you anything,' said Nick. He looked at me closely for a few moments. 'There's no charge, sir. The chablis is on us.' He offered me his hand and I shook it. 'I think you gave it your best shot.'

I looked up to see Gene and Claudia arriving. They were holding hands. I had not seen them do this for several years.

'Don't tell me we're too late,' said Gene, jovially.

I nodded, then looked back into the restaurant. Rosie was walking quickly towards us.

'Don, what are you doing?' she said.

'Leaving. You said we shouldn't see each other again.'

'Fuck,' she said, then looked at Gene and Claudia. 'What are you doing here?'

'We are summoned to a "Thank you and celebration",' said Gene. 'Happy birthday, Don.'

He gave me a gift-wrapped package, and put his arm around me in a hug. I recognised that this was probably the final step in the male-male advice protocol, indicating acceptance of the advice without damage to our friendship, and managed not to flinch, but could not process the input any further. My brain was already overloaded.

'It's your birthday?' said Rosie.

'Correct.'

'I had to get Helena to look up your birth date,' said Gene, 'but "celebration" was a clue.'

I normally do not treat birthdays differently from other days, but it had struck me as an appropriate occasion to commence a new direction.

Claudia introduced herself to Rosie, adding, 'I'm sorry, it seems we've come at a bad time.'

Rosie turned to Gene. 'A "thank you"? Thank *you*? Shit. It wasn't enough to set us up—you had to coach him. You had to turn him into you.'

Claudia said, quietly, 'Rosie, it wasn't Gene's—'

Gene put a hand on Claudia's shoulder and she stopped.

'No, it wasn't,' he said. 'Who *asked* him to change? Who said that he'd be *perfect* for her if he was *different*?'

Rosie was now looking very upset. All of my friends (except Dave the Baseball Fan) were fighting. *This was terrible.* I wanted to roll the story back to New York and make better decisions. But it was impossible. Nothing would change the fault in my brain that made me unacceptable.

Gene hadn't stopped. 'Do you have any idea what he did for you? Take a look in his office sometime.' He was presumably referring to my schedule and the large number of Rosie Project activities.

Rosie walked out of the restaurant.

Gene turned to Claudia. 'Sorry I interrupted you.'

'Someone had to say it,' said Claudia. She looked at Rosie, who was already some distance down the street. 'I think I coached the wrong person.'

Gene and Claudia offered me a lift home, but I did not want to continue the conversation. I started walking, then accelerated to a jog. It made sense to get home before it rained. It also made sense to exercise hard and put the restaurant behind me as quickly as possible. The new shoes were work-able, but the coat and tie were uncomfortable even on a cold night. I pulled off the jacket, the item that had made me temporarily acceptable in a world to which I did not belong, and threw it in a rubbish bin. The tie followed. On an impulse I retrieved the daphne from the jacket and carried it in my hand for the remainder of the journey. There was rain in the air and my face was wet as I reached the safety of my apartment.

34

We had not finished the wine at the restaurant. I decided to compensate for the resulting alcohol deficit and poured a tumbler of tequila. I turned on the television screen and computer and fast-forwarded *Casablanca* for one last try. I watched as Humphrey Bogart's character used beans as a metaphor for the relative unimportance in the wider world of his relationship with Ingrid Bergman's character, and chose logic and decency ahead of his selfish emotional desires. The quandary and resulting decision made for an engrossing film. But this was not what people cried about. *They were in love and could never be together.* I repeated this statement to myself, trying to force an emotional reaction. I couldn't. I didn't care. I had enough problems of my own.

The doorbell buzzed, and I immediately thought *Rosie*, but when I pushed the CCTV button, it was Claudia's face that appeared.

'Don, are you okay?' she said. 'Can we come up?'

'It's too late.'

Claudia sounded panicked. 'What have you done? Don?'

'It's 10.31,' I said. 'Too late for visitors.'

'Are you okay?' said Claudia, again.

'I'm fine. The experience has been highly useful.

New social skills. And final resolution of the Wife Problem. Clear evidence that I'm incompatible with women.'

Gene's face appeared on the screen. 'Don. Can we come up for a drink?'

'Alcohol would be a bad idea.' I still had a half-glass of tequila in my hand. I was telling a polite lie to avoid social contact. I turned off the intercom.

The message light on my home phone was flashing. It was my parents and brother wishing me a happy birthday. I had already spoken to my mother two days earlier when she made her regular Sunday evening call. These past three weeks, I had been attempting to provide some news in return, but had not mentioned Rosie. They were utilising the speaker-phone function, and collectively sang the birthday song—or at least my mother did, strongly encouraging my other two relatives to participate.

'Ring back if you're home before 10.30,' my mother said. It was 10.38, but I decided not to be pedantic.

'It's 10.39,' said my mother. 'I'm surprised you rang back.' Clearly she had expected me to be pedantic, which was reasonable given my history, but she sounded pleased.

'Hey,' said my brother. 'Gary Parkinson's sister saw you on Facebook. Who's the redhead?'

'Just a girl I was dating.'

'Pull the other leg,' said my brother.

The words had sounded strange to me too, but I had not been joking.

'I'm not seeing her anymore.'

'I thought you might say that.' He laughed.

My mother interrupted. 'Stop it, Trevor. Donald, you didn't tell us you were seeing someone. You know you're always welcome—'

'Mum, he was having a lend of you,' said my brother.

'I *said*,' said my mother, 'that *anytime* you want to bring *anyone* to meet us, *whoever* she or *he*—'

'Leave him alone, both of you,' said my father.

There was a pause, and some conversation in the background. Then my brother said, 'Sorry, mate. I was just having a go. I know you think I'm some sort of redneck, but I'm okay with who you are. I'd hate you to get to this age and think I still had a problem with it.'

So, to add to a momentous day, I corrected a misconception that my family had held for at least fifteen years and came out to them as straight.

The conversations with Gene, Phil and my family had been surprisingly therapeutic. I did not need to use the Edinburgh Postnatal Depression Scale to know that I was feeling sad, but I was back from the edge of the pit. I would need to do some disciplined thinking in the near future to be certain of remaining safe, but for the moment I did not need to shut down the emotional part of my brain entirely. I wanted a little time to observe how I felt about recent events.

It was cold and the rain was pouring, but my balcony was under shelter. I took a chair and my glass outside, then went back inside, put on the greasy wool jumper that my mother had knitted for a much earlier birthday and collected the tequila bottle.

I was forty years old. My father used to play a song written by John Sebastian. I remember that it was by

John Sebastian because Noddy Holder announced prior to singing it, 'We're going to do a song by John Sebastian. Are there any John Sebastian fans here?' Apparently there were because there was loud and raucous applause before he started singing.

I decided that tonight I was also a John Sebastian fan and that I wanted to hear the song. This was the first time in my life that I could recall a desire to hear a particular piece of music. I had the technology. Or used to. I went to pull out my mobile phone and realised it had been in the jacket I had discarded. I went inside, booted my laptop, registered for iTunes, and downloaded 'Darling Be Home Soon' from *Slade Alive!*, 1972. I added 'Satisfaction', thus doubling the size of my popular music collection. I retrieved my earphones from their box and returned to the balcony, poured another tequila and listened to a voice from my childhood singing that it had taken a quarter of his life before he could begin to see himself.

At eighteen, just before I left home to go to university, statistically approaching a quarter of my life, I had listened to these words and been reminded that I had very little understanding of who I was. It had taken me until tonight, approximately halfway, to see myself reasonably clearly. I had Rosie, and the Rosie Project to thank for that. Now it was over, what had I learned?

1. I need not be visibly odd. I could engage in the protocols that others followed and move undetected among them. And how could I be sure that other people were not doing the same—playing the game

to be accepted but suspecting all the time that they were different?

2. I had skills that others didn't. My memory and ability to focus had given me an advantage in baseball statistics, cocktail-making and genetics. People had valued these skills, not mocked them.

3. I could enjoy friendship and good times. It was my lack of skills not lack of motivation that had held me back. Now I was competent enough socially to open my life to a wider range of people. I could have more friends. Dave the Baseball Fan could be the first of many.

4. I had told Gene and Claudia that I was incompatible with women. This was an exaggeration. I could enjoy their company, as proven by my joint activities with Rosie and Daphne. Realistically, it was possible that I could have a partnership with a woman.

5. The idea behind the Wife Project was still sound. In many cultures a matchmaker would have routinely done what I did, with less technology, reach and rigour, but the same assumption—that compatibility was as viable a foundation for marriage as love.

6. I was not wired to feel love. And faking it was not acceptable. Not to me. I had feared that Rosie would not love me. Instead, it was I who could not love Rosie.

7. I had a great deal of valuable knowledge—about genetics, computers, aikido, karate, hardware, chess, wine, cocktails, dancing, sexual positions, social protocols and the probability of a fifty-six-game hitting streak occurring in the history of baseball. I knew so much *shit* and I still couldn't fix myself.

As the shuffle setting on my media player selected the same two songs over and over, I realised that my thinking was also beginning to go in circles and that, despite the tidy formulation, there was some flaw in my logic. I decided it was my unhappiness with the night's outcome breaking through, my wish that it could be different.

I watched the rain falling over the city and poured the last of the tequila.

35

I was still in the chair when I woke the next morning. It was cold and raining and my laptop battery had exhausted itself. I shook my head to test for a hangover but it seemed that my alcohol-processing enzymes had done their job adequately. So had my brain. I had unconsciously set it a problem to solve and, understanding the importance of the situation, it had overcome the handicap of intoxication to reach a solution.

I began the second half of my life by making coffee. Then I reviewed the very simple logic.

1. I was wired differently. One of the characteristics of my wiring was that I had difficulty empathising. This problem has been well documented in others and is, in fact, one of the defining symptoms of the autism spectrum.
2. A lack of empathy would account for my inability to respond emotionally to the situations of fictional characters in films. This was similar to my inability to respond as others did to the victims of the World Trade Center terrorist attacks.

But I did feel sorry for Frank the fire-fighter guide. And for Daphne, my sister, my parents when my sister died, Carl and Eugenie because of the Gene–Claudia marriage crisis, Gene himself, who wanted to be admired but had achieved the opposite, Claudia, who had agreed to an open marriage but changed her mind and suffered as Gene continued to exploit it, Phil, who had struggled to deal with his wife's infidelity and death and then to win the love of Rosie, Kevin Yu, whose focus on passing the course had blinded him to ethical conduct, the Dean, who had to make difficult decisions under contradictory rules and deal with prejudice about her dress and relationship, Faith Healer, who had to reconcile his strong beliefs with scientific evidence, Margaret Case, whose son had committed suicide and whose mind no longer functioned and, critically, Rosie, whose childhood and now adulthood had been made unhappy by her mother's death and her father problem and who now wanted me to love her. This was an impressive list, and, though it did not include Rick and Ilsa from *Casablanca*, it was clear evidence that my empathy capability was not entirely absent.

3. An inability (or reduced ability) to empathise is not the same as an inability to

love. Love is a powerful feeling for another person, often defying logic.
4. Rosie had failed numerous criteria on the Wife Project, including the critical smoking question. My feelings for her *could not be explained by logic*. I did not care about Meryl Streep. But I was in love with Rosie.

I had to act quickly, not because I believed the situation with Rosie was likely to change in the immediate future, but because I needed my jacket, which was, I hoped, still in the rubbish bin where I had thrown it. Luckily I was already dressed from the previous evening.

It was still raining when I arrived at the bin, just in time to see it emptied into a garbage truck compactor. I had a contingency plan, but it was going to take time. I turned the bike around to head for home and crossed the road. Slumped in a shop doorway, out of the rain, was a hobo. He was fast asleep, and he was wearing my jacket. I carefully reached into the inside pocket and extracted the envelope and my phone. As I remounted my bike, I saw a couple on the other side of the street watching me. The male started to run towards me, but the woman called him back. She was making a call on her mobile phone.

It was only 7.48 a.m. when I arrived at the university. A police car approached from the opposite direction, slowed as it passed me, then signalled a U-turn. It occurred to me that it could have been summoned to deal with my apparent theft from the hobo. I turned quickly down the bicycle path, where I could not be followed by a motor vehicle, and headed towards the Genetics building to find a towel.

As I opened the unlocked door of my office it was obvious that I had had a visitor, and who that visitor had been. The red roses were lying on my desk. So was the Father Project file, which had been removed from its home in the filing cabinet. The list of father-candidate names and sample descriptions was on the desk beside it. Rosie had left a note.

Don, I'm sorry about everything. But I know who Table-Napkin Man is. I've told Dad. I probably shouldn't have but I was very upset. I tried to call you. Sorry again. Rosie.

There was a lot of crossed-out writing between *Sorry again* and *Rosie*. But this was a disaster! I needed to warn Gene.

His diary indicated a breakfast meeting at the University Club. I checked the PhD area, and Stefan was there, but not Rosie. Stefan could see that I was highly agitated, and followed me.

We reached the club, and located Gene at a table with the Dean. But at another table, I saw Rosie. She was with Claudia and seemed very distressed. I realised that she could be sharing the news about Gene, even prior to a DNA ratification. The Father Project was ending in total disaster. But I had come for something else. I was desperate to share my revelation. We could resolve the other problem later.

I ran to Rosie's table. I was still wet as a result of forgetting to dry myself. Rosie was obviously surprised to see me. I dispensed with formalities.

'I've made an incredible mistake. I can't believe

I've been so stupid. Irrational!' Claudia made signals for me to stop, but I ignored them. 'You failed almost every criterion of the Wife Project. Disorganised, mathematically illiterate, ridiculous food requirements. Incredible. I considered sharing my life with a smoker. Permanently!'

Rosie's expression was complex, but appeared to include sadness, anger and surprise. 'It didn't take you long to change your mind,' she said.

Claudia was frantically waving at me to stop, but I was determined to proceed according to my own plan.

'I haven't changed my mind. That's the point! I want to spend my life with you even though it's totally irrational. And you have short earlobes. Socially and genetically there's no reason for me to be attracted to you. The only logical conclusion is that I must be in love with you.'

Claudia got up and pushed me into her chair.

'You don't give up, do you?' said Rosie.

'I'm being annoying?'

'No,' said Rosie. 'You're being incredibly brave. I have the best fun with you, you're the smartest, funniest person I know, you've done all these things for me. It's everything I want and I've been too scared to grab it because—'

She stopped but I knew what she was thinking. I finished her sentence for her.

'Because I'm weird. Perfectly understandable. I'm familiar with the problem because everyone else seems weird to me.'

Rosie laughed.

I tried to explain.

'Crying over fictitious characters, for example.'

'Could you live with me crying in movies?' said Rosie.

'Of course,' I said. 'It's conventional behaviour.' I stopped as I realised what she had said.

'You're offering to live with me?'

Rosie smiled.

'You left this on the table,' she said, and pulled the ring container from her bag. I realised that Rosie had reversed her decision of the previous night, and was in effect rolling back time to allow my original plan to proceed at an alternative location. I extracted the ring and she held out her finger. I put it on and it fitted. I felt a major sense of relief.

I became aware of applause. It seemed natural. I had been living in the world of romantic comedy and this was the final scene. But it was real. The entire University Club dining room had been watching. I decided to complete the story according to tradition and kissed Rosie. It was even better than the previous occasion.

'You'd better not let me down,' said Rosie. 'I'm expecting constant craziness.'

Phil walked in, his nose in a plaster cast, accompanied by the club manager. She was followed by two police. The manager pointed Gene out to Phil.

'Oh shit,' said Rosie. Phil walked over to Gene, who stood up. There was a brief conversation and then Phil knocked him to the floor with a single punch to the jaw. The police rushed forward and restrained Phil, who did not resist. Claudia ran up to Gene, who was slowly rising. He appeared not to be seriously injured. I realised that under the traditional rules of romantic behaviour, it was correct for Phil to assault Gene, assuming he had in fact seduced Rosie's mother when she was Phil's girlfriend.

However, it was not certain that Gene was the culprit. On the other hand, numerous men were probably entitled to punch Gene. In this sense, Phil was dispensing romantic justice on their behalf. Gene must have understood, because he appeared to be reassuring the police that everything was okay.

I redirected my attention to Rosie. Now that my previous plan had been reinstated, it was important not to be distracted.

'Item Two on the agenda was your father's identity.'

Rosie smiled. 'Back on track. Item One: let's get married. Okay, that's sorted. Item Two. This is the Don I've grown to know and love.'

The last word stopped me. I could only look at Rosie as I took in the reality of what she had said. I guessed she was doing the same, and it was several seconds before she spoke.

'How many positions in that book can you do?'

'The sex book? All of them.'

'Bullshit.'

'It was considerably less complex than the cocktail book.'

'So let's go home,' she said. 'To my place. Or your place if you've still got the Atticus Finch outfit.' She laughed.

'It's in my office.'

'Another time. Don't throw it out.'

We got up, but the police, one man and one woman, blocked our path.

'Sir,' said the woman (age approximately twenty-eight, BMI twenty-three), 'I'm going to have to ask you what's in your pocket.'

I had forgotten the envelope! I pulled it out and waved it in front of Rosie.

'Tickets! Tickets to Disneyland. All problems solved!' I fanned out the three tickets, took Rosie's hand and we walked towards Phil to show him.

36

We went to Disneyland—Rosie, Phil and I. It was great fun and appeared to be a success in improving all relationships. Rosie and Phil shared information and I learned a lot about Rosie's life. It was important background for the difficult but essential task of developing a high level of empathy for one person in the world.

Rosie and I were on our way to New York, where being weird is acceptable. That is a simplification of the rationale: in reality what was important for me was to be able to make a new start with my new skills, new approach and new partner, without being held back by others' perceptions of me—perceptions that I had not only deserved but encouraged.

Here in New York, I am working in the Department of Genetics at Columbia University, and Rosie is in the first year of the Doctor of Medicine program. I am contributing to Simon Lefebvre's research project remotely, as he insisted on it as a condition of providing funding. I consider it a form of moral payback for using the university's equipment for the Father Project.

We have an apartment in Williamsburg, not far from the Eslers, whom we visit regularly. The Cellar Interrogation is now a story that Isaac and I both tell on social occasions.

We are considering reproducing (or, as I would say in a social encounter, 'having children'). In order to prepare for this possibility, Rosie has ceased smoking, and we have reduced our alcohol intake. Fortunately we have numerous other activities to distract us from these addictive behaviours. Rosie and I work in a cocktail bar together three evenings a week. It is exhausting at times, but social and fun, and supplements my academic salary.

We listen to music. I have revised my approach to Bach, and am no longer trying to follow individual notes. It is more successful, but my music tastes seem to have been locked in in my teens. As a result of failing to make my own selections at that time, my preferences are those of my father. I can advance a well-reasoned argument that nothing worth listening to was recorded after 1972. Rosie and I have that argument frequently. I cook, but reserve the meals of the Standardised Meal System for dinner parties.

We are officially married. Although I had performed the romantic ritual with the ring, I did not expect Rosie, as a modern feminist, to want to actually get married. The term 'wife' in Wife Project had always meant 'female life partner'. But she decided that she should have 'one relationship in my life that was what it was supposed to be'. That included monogamy and permanence. An excellent outcome.

I am able to hug Rosie. This was the issue that caused me the most fear after she agreed to live with me. I generally find body contact unpleasant, but sex is an obvious exception. Sex solved the body contact problem. We are now also able to hug without having sex, which is obviously convenient at times.

Once a week, in order to deal with the demands of living with another person, and to continue to improve my skills in this sphere, I spend an evening in therapy. This is a small joke: my 'therapist' is Dave and I provide reciprocal services to him. Dave is also married and, considering that I am supposedly wired differently, our challenges are surprisingly similar. He sometimes brings male friends and colleagues from work, where he is a refrigeration engineer. We are all Yankees fans.

For some time, Rosie did not mention the Father Project. I attributed this to the improved relationship with Phil and the distraction of other activities. But, in the background, I was processing some new information.

At the wedding, Dr Eamonn Hughes, the first person we had tested, asked to speak to me privately.

'There's something you should know,' he said. 'About Rosie's father.'

It seemed entirely plausible that Rosie's mother's closest friend from medical school would know the answer. Perhaps we had only needed to ask. But Eamonn was referring to something else. He pointed to Phil.

'Phil's been a bit of a screw-up with Rosie.'

So it wasn't only Rosie who thought Phil was a poor parent.

'You know about the car accident?'

I nodded, although I had no detailed information. Rosie had made it clear that she did not want to discuss it.

'Bernadette was driving because Phil had been drinking.'

I had deduced that Phil was in the car.

'Phil got out, with a broken pelvis, and pulled Rosie out.' Eamonn paused. He was obviously distressed. 'He pulled Rosie out first.'

This was truly an awful scenario, but as a geneticist my immediate thought was 'of course'. Phil's behaviour, in pain and under extreme pressure, would surely have been instinctual. Such life-and-death situations occur regularly in the animal kingdom and Phil's choice was in line with theory and experimental results. While he had presumably revisited that moment many times in his mind, and his later feelings towards Rosie may have been severely affected by it, his actions were consistent with the primitive drive to protect the carrier of his genes.

It was only later that I realised my obvious error. As Rosie was not Phil's biological daughter, such instincts would not have been applicable. I spent some time reflecting on the possible explanations for his behaviour. I did not share my thoughts or the hypothesis I formed.

When I was established at Columbia, I requested permission to use the DNA-testing facilities for a private investigation. They were willing to let me do so. It would not have been a problem if they had refused. I could have sent my remaining samples to a commercial laboratory and paid a few hundred dollars for the tests. This option had been available to Rosie from the beginning of the Father Project. It is now obvious to me that I did not alert Rosie to that option because I was subconsciously interested in a relationship with her even then. Amazing!

I did not tell Rosie about the test. One day I just packed my bag with the samples that I had brought with me to New York.

I started with the paranoid plastic surgeon,

Freyberg, who was the least likely candidate in my assessment. A green-eyed father was not impossible, but there was no other evidence making him more probable than any of the previous candidates. His reluctance to send me a blood sample was explained by him being a generally suspicious and unhelpful person. My prediction was correct.

I loaded Esler's specimen, a swab from a fork that had travelled more than halfway around the world and back again. In his darkened basement, I had been certain he was Rosie's father. But afterwards I had come to the conclusion that he could have been protecting a friend or the memory of a friend. I wondered if Esler's decision to become a psychiatrist had been influenced by the suicide of the best man at his wedding, Geoffrey Case.

I tested the sample. Isaac Esler was not Rosie's father.

I picked up Gene's sample. *My* best friend. He was working hard on his marriage. The map was no longer on his wall when I went in to submit my resignation to the Dean. But I had no recollection of seeing a pin in Ireland, Rosie's mother's birthplace. There was no need to test the table napkin. I tossed it in the waste bin.

I had now eliminated every candidate except Geoffrey Case. Isaac Esler had told me that he knew who Rosie's father was and that he was sworn to secrecy. Did Rosie's mother—and Esler—not want Rosie to know that there was a family history of suicide? Or perhaps a genetic predisposition to mental illness? Or that Geoffrey Case had possibly killed himself in the wake of the news that he was Rosie's father and that her mother had decided to remain with Phil? These were all good reasons—good enough that I considered it highly likely that Rosie's mother's one-night encounter had been with Geoffrey Case.

I reached into my bag and pulled out the DNA sample that fate had delivered to me without Rosie's knowledge. I was now almost certain that it would confirm my hypothesis as to her paternity.

I cut a small portion of the cloth, poured over the reagent, and let it sit for a few minutes. As I watched the fabric in the clear solution, and mentally reviewed the Father Project, I became more and more confident in my prediction. I decided that Rosie should join me for this result, regardless of whether I was right or wrong. I texted her. She was on campus and arrived a few minutes later. She immediately realised what I was doing.

I put the processed sample in the machine, and waited while the analysis proceeded. We watched the computer screen together until the result came up. After all the blood-collecting, cheek-swabbing, cocktail-shaking, wall-climbing, glass-collecting, flying, driving, proposal-writing, urine-mopping, cup-stealing, fork-wiping, tissue-retrieving, toothbrush-stealing, hairbrush-cleaning and tear-wiping, we had a match.

Rosie had wanted to know who her biological father was. Her mother had wanted the identity of the man she had sex with, perhaps only once, on an occasion of emotion-driven rule-breaking, to remain a secret forever. I could now fulfil both of their wishes.

I showed her the remains of the blood-stained singlet from Jarman's Gym with the sample square cut out of it. There would be no need to test the handkerchief that had wiped Margaret Case's tears.

Ultimately, the entire father problem was caused by Gene. He almost certainly taught the medical students an oversimplified model of the inheritance of common traits. If Rosie's mother had known that eye colour was not a reliable indicator of paternity, and organised a DNA test to confirm her suspicions, there would have been no Father Project, no Great Cocktail Night, no New York Adventure, no Reform Don Project—and no Rosie Project. Had it not been for this unscheduled series of events, her daughter and I would not have fallen in love. And I would still be eating lobster every Tuesday night.

Incredible.

Acknowledgements

The Rosie Project was written quickly. I poked my head up for just long enough to consult with my writer wife Anne, daughter Dominique and my novel-writing class at RMIT, led by Michelle Aung Thin.

After being adopted by Text Publishing, the manuscript benefited enormously from the attentions of my editor, Alison Arnold, who understood exactly what I was aiming for, and the passionate support of Michael Heyward and his team, in particular Jane Novak, Kirsty Wilson, Chong Weng Ho and Michelle Calligaro. Anne Beilby's efforts in bringing *Rosie* to the attention of international publishers have ensured that Don and Rosie's story will be told in thirty languages.

But the underlying story has a longer pedigree. It began as a screenplay, developed during screenwriting studies at RMIT. Anne, my son Daniel and I workshopped the original plot during a walk in New Zealand. A work-up for the characters was published as *The Klara Project: Phase 1* in *The Envelope Please* in 2007 and I completed the first draft of the screenplay, with a different plot and a nerdy Hungarian Klara instead of Rosie, in 2008, having taken some time to decide that it was a comedy rather than a drama. The story changed significantly over five years, very much for the better, and for that I have to thank the many people who encouraged, criticised, and pushed me not to be satisfied with what I had.

The faculty at RMIT taught me the principles of story-telling, as well as offering specific advice on the script. Special mentions are due to Clare Renner, Head of School; Tim Ferguson, comedy legend; David Rapsey and Ian Pringle, seasoned film producers who did not stint on the tough love; and Boris Trbic who gave me an appreciation for the screwball comedy. Cary Grant would have made a perfect Don. Jo Moylan was my writing buddy through a year of the most radical changes. Making short films with the audiovisual students, under the leadership of Rowan Humphrey and Simon Embury, taught me much about what worked and what didn't. As I watched my extraneous dialogue hit the digital equivalent of the cutting-room floor, I learned a lot about writing economically. Kim Krejus of 16th Street Actors Studio organised talented actors for an enlightening reading.

I am fortunate to belong to a talented and hard-working writers' group: Irina Goundortseva, Steve Mitchell, Susannah Petty and May Yeung. *Rosie* was regularly on the agenda, and Irina's enthusiasm for the short story was instrumental in my taking it further. Later, Heidi Winnen was the first person outside my family to suggest that the novel might have potential.

The script benefited from the astute feedback of screenwriting gurus Steve Kaplan and Michael Hauge. Their involvement was in turn made possible by Marcus West of Inscription and the Australian Writers' Guild who sponsored a prize for romantic comedy writing in

2010. Producers Peter Lee and Ros Walker and director John Paul Fischbach also offered valuable criticism.

The path to publication began when *The Rosie Project* won the Victorian Premier's Literary Award for an unpublished manuscript in 2012, and I acknowledge the Victorian State Government and the Wheeler Centre for sponsoring and administering the award. I also thank the judges, Nick Gadd, Peter Mews, Zoe Dattner and Roderick Poole, for their brave choice.

Many other people have supported *Rosie* and me on the six-year journey from concept to published novel, notably Jon Backhouse, Rebecca Carter, Cameron Clarke, Sara Cullen, Fran Cusworth, Barbara Gliddon, Amanda Golding, Vin Hedger, Kate Hicks, Amy Jasper, Noel Maloney, Brian McKenzie, Steve Melnikoff, Ben Michael, Helen O'Connell, Rebecca Peniston-Bird, April Reeve, John Reeves, Sue and Chris Waddell, Geri and Pete Walsh, and my fellow students at RMIT.

Don's lobster salad is based on a recipe from Teage Ezard's *Contemporary Australian Food*. Perfect for a romantic evening on a balcony with a bottle of Drappier rosé champagne.